WAR CRIMES

Peter Carey grew up in Bacchus Marsh, Victoria. His first, bestselling book, *The Fat Man in History*, was followed by *War Crimes*, which won the New South Wales Premier's Award in 1980. *Bliss* won the same award in 1982 as well as the Miles Franklin and National Book Council awards. The film *Bliss*, based on the novel, won three Australian Film Institute awards in 1985, including best feature film. His novel *Illywhacker* (1985) won the Victorian Premier's Award, the *Age* Book of the Year Award, the NBC Award for Australian Literature, the FAW Barbara Ramsden Award, and was shortlisted for the Booker Prize. *Oscar and Lucinda*, Peter Carey's bestselling novel, won the 1988 Booker Prize and many other awards including the 1989 Miles Franklin. *The Tax Inspector* is his most recent novel.

PETER CAREY

WAR CRIMES

University of Queensland Press

First published 1979 by University of Queensland Press
Box 42, St Lucia, Queensland 4067 Australia
Reprinted in paperback 1981, 1984, 1988, 1991

Printed in Australia by The Book Printer, Melbourne

Cataloguing in Publication Data
National Library of Australia

Carey, Peter, 1943-
    War crimes.

    I. Title.

A823'.3

ISBN 0 7022 1649 6

Contents

Acknowledgments

Some of these stories have appeared before:
"Do You Love Me?" in *Tabloid Story*
"Fragrance of Roses" in *Nation Review*
"The Last Days of a Famous Mime" in *Stand*

The Journey of a Lifetime

1.

How I have waited for the train, dreamed about it, studied its every detail. It has been my ambition, my obsession, a hope too far-fetched for one of my standing. My poor, dimly lit room is lined with newspaper cuttings, postcards, calendars (both cheaply and expensively printed) celebrating its glories, the brutal power of its locomotive, the velvety luxury of its interiors.

On stifling summer nights I have lain on my bed and lingered over the pages of my beautiful scrapbooks, particularly the one titled "Tickets, Reservations, etc". Possibly it is the best collection of its type. I do not know. But I have been fortunate indeed to have superiors who have not only known of my interest but have been thoughtful enough to hand on what bits and pieces have come their way.

I imagine them at dinner parties: the clink of fine crystal, the witty conversation, the French wines and white-shouldered women.

"Ah," one would say, "so you have been north on the train?"

"Yes," said nonchalantly, as if the train were nothing, a bicycle, a bowl of soup.

"I wonder perhaps if I may have your tickets. I have a clerk who has an interest . . ."

Even now, imagining this conversation I hold my

breath. I wait on tenterhooks. Have the tickets been thrown away? Have they been kept? If so will my superior remember to ask about dining room reservation cards, a menu, baggage tickets?

"Well yes, I believe I have them still."

Will he get them now? Or will he merely intend to fetch them but stay talking for a moment and then, finally, forget the matter entirely.

No. No. He stands. A tall man, very white-skinned, a rather cruel aristocratic nose. A kindly smile flickers around his thin lips. "Best to get it now," he says, "lest one forget."

It is a large house of course and he is away some time. He walks lightly up the great curving staircase where he passes maids in black dresses and white aprons. He greets them kindly, knowing each one by name. I follow him down wide corridors and into a study, book-lined, a large green lamp hanging over a cedar table on which sits a stamp collection in eight leather-bound volumes. One album lies open revealing blue stamps, almost identical, but with slight differences in printing.

He fossicks in the drawer of a mahogany desk. I cannot make out what he has. Ah, an envelope. Now, down the corridors. Oh the agony of waiting. On the staircase he stops to talk with a servant, inquiring about the man's father. The conversation drags on. It seems as if we will be here all night. But no, no, it is over. The servant proceeds upstairs, his master downstairs.

Finally at the dinner table the envelope is presented to my superior. He opens it. Thank God. I thought for a moment he was going to put it in his pocket without even looking.

And oh what treasures we have.

First, two small blue first class tickets. The blue denotes a journey in excess of one thousand miles. Rare enough, but across the blue is a faint green stripe which denotes the Family Saloon. I imagine the saloon, recalling the colour gravure calendar which displays its glories. The oak door leading to the observation platform. The high arched roof with the clerestory windows. The two quilted chairs upholstered in rich rust-coloured velvet. There is also a couch with two loose cushions, one with tassels, one bearing an insignia the nature of which remains mysterious to me. There is a writing table with a lamp of graceful design. The windows of the carriage are large, affording a panorama of the most spectacular scenery by day, curtained by ingenious blinds at night.

In addition the envelope contains reservations for the dining car, a lavishly printed menu and two unusual luggage labels denoting the high rank of the traveller.

They will go into my scrapbook, of course, and be held there not by anything as coarse as glue, but by the small transparent hinges used by stamp collectors. The scrapbook shall lie under my bed as always. On a hot night I will lean down and take it out, and slowly, having all the time in the world, I will peruse its contents.

If the fat bitch in the next room roars and moans in her stinking lust I will not become distressed. I will not even hear her. While her organ grips and slides over her latest lover's aching penis, I will be far away. Nothing will touch me. I will not hammer on the wall in rage. Nor will I be so base as to press

3

my ear closer to catch the obscenities she mutters or the details of the perversions she commands him to perform.

I will travel first through the old tickets, pale gold with ornate copperplate, then over the commemorative journeys with their ornamental insignia, their laurels, crests and specially commissioned engravings. The list, although not endless, is certainly long. There are five hundred and thirty-three separate tickets.

If the following day is a Sunday I will wake early and travel by blue bus to the Central Station. It is not permitted to visit the platform itself but one can look through the wire grille and watch the activity. The passengers, beautifully dressed, occasionally accompanied by servants, stroll to and fro on the platform. One may also catch a glimpse of a courtesan, white-skinned and dark-eyed, her position in life denoted by the small white umbrella she holds in one small gloved hand. Porters bustle. Waiters in red uniform, their faces as empty of expression as the glass window they stand behind, examine the status of those whom they will shortly serve. At one time a string quartet was established in a long white carriage and when the train at last departed it was possible to hear the sweet music of a cello above the muscular sound of the locomotive.

Doubtless you think me a poor fellow, forever watching, never travelling, my red hands gripped around the wire mesh, doomed to be left behind, to watch from cuttings, to peer from bridges, to stand amongst thistles in driving rain whilst the train passes me by and leaves me to walk two miles through muddy paddocks and wait for a bus to take me back to my room. If you think me pitiful, you are not alone. My co-workers have belittled me, taken every opportunity to play some cruel trick on me and in general have acted as if they are in some way superior and all the while they have complained about their own lot, the monotony of their lives, the injustice of the state, the cruelty of their superiors. Little did they know how I pitied them, how I laughed at their presumption that they might one day control their own destiny.

But I, I have not complained. I have worked day in, day out, forever filing away the mountains of paper which record the business of the state: births, deaths, marriages, all tucked away in the right place so they can easily be found when needed. I have filed acts of parliament, executions, stays of execution, punishments of greater and lesser degree, exhumations, cremations, promotions and so on. When my clothes have become worn I have spent my precious savings in order that I might do honour to my lowly position and not disgrace my superiors.

My colleagues' frayed cuffs and stained suits have appalled me. Their scuffed shoes, their dirty hair, their missing buttons have affronted me day in and day out for nearly thirty years.

They have thought me vain, foolish, lonely, pathetic but they, like you, do not know everything, and when they hear of my reward, my gift, my privilege we will see who is laughing at who.

For I, Louis Morrow Baxter Moon, am to travel on the train on official business.

Ha.

Today I have been to the bank and withdrawn

my savings, every penny. I have purchased a new suit, a pair of shoes, one pair of dark socks, and I still have some not insubstantial amount left to cover such items as tips and wine. The state, of course, will pay normal expenses but I do not intend to travel as a lackey.

In addition I intend to drink gin and tonic.

2.

The ticket is palest pink, denoting a journey of two thousand miles. A black diagonal line across the corner entitles me to a private salon of the second rank which, humble as it may sound to the un-initiated, is more sumptuous than anything my co-workers will experience if they live to be three hundred years old.

The ticket is held between two gloved fingers. I hand it to the man on the gate. He looks at me quizzically. Does he remember me? Has he seen me here on Sunday mornings and is he now indignant that I shall at last pass through his gate? I stare him down. He waves me through and I enter the platform with my heavy suitcase.

I had expected a porter to rush to my service, but this is not the case. All around porters carry cases belonging to other passengers. Perhaps my dress is not of the style normally worn by travellers. I carry my case without complaint. In any case it will save me the difficulty of tipping. I would rather save the money for other things.

I experience a strange sense of unreality, perhaps explained by my sleepless night, the curious nature of the mission that has been given me, the experience of walking, after so many years, on the platform itself. How often have I dreamed of just this moment: seeing myself reflected in the large windows of the carriages, a ticket in my hand, ready to board the train.

Through the windows of the dining car I see maids laying tables with fine silver. Three wine glasses are with each setting and do not think that when the time comes I will not use at least two of them.

I present myself at car 23 and hand my ticket to the steward.

"Who is this for?" he asks. He is red haired and freckled faced. His elegant uniform does not disguise his common upbringing. I do not like his tone.

"It is for me. Mr Moon. A booking made on the account of the State on whose business I am travelling."

"Ah yes, I see." He seems almost disappointed to have found my name in his register. His manner is not what I would have expected.

He allocates me the salon next to his office.

"Here we are."

"Is this over the wheels?" I ask this as planned. It is well known that a salon directly over the wheels is less comfortable than one between the wheels even though the rails are now laid in quarter-mile sections, thus eliminating the clickety-clack commonly associated with trains.

"It don't float on air," he says and somehow thinks that he has made a great joke. He leaves, laughing loudly, and in my confusion I forget to open the envelope I had marked "Tips".

Any feeling (and I will admit to the presence of certain feelings) that he has somehow given me an inferior salon soon disappear as I investigate.

3.

The salon, in fact, was roughly the same size as my room. But there the similarity ended. The floor, to begin at the bottom, was covered with a plush burgundy carpet so soft and luxurious that I removed my shoes and socks immediately. There were two couches, not velvet as I had expected, but upholstered with soft old leather and studded along the fronts with brass brads, each one gleaming and newly polished. The bed stood along one wall, a majestic double bed with high iron ends in which I discovered porcelain plaques depicting rural scenes. The bed, of course, could be curtained off from the rest of the salon and one reached the toilet and shower through a small door disguised as panelling. The wallpaper was a rich wine red, embossed with fleurs-de-lys.

I placed my case high on the rack above the bed, put my shoes and socks back on, and retired to the leather couch. From this privileged position I could watch the other passengers pass by my window without appearing in the least inquisitive. Then, remembering the matter of the tip, I removed two notes from the envelope in my breast pocket, folded them, and slipped them lightly into my side pocket. Then I rang the bell.

He took long enough to come.

"Yes?" He just stood at the door, staring in. I would have no more of this.

"Please enter."

He entered reluctantly, tapping a pencil against his leg with obvious impatience.

First, the tip. I'm afraid the manoeuvre was not gracefully executed. Perhaps he thought I wished to hold his hand, how can I tell? But he stepped away. I clutched after him, missed, and finally stood up. Abandoning all pretence at subtlety I displayed the notes. His manner changed.

"Now," I said, retiring to the couch, "there are services I shall require."

"Yes sir."

It would be an exaggeration to say that there was respect in his voice, but at least he used the correct form of address.

"For a start I will be drinking gin and tonic."

"Gin and tonic, sir."

"And I wish there to be plenty of ice. On occasions I believe the ice can run out very early, is this so?"

"You don't need to worry, sir."

"Then I shall require a reservation in the dining car and after dinner I wish a . . ." and here, I blush to remember, I hesitated. I had been so intent on not hesitating that I did.

"You wish, after dinner?"

"A courtesan."

"A what, sir?"

"A courtesan."

"You mean a woman, sir?" I swear he smirked. He had me there. Perhaps the term courtesan was not in common use amongst the lower classes from which he came.

"A woman, a courtesan," I insisted.

"And ice."

"And ice."

"Will that be all, sir?"

"That will be all."

He left me. Was he smiling? I couldn't be sure.

My pleasure in the train's departure was marred by my embarrassment over this incident, but as the train passed through the slums I called for my first gin and tonic. The ice was clear and cold and the drink quickly restored my good spirits.

I sat back deep in the couch and prepared to enjoy the journey of a lifetime.

4.

How to describe the afternoon? A long slow dream in which everything was as it should be. I perused my "Tickets" album and resisted the temptation to place my current ticket in it although I had brought hinges for just this purpose. I drank gin and tonic as planned and had a light lunch brought to my salon. The train left the city very quickly, edged slowly around Mount Speculation, and by three o'clock we were already entering that poor dry country which marks the edges of the Great Eastern Desert. Here and there I saw bands of prisoners working on some task, guarded by soldiers and I was reminded, against my will, of the mission that awaited me two thousand miles hence. I will confess that I drank a little more than might be considered correct and by four o'clock I was sound asleep.

I woke at five-thirty, feeling a little the worse for wear, showered, dressed, and, with nothing else planned, decided on an early visit to the dining car.

This was not the right thing to do. My impatience got the better of me. For had I not imagined this moment for so many years, the moment I would take my place beside my superiors at dinner. To remain sitting in my salon was thus beyond my power.

Yet, as I said, this was a mistake. The dining car was practically empty and I thought at first that I had mistaken the hour. However I soon noticed, at the far end of the carriage, an old gentleman already eating. I thought to join him, to engage in traveller's conversation, but the waiter, resplendent in red coat and black trousers, escorted me to an obscure corner behind the dessert trolley where, as he pointed out, I could enjoy some privacy.

Here is not perhaps the place to record the meal for it is all entered in the menu which I quietly slipped into my jacket. But I would wish to record that I drank a bottle of Château Smith Haut-Laffite which many consider one of the finest wines in the world, although it did have the unfortunate effect of drying my mouth and making my tongue a trifle furry.

I retired without enjoying a cigar and, feeling a little below par, decided to cancel the courtesan.

The wine cannot be held responsible for the violent sickness which beset me during the night. Doubtless it was due to overexcitement on my part. But here again, even in the midst of such upheaval,

I appreciated the little luxuries the train provided, for the toilet was but a short step from my bed.

5.

The morning revealed the truth which our most experienced travellers have so often related: that there is a certain monotony in a long journey through the desert. I was pleased to find that my view coincided with that of my superiors.

We were well and truly in the desert now and even a cluster of poor rocks was welcomed as something new, eagerly awaited, studied on arrival, and reluctantly farewelled.

I strolled the corridors a little and, not feeling up to much conversation, merely nodded to those ladies and gentlemen I met. Their smiles were in no way condescending.

In the afternoon I composed my instructions to the courtesan which I took great care over, drafting them several times and, to be honest, feeling not a little aroused by the activities I described. She was to visit me before dinner. I had the money in an envelope marked "Courtesan". I placed it under the pillow where I considered it would be easily reached when the time came.

6.

"And this is what you want?" she said. She was so beautiful I could barely look at her.

"Yes."

"You have written it all by hand."

"Yes." I wore my dressing gown, explaining that I had just had a shower. And in fact I had wet my hair a little just to go along with the story. All this was as planned.

She wore a long blue dress, very low cut at the front. Her skin was white, so very, very white, and she smelt like a garden of flowers. A little smile played around her full lips.

"You have very beautiful handwriting," she said.

"Thank you."

"Shall we start then?"

"Very well."

"You want to start with," she consulted the instructions, paused, smiled, "number one."

"Yes."

"Oh master," she began. And fell upon my ear, licking it furiously.

"Not ears," I shouted, "not ears."

She consulted the list again and soon realized her mistake. After that she seemed to become more familiar with my handwriting.

7.

At dinner I was strangely pleased to hear that the dining car had run out of ice. Yet I had enjoyed ice aplenty in the gin and tonic I had ordered in my salon just fifteen minutes before. The practice of tipping had brought me rewards and I felt immensely pleased with myself in every respect.

After dinner I took a constitutional, walking the complete length of the train several times, feeling very much at peace with the world. True, the nature of my mission sometimes clouded this perfect happiness but there were so many things to observe, so many small memorabilia to collect, that the clouds soon passed.

It was near car 33 that I passed a large storage compartment and looking in saw the steward, my steward from car 23. He was bent over a cabinet, or so I thought it, scooping ice into a silver bucket.

"Ah," I thought, "the devil has his own supply." And seeking to congratulate him on his initiative I stepped inside.

"Good evening," I said, and smiled to see him jump with fright, for he had not noticed my presence.

My smile, alas, was short lived. For as he turned I looked into the cabinet and found it to be not a cabinet at all, but rather a coffin of sorts. To my horror I saw a man's naked corpse inside and, packed around his pale corpulence, great quantities of ice floating in water. So this was the ice the rascal had been giving me.

I said not a word, but turned on my heel.

As I hurried along the corridor I heard him coming after me. I went into my salon and locked the door. I did not answer when he knocked, and in fact was unable to, for I was in the toilet, my stomach rent with uncontrollable spasms.

8.

How can it be that our dreams are so vulnerable, so tender, so frail that the spasms of the body can

14

serve to rip them apart in so short a time. For that is what occurred in the long night that followed. It was as if every cell in my body rebelled against the train, its motion, its food, its passengers, its wine, and most particularly my mission which floated before me, pale, bloated and surrounded by ice.

My stomach was emptied but my body produced a green poison in order that there should be something to expel. Near as the cabinet was it was not always possible to arrive in time. And what dreams, what visions came to assail me: wide staring eyes, matted hair, pale hands floating in cold water. The taste of gin, foul and perfumed, surrounded me. I prayed to God that the spasms would stop and wished for nothing more than to be home in my poor bed.

But my prayers were shunned and all night the blackness was sliced into sickening strips by the hiss of a guillotine.

9.
The train moved like a merciless juggernaut, dragging my dead weight from grey dawn to pale day. I did not welcome it. For now I could see only the price which I, in my madness, had agreed to pay for this journey.

I wanted the courtesan, dreamed of her for so many years, wanted her breasts in my mouth, her legs wrapped around me, but when it was done, it was done and I couldn't wait to get her out of my salon. So too it was with the train: I had had it and wanted it no more. But now the price I had agreed to in passion and lust must be paid on this cold grey morning when my lust seemed ugly and the blindfold of desire had been ripped away.

The assignment I had accepted was to be the executioner (I! Executioner!) of Frederick Myrdal, a man whom even the professional executioner shrank from killing.

Even now they will be waiting for me on the platform in their grey suits and long coats.

I will step onto the platform.

"Please sir," they will say, "come this way."

"Do You Love Me?"

1. *The Role of the Cartographers*

Perhaps a few words about the role of the Cartographers in our present society are warranted.

To begin with one must understand the nature of the yearly census, a manifestation of our desire to know, always, exactly where we stand. The census, originally a count of the population, has gradually extended until it has become a total inventory of the contents of the nation, a mammoth task which is continuing all the time — no sooner has one census been announced than work on another begins.

The results of the census play an important part in our national life and have, for many years, been the pivot point for the yearly "Festival of the Corn" (an ancient festival, related to the wealth of the earth).

We have a passion for lists. And nowhere is this more clearly illustrated than in the Festival of the Corn which takes place in midsummer, the weather always being fine and warm. On the night of the festival, the householders move their goods and possessions, all furniture, electrical goods, clothing, rugs, kitchen utensils, bathrobes, slippers, cushions, lawnmowers, curtains, doorstops, heirlooms, cameras, and anything else that can be moved into the street so that the census officials may the more easily check the inventory of each household.

The Festival of the Corn is, however, much more than a clerical affair. And, the day over and the night come, the householders invite each other to view their possessions which they refer to, on this night, as gifts. It is like nothing more than a wedding feast — there is much cooking, all sorts of traditional dishes, fine wines, strong liquors, music is played loudly in quiet neighbourhoods, strangers copulate with strangers, men dance together, and maidens in yellow robes distribute small barley sugar corn-cobs to young and old alike.

And in all this the role of the Cartographers is perhaps the most important, for our people crave, more than anything else, to know the extent of the nation, to know, exactly, the shape of the coastline, to hear what land may have been lost to the sea, to know what has been reclaimed and what is still in doubt. If the Cartographers' report is good the Festival of the Corn will be a good festival. If the report is bad, one can always sense, for all the dancing and drinking, a feeling of nervousness and apprehension in the revellers, a certain desperation. In the year of a bad Cartographers' report there will always be fights and, occasionally, some property will be stolen as citizens attempt to compensate themselves for their sense of loss.

Because of the importance of their job the Cartographers have become an elite — well-paid, admired, envied, and having no small opinion of themselves. It is said by some that they are over-proud, immoral, vain and foot-loose, and it is perhaps the last charge (by necessity true) that brings about the others. For the Cartographers spend their years travelling up and down the coast, along the great rivers, traversing great mountains and vast deserts. They travel in small parties of three, four, sometimes five, making their own time, working as they please, because eventually it is their own responsibility to see that their team's task is completed in time.

My father, a Cartographer himself, often told me stories about himself or his colleagues and the adventures they had in the wilderness.

There were other stories, however, that always remained in my mind and, as a child, caused me considerable anxiety. These were the stories of the nether regions and I doubt if they were known outside a very small circle of Cartographers and government officials. As a child in a house frequented by Cartographers, I often heard these tales which invariably made me cling closely to my mother's skirts.

It appears that for some time certain regions of the country had become less and less real and these regions were regarded fearfully even by the Cartographers, who prided themselves on their courage. The regions in question were invariably uninhabited, unused for agriculture or industry. There were certain sections of the Halverson Ranges, vast stretches of the Greater Desert, and long pieces of coastline which had begun to slowly disappear like the image on an improperly fixed photograph.

It was because of these nebulous areas that the Fischerscope was introduced. The Fischerscope is not unlike radar in its principle and is able to detect the presence of any object, no matter how dematerialized or insubstantial. In this way the Cartographers were still able to map the questionable parts of the nether regions. To have returned with blanks on the maps would have created such public anxiety that no one dared think what it might do to the stability of our society. I now have reason to believe that certain areas of the country disappeared so completely that even the Fischerscope could not detect them and the Cartographers, acting under political pressure, used old maps to fake-in the missing sections. If my theory is grounded in fact, and I am sure it is, it would explain my father's cynicism about the Festival of the Corn.

2. *The Archetypal Cartographer*

My father was in his fifties but he had kept himself in good shape. His skin was brown and his muscles still firm. He was a tall man with a thick head of grey hair, a slightly less grey moustache and a long aquiline nose. Sitting on a horse he looked as proud and cruel as Ghenghis Khan. Lying on the beach clad only in bathers and sunglasses he still managed to retain his authoritative air.

Beside him I always felt as if I had betrayed him. I was slightly built, more like my mother.

It was the day before the festival and we lay on the beach, my father, my mother, my girlfriend and I. As was usual in these circumstances my father addressed all his remarks to Karen. He never considered the members of his own family worth talking to. I always had the uncomfortable feeling that he was flirting with my girlfriends and I never knew what to do about it.

People were lying in groups up and down the beach. Near us a family of five were playing with a large beach ball.

"Look at those fools," my father said to Karen.

"Why are they fools?" Karen asked.

"They're fools," said my father. "They were born fools and they'll die fools. Tomorrow they'll dance in the streets and drink too much."

"So," said Karen triumphantly, in the manner of one who has become privy to secret information. "It will be a good Cartographers' report?"

My father roared with laughter.

Karen looked hurt and pouted. "Am I a fool?"

"No," my father said, "you're really quite splendid."

3. *The Most Famous Festival*

The festival, as it turned out, was the greatest disaster in living memory.

The Cartographers' report was excellent, the weather was fine, but somewhere something had gone wrong.

The news was confusing. The television said that, in spite of the good report, various items had been stolen very early in the night. Later there was a news flash to say that a large house had completely disappeared in Howie Street.

Later still we looked out the window to see a huge band of people carrying lighted torches. There was a lot of shouting. The same image, exactly, was on the television and a reporter was explaining that bands of vigilantes were out looking for thieves.

My father stood at the window, a martini in his hand, and watched the vigilantes set alight a house opposite.

My mother wanted to know what we should do.

"Come and watch the fools," my father said, "they're incredible."

4. The I.C.I. Incident

The next day the I.C.I. building disappeared in front of a crowd of two thousand people. It took two hours. The crowd stood silently as the great steel and glass structure slowly faded before them.

The staff who were evacuated looked pale and shaken. The caretaker who was amongst the last to leave looked almost translucent. In the days that followed he made some name for himself as a mystic, claiming that he had been able to see other worlds, layer upon layer, through the fabric of the here and now.

5. Behaviour when Confronted with Dematerialization

The anger of our people when confronted with acts of theft has always been legendary and was certainly highlighted by the incidents which occurred on the night of the festival.

But the fury exhibited on this famous night could not compare with the intensity of emotion displayed by those who witnessed the earliest scenes of dematerialization.

The silent crowd who watched the I.C.I. building erupted into hysteria when they realized that it had finally gone and wasn't likely to come back.

It was like some monstrous theft for which punishment must be meted out.

They stormed into the Shell building next door and smashed desks and ripped down office partitions. Reporters who attended the scene were rarely impartial observers, but one of the cooler headed members of the press remarked on the great number of weeping men and women who hurled typewriters from windows and scattered files through crowds of frightened office workers.

Five days later they displayed similar anger when the Shell building itself disappeared.

6. *Behaviour of Those Dematerializing*

The first reports of dematerializing people were not generally believed and were suppressed by the media. But these things were soon common knowledge and few families were untouched by them. Such incidents were obviously not all the same but in many victims there was a tendency to exhibit extreme aggression towards those around them. Murders and assaults committed by these unfortunates were not uncommon and in most cases they exhibited an almost unbelievable rage, as if they were the victims of a shocking betrayal.

My friend James Bray was once stopped in the street by a very beautiful woman who clawed and scratched at his face and said: "You did this to me you bastard, you did this to me."

He had never seen her before but he confessed that, in some irrational way, he felt responsible and didn't defend himself. Fortunately she disappeared before she could do him much damage.

7.   *Some Theories that Arose at the Time*

1.   The world is merely a dream dreamt by god who is waking after a long sleep. When he is properly awake the world will disappear completely. When the world disappears we will disappear with it and be happy.

2.   The world has become sensitive to light. In the same way that prolonged use of say penicillin can suddenly result in a dangerous allergy, prolonged exposure of the world to the sun has made it sensitive to light.

The advocates of this theory could be seen bustling through the city crowds in their long, hooded black robes.

3.   The fact that the world is disappearing has been caused by the sloppy work of the Cartographers and census takers. Those who filled out their census forms incorrectly would lose those items they had neglected to describe. People overlooked in the census by impatient officials would also disappear. A strong pressure group demanded that a new census be taken quickly before matters got worse.

8. *My Father's Theory*

The world, according to my father, was exactly like the human body and had its own defence mechanisms with which it defended itself against anything that either threatened it or was unnecessary to it. The I.C.I. building and the I.C.I. company had obviously consititued some threat to the world or had simply been irrelevant. That's why it had disappeared and not because some damn fool god was waking up and rubbing his eyes.

"I don't believe in god," my father said. "Humanity is god. Humanity is the only god I know. If humanity doesn't need something it will disappear. People who are not loved will disappear. Everything that is not loved will disappear from the face of the earth. We only exist through the love of others and that's what it's all about."

9. *A Contradiction*

"Look at those fools," my father said, "they wouldn't know if they were up themselves."

10. *An Unpleasant Scene*

The world at this time was full of unpleasant and disturbing scenes. One that I recall vividly took place in the middle of the city on a hot, sultry Tuesday afternoon. It was about one-thirty and I was waiting for Karen by the post office when a man of forty or so ran past me. He was dematerializing rapidly. Everybody seemed to be deliberately looking the other way, which seemed to me to make him dematerialize faster. I stared at him hard, hoping that I could do something to keep him there until help arrived. I tried to love him, because I believed in my father's theory. I thought, I must love that man. But his face irritated me. It is not so easy to love a stranger and I'm ashamed to say that he had the small mouth and close-together eyes that I have always disliked in a person. I tried to love him but I'm afraid I failed.

While I watched he tried to hail taxi after taxi. But the taxi drivers were only too well aware of what was happening and had no wish to spend their time driving a passenger who, at any moment, might cease to exist. They looked the other way or put up their NOT FOR HIRE signs.

Finally he managed to way-lay a taxi at some traffic lights. By this time he was so insubstantial that I could see right through him. He was beginning to shout. A terrible thin noise, but penetrating nonetheless. He tried to open the cab door, but the driver had already locked it. I could hear the man's voice, high and piercing: "I want to go home." He repeated it over and over again. "I want to go home to my wife."

The taxi drove off when the lights changed. There was a lull in the traffic. People had fled the corner and left it deserted and it was I alone who saw the man finally disappear.

I felt sick.

Karen arrived five minutes later and found me pale and shaken. "Are you alright?" she said.

"Do you love me?" I said.

11. *The Nether Regions*

My father had an irritating way of explaining things to me I already understood, refusing to stop no matter how much I said "I know" or "You told me before".

Thus he expounded on the significance of the nether regions, adopting the tone of a lecturer speaking to a class of particularly backward children.

"As you know," he said, "the nether regions were amongst the first to disappear and this in itself is significant. These regions, I'm sure you know, are seldom visited by men and only then by people like me whose sole job is to make sure that they're still there. We had no use for these areas, these deserts, swamps, and coastlines which is why, of course, they disappeared. They were merely possessions of ours and if they had any use at all it was as symbols for our poets, writers and film makers. They were used as symbols of alienation, lovelessness, lone-liness, uselessness and so on. Do you get what I mean?"

"Yes," I said, "I get what you mean."

"But do you?" My father insisted. "But do you really, I wonder." He examined me seriously, musing on the possibilities of my understanding him. "How old are you?"

"Twenty," I said.

"I knew, of course," he said. "Do you understand the significance of the nether regions?"

I sighed, a little too loudly and my father narrowed his eyes. Quickly I said: "They are like everything else. They're like the cities. The cities are deserts where people are alone and lonely. They don't love one another."

"Don't love one another," intoned my father, also sighing. "We no longer love one another. When we realize that we need one another we will stop disappearing. This is a lesson to us. A hard lesson, but, I hope, an effective one."

My father continued to speak, but I watched him without listening. After a few minutes he stopped abruptly: "Are you listening to me?" he said. I was surprised to detect real concern in his voice. He looked at me questioningly. "I've always looked after you," he said, "ever since you were little."

12. *The Cartographers' Fall*

I don't know when it was that I noticed that my father had become depressed. It probably happened quite gradually without either my mother or me noticing it.

Even when I did become aware of it I attributed it to a woman. My father had a number of lovers and his moods usually reflected the success or failure of these relationships.

But I know now that he had heard already of Hurst and Jamov, the first two Cartographers to disappear. The news was suppressed for several weeks and then, somehow or other, leaked to the press. Certainly the Cartographers had enemies amongst the civil servants who regarded them as overproud and overpaid, and it was probably from one of these civil servants that the press heard the news.

When the news finally broke I understood my father's depression and felt sorry for him.

I didn't know how to help him. I wanted, badly, to make him happy. I had never ever been able to give him anything or do anything for him that he couldn't do better himself. Now I wanted to help him, to show him I understood.

I found him sitting in front of the television one night when I returned from my office and I sat quietly beside him. He seemed more kindly now and he placed his hand on my knee and patted it.

I sat there for a while, overcome with the new warmth of this relationship and then, unable to contain my emotion any more, I blurted out: "You could change your job."

My father stiffened and sat bolt upright. The pressure of his hand on my knee increased until I yelped with pain, and still he held on, hurting me terribly.

"You are a fool," he said, "you wouldn't know if you were up yourself."

Through the pain in my leg, I felt the intensity of my father's fear.

13. *Why the World Needs Cartographers*

My father woke me at 3 a.m. to tell me why the world needed Cartographers. He smelled of whisky and seemed, once again, to be very gentle.

"The world needs Cartographers," he said softly, "because if they didn't have Cartographers the fools wouldn't know where they were. They wouldn't know if they were up themselves if they didn't have a Cartographer to tell them what's happening. The world needs Cartographers," my father said, "it fucking well needs Cartographers."

14. *One Final Scene*

Let me describe a final scene to you: I am sitting on the sofa my father brought home when I was five years old. I am watching television. My father is sitting in a leather armchair that once belonged to his father and which has always been exclusively his. My mother is sitting in the dining alcove with her cards spread across the table, playing one more interminable game of patience.

I glance casually across at my father to see if he is doing anything more than stare into space, and notice, with a terrible shock, that he is showing the first signs of dematerializing.

"What are you staring at?" My father, in fact, has been staring at me.

"Nothing."

"Well, don't."

Nervously I return my eyes to the inanity of the television. I don't know what to do. Should I tell my father that he is dematerializing? If I don't tell him will he notice? I feel I should do something but I can feel, already, the anger in his voice. His anger is nothing new. But this is possibly the beginning of a tide of uncontrollable rage. If he knows he is de-materializing, he will think I don't love him. He will blame me. He will attack me. Old as he is, he is still considerably stronger than I am and he could hurt me badly. I stare determinedly at the television and feel my father's eyes on me.

I try to feel love for my father, I try very, very hard.

I attempt to remember how I felt about him when I was little, in the days when he was still occasionally tender towards me.

But it's no good.

Because I can only remember how he has hit me, hurt me, humiliated me and flirted with my girl-friends. I realize, with a flush of panic and guilt, that I don't love him. In spite of which I say: "I love you."

My mother looks up sharply from her cards and lets out a surprised cry.

I turn to my father. He has almost disappeared. I can see the leather of the chair through his stomach.

I don't know whether it is my unconvincing declaration of love or my mother's exclamation that makes my father laugh. For whatever reason, he begins to laugh uncontrollably: "You bloody fools," he gasps, "I wish you could see the looks on your bloody silly faces."

And then he is gone.

My mother looks across at me nervously, a card still in her hand. "Do you love me?" she asks.

The Uses of
Williamson Wood

1.

The mornings in the Lost and Found were better
than the afternoons. In the mornings she didn't
think about the afternoons, yet the knowledge of
their coming hung behind her eyes like great grey
cloud banks that would soon blot out the sky.

Few people came to the Lost and Found at any
time. Sometimes in the mornings they would have a
businessman looking for an umbrella or a schoolgirl
looking for a lost coat. But few came to collect the
great library of treasure that was stacked in its high
dusty canyons. Sometimes in the mornings she
would simply wander through the great grey alley-
ways between the metal shelves and then she would
visit her favourite objects: the cases of butterflies
that were stacked in the high shelves above the
railway goods yards, the old gardening books on the
top of the ancient gramophone, the strange and
beautiful building materials that lay in a tangled
heap just near the loading dock. She would sit here
sometimes, perched on a bag of concrete looking at
the big lumps of four by two and imagining what
she might do with them if she had a chance. The
wood was grey and heavy, each piece marked with
the name "Williamson" and she often wondered
who Williamson had been and how anyone could be
so careless as to misplace such a wonderful treasure.

She longed to steal that four by two, to grow even taller than her five feet ten inches and somehow put it under an overcoat and walk out with it in the same way that Jacobs walked out each day with watches and transistors and small items of value. Mr Jacobs used the Lost and Found as a private business, as if the whole saw-tooth roofed warehouse had been built by the government for the express purpose of making Mr Jacobs rich.

Mr Jacobs didn't give a damn for butterflies or books or four by two. He cared solely for money, and he cared for it with a fierce energy that she found alien and disturbing.

In the mornings when he spoke to her he often talked about money, its value, its uses, the freedom he would purchase with it. In two years, he predicted, he would no longer use his battered brown briefcase to smuggle goods from the Lost and Found, but instead use it to collect rents in the afternoons. In the mornings he planned to stay in bed.

Mr Jacobs was a small neat man who combed his hair flat with Californian Poppy hair oil. In his grey dustcoat he could look almost frail. In fewer clothes he revealed the alarming strength of his muscular forearms, disproportionate arms that belonged to a far bigger body than his. Sometimes she saw the arms in nightmares. Yet when he arrived in the morning wearing a suit and carrying a briefcase he looked to her like a respectable businessman. She was always shocked, in the mornings, to see how respectable he looked, and how his eyes, peering behind his rimless glasses, had a soft, almost mouse-like quality. He looked like a character from one of those cartoons which feature hen-pecked husbands. If you hadn't known Mr Jacobs you could have imagined him saying "Yes dear, no dear", but then you wouldn't have known about the forearms, nor the afternoons, nor his angry bachelorhood. A wife, Mr Jacobs said, was a waste of money.

She had never known anyone like Mr Jacobs, but she had little experience of people. When she was a child they had lived in a poor mining area where her mother's lovers had tried to gouge some unknown wealth from a bleak clay-white landscape. Around their tin shack were the high white clay piles of other men's attempts. The ground was dotted with deep shafts and for her first four years she had only been able to play in a special leather harness which was strapped to a length of fencing wire. She had run up and down the wire like a dog on a chain, safe from the dangers of mine shafts. It must have been there, in that white hot place, that she had learned how to go somewhere else, to dream of green places and cool clear rain, to ignore what her eyes saw or her body felt.

People do not love those whose eyes show that they are somewhere else. Her mother had not liked it. Her mother's lovers, in varying degrees, had been enraged or irritated by her withdrawals. She had learned not to hear their words or feel their blows. Now, at nineteen, her long thin legs still bore the ghost of their rages, the stripe of a heavy piece of wire, the spot of a cigarette. Yet they had not touched her.

Now it was morning in the Lost and Found and Mr Jacobs was talking about money again. He was sitting at his desk behind the great grimy counter and she was leaning against the wall, hugging herself with her thin arms, her head on one side, her waving fair hair falling over one eye as she watched Mr Jacobs with curiosity. She asked her ritual question with the untiring curiosity of a child who wants to be told the same frightening story once again.

"Mr Jacobs, would you really do anything for money, really?"

"You bet." He lit a long thin cigar and put his feet on the desk. Each time he put the cigar to his mouth the terrible forearms emerged from his grey dustcoat. She thought of octopuses lurking beneath rocks in shallow pools.

"Would you walk naked in the street for a thousand dollars?"

"I'd do it for five hundred, doll."

"You'd go to jail."

"No, I'd be fined. I could pay the fine and still make a profit."

"Would you drink, you know . . ." she faded off, suddenly embarrassed by what she had said.

"No, I don't know." He smirked. She hated his smirk. He knew what she meant because he had said he would do it before. He had said he would drink piss if there were money in it. She wanted to hear him say it again.

"You know, drink 'it'."

"Piss, would I drink piss for money?"

"Yes." Her pale face burned. "That."

"How much piss?"

"A teaspoonful."

"Forty dollars." It was strange the way he said that, the same tone of voice that he used when he was quoting a price for unredeemed property. It meant he was cheating. It meant, she thought, that he would probably do it for ten dollars.

"I'd do a pint for eighty."

"What about the other?"

"What 'other'?"

"You know."

"Shit?"

She nodded.

"That'd be more expensive. I'd want a hundred and fifty for that."

"What about dog's stuff?"

"Two hundred."

She shook her head appalled at the thought of it.

"You don't believe me?"

"I believe you." She pulled a face. She couldn't help it. The thought of it. The strange respectable little face, the neat clipped moustache smeared with stinking muck.

"Don't pull faces at me young lady." She heard the tone in the voice and began to drift away. It was the nasty voice.

"I wasn't," she said, and then seeing the rage growing on his face, corrected herself. "I was, but I'm sorry. I can't help it."

The confession pacified him. "Look sweetheart, you don't live in the real world. In two years' time I'll be free, just collecting rent."

"Who'll come here then?" Maybe, she thought, there will be someone nice. The thought cheered her. It had never occurred to her before.

"I'm fucked if I know. Somebody. You'll be stuck here and I'll be free just going around collecting rent."

"Oh," she said, "I won't be here either."

He laughed then. "You'll be here my little biddy until you're a shrunken-up old woman. How will you get out?"

She smiled then, so secretly that he started to get angry again.

"What are you smiling about?" He took his feet down off the desk.

"It's nothing," she said, but she was already edging her way along the wall, trying to escape. She couldn't tell him.

"Tell me." He was standing now, and moving towards her. There was really no point in running. She would have to tell him something. Tell him anything.

"Tell me." He was beside her now. His hand took her wrist. What would he do? She began to retreat. She started collecting coloured stones underwater. She liked doing that. Swimming through the pale green water with the bucket, a beautiful turquoise bucket. The stones lay on the bright sandy bottom.

He was twisting her wrist. It was called "A Chinese Burner". He had told her that before. He put two hands around her wrist and twisted different ways.

"I'll get married," she lied, picking up a glowing ruby-coloured stone, "and go away and have children."

That satisfied him. He believed in confessions under pain. He believed in pain as he believed in money. He released her wrist and went back to sit behind his desk. Soon he would make a few false entries in the book, then he would go out to lunch, and then it would be afternoon.

During lunch she retreated into the depths of the Lost and Found. She crouched on the floor, reading in the dusty light: "Harvesting is not easy in a large mango tree, for the fruit must be picked carefully and placed gently into the picking boxes."

There were no photographs of mangoes and she had never seen one.

She waited for the afternoon, placing glowing blue fruit into a pine wood box. She dropped pink tissues into the box and bedded the blue mangoes into it. She loved the feel of them, as soft and gentle as a baby's cheek.

2.

It was afternoon and he stank of drink. He did not want it straight away. He made some phone calls and she waited, desperately flying through dusty corridors looking for beautiful things.

There was so much ugliness.

She saw shelves of dog turds lined up like buns in a bakery. She saw lengths of electrical flex hanging like whips. She looked for coloured stones but when she picked them up they were warm and squelchy in her hands and smelt of unmistakeable filth. She searched on while he talked, looking for the forest, finding at last cool green paths below dripping trees. In the distance the bright blue mangoes shone like magic things and now she walked towards them, her bare feet caressed by a soft sandy path.

He was taking her hand now and leading her into the warehouse.

He wanted her to talk. He tugged at her clothes.

The smell of liquor assailed her. She saw the bottled snake in her mind, soaked in formaldehyde. She hated the smell of the drink.

"Tell me you want to fuck me."

"I want to fuck you."

She said it. She shed her clothes and stood shivering. She didn't see him. She tried to walk down the sandy path and reach the mangoes.

She felt the blow. He liked to hit her. They all liked to hit her. Why did they like it? Why did they always want to hit her? They didn't like her walking down sandy paths. They were jealous and could not see the mangoes.

"I want to fuck you." She tried to say it better. She tried to look at his hard brown eyes which glinted at her behind the horrible spectacles. She felt the moustache on her lips, trying to eat her alive, and she thought of it covered with muck.

He grunted above her now but she was able to feel nothing. She said the words he wanted her to say.

When it was over she remained lying on the old pile of carpet looking up through the canyons of shelves towards the distant skylights.

He stood above her, pulling his trousers on.

"You've go no tits," he said, "it's like fucking a bean pole." He threw her clothes at her. "Get dressed for Chrissakes, I can't stand looking at you."

The clothes fell on her and she smiled at him. "Could I take home some of that wood?"

"Which bloody wood?" He was embarrassed now. He always was. If she smiled it made it worse.

"The four by two."

"How will you get it out?"

"I'll just cut a piece off."

"Alright," he said, "I'll cut it for you."

She'd rather have cut it herself, but she let him do it.

"What do you want it for?"

"I just want it," she said.

"Well get dressed."

As she got dressed she listened to him sawing the wood. He would saw it crooked but it didn't matter, she only wanted it for practice.

3.

It was late at night.

She lay in her narrow bed in her YWCA room, her wide pale eyes following the footsteps in the corridor above. On the floor beside the bed were several very short sawn pieces of the four by two. She had cut the pieces as thin as possible, eking out her length of "Williamson" wood.

She gazed down at the cut pieces, reached down a long arm and picked one up. The cut was straight, but not straight enough. She got out of bed and picked up a piece of Williamson wood again, putting it over the edge of the dressing table. This one would be perfect. She drew the pencil lines using the set square she had bought at the newsagent's. Then, very quietly, she began to saw. Sometimes the wood slipped but when she had finished she looked at the cut she had made. The faintest trace of grey pencil line was visible around it. It was a beautiful cut. She smiled at it with satisfaction.

The rest of the Williamson could be used for nailing.

She took the pillow from the bed and placed it on the dresser. Then she placed the wood on the pillow and began to drive in a three-inch nail. The pillow deadened the noise a little, but didn't make the hammering any easier.

They were knocking on the wall but she finished six nails before she got into bed, taking the hammer and saw and cut pieces of wood with her.

Soon the floor superintendent would be there to complain. She would be sound asleep then, and their voices would not be able to reach her.

4.

He had taken to hitting her more lately, as if he had tapped a new and extraordinary vein of pleasure. While he grunted above her he called her horrible names, names so vile that they broke through the soft pink walls of her jungle dreams and hurt her even there. The passionate blows lay on jungle paths like brightly coloured snakes and their fangs sawed and ripped at her running legs. They would not leave her alone. She built houses on high stilts and climbed into the leafy heart of the mango tree but they were everywhere and pain oozed through the air, covering everything with its black ink.

Her sanctuary was violated. The blue sky was torn to ribbons.

Afterwards she retired deep into the recesses of the Lost and Found, like a hurt animal in search of a place to recuperate. He left her alone then and went to smoke cigars in the front office. She climbed the high steel ladders and lay stretched out on shelves twenty feet from the concrete floor. It was on one of these shelves that she found the old pillow. She placed it under her aching head and stared at the grey metal of the shelf above, dimly recognizing that she had come to a crisis from which she could not escape.

If only there could be another job, but there were no other jobs to be had. Even as he assaulted her, he liked to remind her of this. Even as he bent her arms behind her back, he increased his pleasure by taunting with this hard steel fact, as cruel as a serrated knife.

If he threatened the peace of her private places she would have to fight him. She had never fought. She did not know how. She had been a tree, or a rock, and hate and anger were strange to her. Storms had assailed her, rivers washed over her, but they had not hurt her. Now she lay on the uncomfortable pillow and felt the hate come, like a visit to the toilet too long postponed because of other business. She was surprised at the pleasure it gave her. It came from her in a long slow flood and she felt suffused by a lovely warmth which she kindled with puzzlement and wonder.

Her revenges were far fetched and extravagant but they began to radiate the blue light of her beloved mangoes.

5.

She hid from pain. Twice she avoided him for a whole afternoon, lying on the high shelf just below the ceiling. She lay in dread, barely moving while he bellowed with rage in the canyons below. He screamed her name and threatened her with horrible pains. He shouted tortures through the air and chanted the chilling litanies of dismissal.

Yet in the mornings he was a quiet respectable man with a briefcase. He pretended nothing had happened. She sensed a strange embarrassment about him, as if he knew that he had behaved badly. But that did nothing to stop the tangled schemes she continually constructed for his punishment.

It was on a third afternoon, lying in her hiding place, that her nervous fingers began to explore the peculiarly uncomfortable stuffing in the pillow. As Mr Jacobs began to climb other ladders and look into high shelves three rows away, her closely bitten fingernails plucked at the threads of the pillow. She explored the soft kapok interior more through agitation than curiosity and when her hands touched the bank notes she played with them for a while before she thought to pull them out and see what they were.

There were five hundred and six of them, all single dollar notes.

While Mr Jacobs threatened death, she calmly counted them.

When she had finished, she counted again.

6.

She lay the notes across her bed so they were like a patchwork quilt.

She put them in one single pile and wrapped them in tissue paper.

She spent three of them on a chisel.

She bought a three-foot section of four by two.

She stood outside the bank for half an hour before she got the courage to go in and then she told them what she wanted.

When she emerged fifteen minutes later she had deposited two hundred dollars in a savings account and she had a withdrawal form with her.

7.

It was morning. Mr Jacobs sat at his desk smoking his thin black cigar. She leant, as usual, against the wall. But this was not usual. Nothing was usual. She trembled with excitement at the impossible thing she was going to do. She watched him closely, her heart beating wildly, her fear dominating all other emotions.

Today she would teach him to leave her alone. Today she had money.

"What's the matter with you, stupid?"

"Nothing," she said. She was going to have to say something else soon. Say it now, she thought, say it now.

"What is it?" The voice was already becoming blotched with anger. She was not prepared for a Chinese Burner. She was the one who would give Chinese Burners today.

It was time to say.

"Mr Jacobs, would you really eat dog's poo for two hundred dollars?" She said it as she always said it, with innocent curiosity.

"I told you I would."

"I bet you wouldn't." There. She had started. She had never doubted him before.

"Listen, doll, I said I would, I meant I would. What's the matter with you? What the fuck are you smiling about?"

She had it behind her back, wrapped in a little piece of clear thin plastic film. Now she held it out.

"There it is," she smiled.

He looked at her in disbelief. He took the cigar out of his mouth and put it on the ashtray. He wasn't looking properly and the cigar rolled off the ashtray and lay on the desk, quietly blistering the varnish.

"What's that?"

"Dog's poo."

"Pull the other leg, honey." But his eyes were riveted on the strange little parcel.

She walked over to his desk and unwrapped it gently. It wasn't a very big piece, about three inches long and three quarters of an inch in diameter.

"You dirty little bitch," he was staring at her with astonishment.

"Will you eat it?" She was surprised how controlled her voice was, how quiet and firm and reasonable.

"Two hundred dollars," he said, but the voice trailed off at the end and lacked conviction. He was staring at the turd which lay on the desk in front of him. The neglected cigar was making a strange smell but he didn't seem to notice.

She took the bank book and withdrawal form and placed it beside the turd. She saw then just how little he wanted to eat it.

"It's alright," she goaded him softly, "I knew you wouldn't."

"Sign the form," Jacobs said thickly.

"I'll sign it when you've eaten it."

"Sign it now."

"No. Afterwards."

There was silence then. She picked up the cigar and put it in the ashtray. Jacobs stared at the turd and poked at it with a pencil.

"I didn't think you would," she said.

He didn't say anything for a moment and when he looked up his eyes looked strange and dead. "Get me a glass of water."

She got him the glass of water and placed it beside the turd.

Now when she realized that he was going to do what she hoped, she no longer wanted him to. She saw the flaws in her revenge. She saw that it would solve nothing. It would make it worse. She felt that she had a tiger pinned to the ground and her triumph was fractured by the knowledge that sooner or later she would have to let it go.

"Don't," she pleaded, "please don't, Mr Jacobs."

"Piss off." His little eyes glinted behind his spectacles and he passed his tongue nervously over his lower lip. He bit his neatly trimmed moustache. He daintily pulled back the sleeves of his grey dustcoat. He looked like a high-jumper about to make his run.

"No," she said, "please. I didn't mean it. It was a joke."

His eyes were alight with triumph. "I'll do it, damn you. I'll take your fucking money." But still he didn't touch it. She stared in horror.

It was not what she wanted. It was not what she thought. There would be no pleasure here.

He took the turd like an old lady picking up a lamington, and bit it.

She retched first.

When Jacobs retched nothing came up. He drank the water and smeared the glass. Then he bit again, and swallowed. She could not stand it. It was not what she wanted. She only wanted peace. She only wanted to be somewhere else, to walk soft sandy paths, to build a little house in a warm tropical place. She had wasted her money. She had thrown it away.

Mr Jacob's face was contorted in a horrible grimace. He stood and knocked over his chair and then rushed from the room. She could hear him vomiting.

When he came back he was wiping his face with the back of his hand.

"Now," he said, "sign the form."

She signed it, full of dread. His voice had been like a surgical instrument.

"Now," he said, "give me a kiss."

She ran then, darting around him and fleeing into the doorway that led to her great shelved refuge. He was behind her. There was no hiding. She came to a ladder. It was not her ladder. It led to no refuge, merely to piles of cement bags. She was high up the ladder when he reached the bottom. She didn't look down. She could hear his breathing.

She tried to be somewhere else. She had to be somewhere else. When she dropped the cement bag down the ladder she was already walking down the sandy path to the mango tree. Somewhere far away, she heard a grunt. As she dropped the second bag she knew that the grunt had come from a tangled mess of the bright painful snakes.

"No snakes here," she said.

She descended the ladder beside the path and found the snakes snapping around her ankles.

"Go away," she said, "or I will have to kill you. No snakes here."

But the snakes would not go away and writhed and twisted about each other making their nasty sounds.

It took her a while to mix the cement with sand and carry enough water, but soon she had it mixed and she buried the groaning snakes in concrete where they would do no more harm.

When she looked at the concrete, trowelled neatly and squared off, she realized that it was as good a place as any to build.

She walked off down the path towards the mango tree. There she found some pieces of wood with "Williamson" written on them.

She started sawing then, and by the time dusk came she had built the beginning of her new home.

That night she slept on a high platform above the path, but two nights later she was asleep within her new house.

The moon shone through the saw-toothed sky and she dreamed that she was trapped in a white arid landscape, strapped in a harness and running helplessly up and down on a wire, but that was only a dream.

The Last Days of a Famous Mime

1.

The Mime arrived on Alitalia with very little luggage: a brown paper parcel and what looked like a woman's handbag.

Asked the contents of the brown paper parcel he said, "String."

Asked what the string was for he replied: "Tying up bigger parcels."

It had not been intended as a joke, but the Mime was pleased when the reporters laughed. Inducing laughter was not his forte. He was famous for terror.

Although his state of despair was famous throughout Europe, few guessed at his hope for the future. "The string," he explained, "is a prayer that I am always praying."

Reluctantly he untied his parcel and showed them the string. It was blue and when extended measured exactly fifty-three metres.

The Mime and the string appeared on the front pages of the evening papers.

2.

The first audiences panicked easily. They had not been prepared for his ability to mime terror. They fled their seats continually. Only to return again.

Like snorkel divers they appeared at the doors outside the concert hall with red faces and were puzzled to find the world as they had left it.

3.

Books had been written about him. He was the subject of an award-winning film. But in his first morning in a provincial town he was distressed to find that his performance had not been liked by the one newspaper's one critic.

"I cannot see," the critic wrote, "the use of invoking terror in an audience."

The Mime sat on his bed, pondering ways to make his performance more light-hearted.

4.

As usual he attracted women who wished to still the raging storms of his heart.

They attended his bed like highly paid surgeons operating on a difficult case. They were both passionate and intelligent. They did not suffer defeat lightly.

5.

Wrongly accused of merely miming love in his private life he was somewhat surprised to be confronted with hatred.

"Surely," he said, "if you now hate me, it was you who were imitating love, not I."

"You always were a slimy bastard," she said. "What's in that parcel?"

"I told you before," he said helplessly, "string."

"You're a liar," she said.

But later when he untied the parcel he found that she had opened it to check on his story. Her understanding of the string had been perfect. She had cut it into small pieces like spaghetti in a lousy restaurant.

6.

Against the advice of the tour organizers he devoted two concerts entirely to love and laughter. They were disasters. It was felt that love and laughter were not, in his case, as instructive as terror.

The next performance was quickly announced. TWO HOURS OF REGRET.

Tickets sold quickly. He began with a brief interpretation of love using it merely as a prelude to regret which he elaborated on in a complex and moving performance which left the audience pale and shaken. In a final flourish he passed from regret to loneliness to terror. The audience devoured the terror like brave tourists eating the hottest curry in an Indian restaurant.

7.

"What you are doing," she said, "is capitalizing

on your neuroses. Personally I find it disgusting, like someone exhibiting their club foot, or Turkish beggars with strange deformities."

He said nothing. He was mildly annoyed at her presumption: that he had not thought this many, many times before.

With perfect misunderstanding she interpreted his passivity as disdain.

Wishing to hurt him, she slapped his face.

Wishing to hurt her, he smiled brilliantly.

8.

The story of the blue string touched the public imagination. Small brown paper packages were sold at the doors of his concerts.

Standing on stage he could hear the packages being noisily unwrapped. He thought of American matrons buying Muslim prayer rugs.

9.

Exhausted and weakened by the heavy schedule he fell prey to the doubts that had pricked at him insistently for years. He lost all sense of direction and spent many listless hours by himself, sitting in a motel room listening to the airconditioner.

He had lost confidence in the social uses of controlled terror. He no longer understood the audience's need to experience the very things he so desperately wished to escape from.

He emptied the ashtrays fastidiously.

He opened his brown paper parcel and threw the small pieces of string down the cistern. When the torrent of white water subsided they remained floating there like flotsam from a disaster at sea.

10.
The Mime called a press conference to announce that there would be no more concerts. He seemed small and foreign and smelt of garlic. The press regarded him without enthusiasm. He watched their hovering pens anxiously, unsuccessfully willing them to write down his words.

Briefly he announced that he wished to throw his talent open to broader influences. His skills would be at the disposal of the people, who would be free to request his services for any purpose at any time.

His skin seemed sallow but his eyes seemed as bright as those on a nodding fur mascot on the back window ledge of an American car.

11.
Asked to describe death he busied himself taking Polaroid photographs of his questioners.

12.
Asked to describe marriage he handed out small cheap mirrors with MADE IN TUNISIA written on the back.

13.

His popularity declined. It was felt that he had become obscure and beyond the understanding of ordinary people. In response he requested easier questions. He held back nothing of himself in his effort to please his audience.

14.

Asked to describe an aeroplane he flew three times around the city, only injuring himself slightly on landing.

15.

Asked to describe a river, he drowned himself.

16.

It is unfortunate that this, his last and least typical performance, is the only one which has been recorded on film.

There is a small crowd by the river bank, no more than thirty people. A small, neat man dressed in a grey suit picks his way through some children who seem more interested in the large plastic toy dog they are playing with.

He steps into the river, which, at the bank, is already quite deep. His head is only visible above the water for a second or two. And then he is gone.

A policeman looks expectantly over the edge, as

if waiting for him to reappear. Then the film stops.

Watching this last performance it is difficult to imagine how this man stirred such emotions in the hearts of those who saw him.

A Schoolboy Prank

1.

It is Monday morning and the prank will not be played until seven o'clock tonight. The backyards are quiet: paling fences, trim grass and gum leaves floating in suburban swimming pools. In the middle of this a man stands crying, gulping in the blue early summer air in huge desperate breaths.

The noise is frightening, like curtains rending in temples, ancient statues falling, the woes of generations in pyres of lace curtains and tinder-dry wood.

A neighbour stands peering from his back steps, standing with the shocked uncertainty of those who witness motor accidents.

Turk Kershaw is weeping.

Turk Kershaw is a large man, hard, gnarled, knurled, lumped like a vine that has been cut and pruned and retained and restrained so that he has grown strong and old against the restrictions placed on him. He has grown around them like a tree grows around fencing wire. He has grown under them and his roots have slid into rock crevices, coarse-armed, fine-haired, searching for soft soil and cool water.

He is red-necked, close-barbered, with a gnome-like forehead, a thick neck and a strong pugnacious chin. The noise he now makes is strange and frightening to him and does not seem to be his. It has erupted from him out of nowhere.

Turk Kershaw is sixty-six years old and his dog, old and worn as a hallway carpet, lies beside his foot, dead.

When Turk wept for the dog he wept for many things. He wept for a man who had died five years before and left his bed cold and empty. He wept for parents who had died twenty years before that. He wept for lost classrooms full of young faces, prayers after meals, the smell of floor polish, blue flowers in a pickle-jar vase. He wept because he was totally alone.

At seven o'clock in the morning Turk Kershaw began digging. The ground was dry and hard, too hard for a spade. He walked slowly back to the house to get a mattock.

2.

It was five o'clock in the afternoon. He waited at the Golden Nugget Bar to see what time had done to his pupils. They had idolized him and wished to please him with their success. He had had meetings like this before and he had always enjoyed the display of their triumphs, achievements as smooth and predictable as hens' eggs.

But today, in the gaudy darkness of the Golden Nugget amidst the cufflinks and the high-heeled shoes, all he could think was that his dog had died. He took a large gulp of the expensive whisky, gritted his teeth and swallowed hard. He was terrified that he might cry again. It was ridiculous. It would be seen to be ridiculous for him to cry because his dog had died. It would not be acceptable to these bright young men who would shortly arrive. Yet he could think of nothing but the emptiness of the house without the dog. There were too many empty things in the house anyway: a bed that was now too large, a pottery kiln that was no longer used, a dining room that had been vacated in favour of the chromium table in the kitchen. And now there was a metal food bowl which the dog had nightly nuzzled into a corner as he had eaten his food. There was an old chipped porcelain bowl still filled with water and, on the kitchen bench, a half-empty packet of dry dog food. He should have thrown them out.

It was ridiculous, it would be seen to be ridiculous. He had loved his dog. A man can love a dog. There was no one to explain this to.

Turk Kershaw was a legend and a character and tears did not form part of his myth.

The waitress who brought him his second scotch, a scotch he couldn't afford, did not treat him as a myth or a legend. She saw only a seedy old man in a tweed sportscoat who might once have been good-looking. He was a large man and his leather-patched sportscoat was a little too small for him. He counted the money for the drink from a small leather purse and as she waited for him to add up the coins she wondered if he was an old queen. Whatever he was, he didn't belong here and she managed to let him know it, tapping her foot impatiently while he provided her with exactly the right money. No tip. Fuck you, she thought, you're going to wait a long time for your next drink. She left him disdainfully, an old man with dandruff on his shoulders who ate Lifesavers with his scotch.

Turk Kershaw barely remembered the students who would meet him today, yet he missed them dreadfully. Somewhere in the midst of the smells of tobacco and perfume he smelt the very distinctive odour of floor polish and he ached for the comforts of boarding school where floor polish was the dominant perfume of innocent romances, crushes and night assignations. He had, of course, not participated in any of this but had enjoyed being amongst them, feeling like an old bull in the midst of nuzzling calves.

It had made him soft, he reflected, reliant on the company of others, left him ill-equipped to handle life on his own, made him place all his weight on a dog so the death of a dog was like the death of a lover or a parent. He could see the craziness of it. He had seen it this morning whilst he dug the grave and placed the body of the little fox terrier in it. But seeing the craziness did not stop the pain.

He needed a drink. He caught the waitress's eye but she turned the other way. He didn't feel up to this meeting. He didn't feel he could be the Turk Kershaw they wanted him to be.

Turk Kershaw had been a tough old bastard and had been loved for it. He had taken thousands of boys through the junior school and changed them from pampered little rich boys into something a little better. He had been obsessed with teaching them the skills of survival. He had taught them how to exist in the bush for a week without fire or prepared foods. He had shown them how to build shelter from the shed bark of giant trees. He had forced the weak to become strong and the strong to become disciplined.

And today, he knew, his success with these boys would frighten him as it had sometimes frightened him on other such meetings. They would appear to him as iron men who control companies and countries. The sons of the rich, the rulers, whom he had equipped so skilfully to defend what they had. He had misunderstood the realities of power and had taught them as he would have taught himself. It would have been better to soften them, to teach them to touch each other gently, to show compassion to the weak, to weep shamelessly over losses. Sometimes it occurred to him that he had been a Frankenstein, obsessively creating the very beings who had the power to crush him totally. For he had not been honest with them. He had tried to remake them so that they wouldn't suffer what he had suffered when there was no likelihood they ever would.

They would not shed tears over the death of dogs. He had taught them how to despise anyone who did.

3.

Sangster found the drink that Turk couldn't. He attracted the waitress with one careless wave of his arm, ordered a scotch for Turk and a bourbon for himself and, after a few polite inquiries about Turk's retirement, proceeded to chronicle his success as a husband, father, and newspaper proprietor.

The newspaper had, of course, been his father's

and had become his with his father's death. Turk hardly listened. He had read it all in the papers. The boardroom battles. The takeover bids. The fierce sackings throughout the company after the younger Sangster took the chair.

He was busy trying to defeat waves of sadness and loss with his third scotch. He tried to remember Sangster before dark whiskers and expensive lunches had forced their attention on his slender, olive-skinned face. Turk recalled the early battles they had had, when Sangster, who was fast and skilful in using his mind and his body, had refused to try. Sangster had wanted to be liked and had feared excellence. Turk had taught him, painfully, to ignore that fear. He had pushed him and bullied him until fear of Turk was a more serious motivating force than fear of his friends' envy.

Looking at the new Sangster, he missed the old one who was languid and lazy and imbued with an easy grace.

4.

Davis and McGregor arrived together. They shook hands eagerly and laughed too much. Turk sensed their disappointment in him. He was different from how they'd remembered him. He was not what they wanted to meet. He remembered the dandruff and brushed his shoulder. McGregor saw him do it. Their eyes met for a second and McGregor got him another scotch.

McGregor, stocky, red-haired, no longer blushed as he had when his name was mentioned in class. He still had his bullish awkwardness but it was now combined with a drawling aggressiveness that Turk found almost unpleasant.

McGregor, now the marketing director of a large company, had no idea what to say to Turk Kershaw. He was shocked by the seediness of the man, his sloppiness, his age, the strange puffy eyes. There was also something funny, almost effeminate, about the way he held his cigarette. And those bloody Lifesavers. He turned to Sangster and began to question him about a case that was being heard by the Trade Practices Commission. It had some relevance to the way advertising space would be bought in newspapers.

Turk Kershaw had no interest in the subject. He felt vaguely contemptuous of McGregor and wished the meeting to be over soon.

Davis, short and meticulous, seemed the one who was most as he had been. His good looks had not become over-ripe as had Sangster's. Neither had success made him as disdainful of Turk as it had McGregor. Whilst Sangster and McGregor continued their conversation with earnest exclusiveness, Davis talked quietly and modestly to Turk about his hospital work. And it was Davis, pointedly ignoring the other conversation, who asked Turk about his dog, a different dog who had been less important to him.

The question almost brought Turk undone.

He had another swallow of scotch before he answered.

"It died," he said.

Davis nodded, sensing the pain, but not understanding it. "How long ago?"

"Ten years," Turk said. "You would have been at university by then." He remembered a story that Davis had written in first form. It came to him then. The ten-year-old boy standing beside his desk reading aloud a work that verged on the erotic. He had read it to a tittering class without embarrassment. Turk had said nothing about the story. He had given it an average mark, yet it had touched him, it had been a strange eruption from a sea of mediocrity. Why had he given it an average mark? Had he been embarrassed too? Why had he wished to discourage him?

McGregor was talking about some ideas he had to stop the problem of dole cheats. Sangster was obviously bored with the conversation. He was staring intently at a Malaysian air hostess who was drinking alone at the next table.

"Did you get another one?" Davis asked.

"Another what . . . I'm sorry." Turk had been watching the air hostess smile at Sangster and had been pleased to note McGregor's annoyance when he saw the same thing.

"Another dog."

The word cut into him. He thought, I must not think of the metal dish. And then immediately he thought of it, and the chipped water bowl and the small grave, and the shed hair on the bedclothes, and the weight of the dog when it came to lie on his bed after the fire had gone cold at night.

He swallowed and sucked in his breath. "It died too, I'm afraid." He looked at Davis. He wondered if Davis understood anything. He had a sensitive face. It was a face his patients would have trusted. Davis listened to Turk, and his dark brown eyes never left his face. "This morning . . . I . . . had to bury him." Turk tried to smile, but he was too distressed and didn't trust himself to say more. He could handle it. He would handle it. He had drunk too much, but he would handle it because there was no way not to handle it. Turk Kershaw did not weep.

He blew his nose and caught Sangster looking at him warily. The air hostess had left. McGregor was talking to the waitress.

Then Davis did something which he had not expected. He put his hand on Turk's shoulder and said, "I'm sorry."

It was because of the concern, the kindness, the surgeon's understanding of the total emptiness that he now felt that his defences crumbled. It was because of this that he now cried, very quietly, holding his snot-wet handkerchief to his eyes.

It did not last long. But when he had put his handkerchief back in his pocket the table had new drinks on it, there was a clean ashtray, and everyone seemed uncomfortable.

The awkwardness of the situation summoned up reserves in Turk that he had thought long gone. With red eyes and a blocked nose he fought his way out of his sentimentality, his loneliness, his empty house, and began to ease the conversation back to normality by helping them talk about what they wanted to talk about: the school, its characters, the people they had all once known.

He was impatient and in a hurry to settle things, and it was this haste which made his first choice such a bad one. For he turned to McGregor and said, "Tell me Mac, do you ever see Masterton?"

It was only when he saw McGregor redden till his face was the bright crimson he had shown so readily at the age of twelve that he realized what he had said and how unacceptable the memory must be to McGregor. Masterton had been several years younger than McGregor, a blonde boy with fine exquisite features, long lashes, and a prettiness of a type that is more commonly admired in females. McGregor had loved him hotly, chastely, with puzzled intensity. Their friendship had been one of those small, delightful scandals but one which had lasted longer than most. Turk had known all this but had never thought anything of it, had enjoyed it all, had watched the young lovers with the protective happiness of a parent. In his haste it had not occurred to him that McGregor might wish to forget it.

Nor had it occurred to him that talk of Masterton and McGregor might make Sangster and Davis more than a little uncomfortable. For they too had had their affairs of the heart and simpler more obvious releases of adolescent lust.

So they found themselves, all three, confronted with things they had no wish to remember. They did not wish to know that they had sucked the cocks of boys who had grown up to be married men or that they had loved other boys in the peculiarly intense way that the marketing director had loved Masterton.

Davis's foot accidently touched Sangster's leg and he withdrew it quickly as if stung.

Sangster, the newspaper proprietor, had no wish to remember that he had coated his cock with vaseline hair tonic and slipped it gently into Davis, the surgeon's, arse. Nor did Davis wish to remember the hot painful wonder of it, the shameful perplexing door of a world he had not known existed.

None of the young men who sat at this table with Turk Kershaw wanted to recall the euphemistic way they had come to proposition one another by saying "Let's inspect the plumbing", which was delightfully ambiguous for them and meant, on the simplest level, crawling beneath the locker rooms, the dark damp space beneath the floor where they made love from curiosity and Sunday boredom and hot adolescent need.

It had been another world, another time, with other rules.

Now in the Golden Nugget Bar they experienced the fear of dreams where you walk naked into crowded churches.

They looked at Turk Kershaw and saw that he was, in spite of his obvious discomfort, smiling. There was a twinkle in his red eyes. And they knew that a hundred pieces of gossip and scandal were contained in that great domed head. He was ridiculous in his dirty old sportscoat. His sleeves were too short. His shirt was not properly ironed. He moved his hands in ways which were not conventionally masculine. If he had not been Turk Kershaw they would never have spoken to him. But there he was, sitting across the table, a glimmer of a smile betraying the dirty secrets he still carried with him. They looked at Turk Kershaw and could not forgive him for being their past.

5.

It was McGregor who was most angry with Turk. He had been made to look a fool and he could not forgive that. He had become the master of both the cudgel and the stiletto, using both of them with equal skill. He had learned the art of the lethal memo and knew how to maximize its effects: who to send copies to and how to list their names in orders both ingratiating and insulting. He had become an expert in detecting weaknesses and never hesitated to hit the weak spots when the moment was right. He had had his predecessor fired and he would be managing director within two years. He no longer remembered that it was Turk himself who had first shown him the benefits of intelligent analysis of your enemies' weaknesses. It was Turk who had coached McGregor's bullish bowling, and had made him look at each batsman as a separate problem. "Pick the weakness," Turk had said, "everybody has a weak point. When you've found it, pound away at it."

So now McGregor waited while the others played "remember when". And when he was ready he took advantage of a natural pause in the conversation. He smiled at Turk and said, "Remember how you used to get the kids doing exercises in the morning, in front of your bedroom window?"

He drew blood. He watched with satisfaction as the colour came into Turk's face. He reacted to the colour like a shark tasting blood in the water. He attacked politely, never once abandoning his perfect manners.

"Why did you get them to do it in front of your

bedroom window? Frankly," he smiled, "I find that curious."

Turk watched him warily. He saw, out of the corner of his eye, Sangster grinning broadly. "I saw no reason to get out of bed simply because you lot couldn't behave yourselves. The punishment was for you, not me."

He looked at Davis. Davis looked away. He looked to Sangster. Was Sangster for him or against him? McGregor folded his arms and smiled complacently.

"Come on Turk," said Sangster, "you've got to admit, it's a bit strange when you look at it. Lying in bed watching twelve-year-old boys doing their exercises. In their underwear."

Even as they spoke they began to wonder if it wasn't true. Was it possible that Turk Kershaw was an old queen? They watched for other clues now, although the thought itself shocked them. For now they remembered how Turk had wrestled with them at night when he had come round to put the lights out, how they had attempted, four or five at a time, to overpower him. They thought of themselves as boys wrestling with an old queen. They felt foolish and disgusted with themselves and it was finally Davis (you too Davis, thought Turk) who said: "You used to like wrestling."

Turk reddened again. He watched their smiling faces and detested them. He thought of their wives whom he had seen in the social pages of *Vogue* which he bought for just this reason. He saw the wives, one as beautiful as the next and almost identical in their style, each reduced to a charming doll in the small black and white photographs. While the men came to show the marks of character and experience on their faces the women paid fortunes so that their experience and pain didn't show, so they looked, each one, like people who had discovered nothing. And when, finally, their lives burst out through the treatments and the creams and showed on their faces they would feel it was the beginning of the end. He felt pity for the wives with their swimming pool parties and charity balls and anger at their husbands who displayed their deeds and emotions so proudly on their faces yet refused to allow their wives the same privileges.

"No," he said slowly with a quietness they all remembered with not some little fear. "No, it was you who enjoyed the wrestling." He watched them, one by one, saw their anger and apprehension, hesitated, and finally decided it wiser not to say the words that were already formed in his mind: your little dicks were stiff with excitement.

They paused then, aware of a new strength in him. They watched him carefully and found no weakness. The wound had closed.

Sangster had none of McGregor's political sense. It had never been necessary for him to have any. So now he continued where the other held back. "Tell us," he said, toying with his drink, "where you buried your dog."

Turk looked at him with narrowed eyes. He felt Davis shift uneasily in his chair. "I buried the dog," he said, "beneath the fig tree in the back yard of my house." His head was perfectly clear now and he would not weep. He was vulnerable to pity or love but not to a crude bullying attack like that.

There was silence at the table then. At other

tables the habitués of the Golden Nugget conducted their business, boasted, made assignations and confessions and went to the telephone to tell lies with complicated plots.

The attack on Turk had lost its momentum and the three students were temporarily marooned in the midst of battle, nervous, embarrassed by what they had done.

But McGregor wouldn't give up. While Turk was looking for his matches McGregor looked across at Sangster and made a limp-wristed caricature of a homosexual.

Turk saw it.

McGregor smiled back insultingly.

Turk stood, slowly, feeling the weight of the whisky for the first time.

McGregor waited.

"McGregor," Turk smiled, "surely, if you're honest, you'll admit that you miss Masterton. He did have such a firm little arse."

He walked from the bar before McGregor could recover, full of rage yet not for a second denying the pleasure he felt in saying the unsayable.

In the bar three successful men in their early thirties stayed to plan their revenge.

It was not a revenge at all, the way they discussed it.

It was a prank.

6.

Sangster's Mercedes arrived at the house before Turk's bus could hope to. Davis, unsure and worried, lost courage at the last moment and sat in the car. He was beginning to feel sick and had no appetite for what was planned. He remembered a childhood afternoon when he had fired air-rifle pellets into a large, slow-moving lizard, only realizing the atrocity he was committing after he had fired twenty slugs into the slow body and saw the blood spots and the open eyes of the terribly silent being which stubbornly refused to die.

He waited in the dark street, fearful of both Turk's arrival and his friends' activity. He considered leaving but he lacked the courage, just as he had lacked the courage to speak against the prank.

In the gloom he saw Sangster and McGregor carrying something. Their laughter was sharp and clear.

They were on the porch now. He heard the giggling, and then the hammering as they nailed the muddy body of Turk's fox terrier to his front door.

They made him come then, to admire the work.

The surgeon in the dark suit walked up the steps of the house where he joined a marketing director and a newspaper proprietor in looking at the body of a dead dog nailed to a door.

At that moment they were not to know that they had made an enduring nightmare for themselves, that the staring eyes of the dead dog would peer into the dirty corners of their puzzled dreams for many years to come.

For the people they continued to make love to in their dreams did not always have vaginas and the dog looked on, its tongue lewdly lolling out, observing it all.

The Chance

1.

It was three summers since the Fastalogians had arrived to set up the Genetic Lottery, but it had got so no one gave a damn about what season it was. It was hot. It was steamy. I spent my days in furies and tempers, half-drunk. A six-pack of beer got me to sleep. I didn't have the money for more fanciful drugs and I should have been saving for a Chance. But to save the dollars for a Chance meant six months without grog or any other solace.

There were nights, bitter and lonely, when I felt beyond the Fastalogian alternative, and ready for the other one, to join the Leapers in their suicidal drops from the roofs of buildings and the girders of bridges. I had witnessed a dozen or more. They fell like over-ripe fruit from the rotten trees of a forgotten orchard.

I was overwhelmed by a feeling of great loss. I yearned for lost time, lost childhoods, seasons for Chrissake, the time when peaches are ripe, the time when the river drops after the snow has all melted and it's just low enough to wade and the water freezes your balls and you can walk for miles with little pale crayfish scuttling backwards away from your black-booted feet. Also you can use a dragonfly larva as live bait, casting it out gently and letting it drift downstream to where big old brown frontation they became much less pleasant, turning curiously evasive while their voices assumed a high-pitched, nasal, wheedling characteristic.)

In appearance they were so much less threatening than the Americans. Their clothes were worn badly, ill-fitting, often with childish mistakes, like buttoning the third button through the fourth buttonhole. They seemed to us to be lonely and puzzled and even while they controlled us we managed to feel a smiling superiority to them. Their music was not the music of an inhuman oppressor. It had surprising fervour, like Hungarian rhapsodies. One was reminded of Bartok, and wondered about the feelings of beings so many light years from home.

Their business was the Genetic Lottery or The Chance, whatever you cared to call it. It was, of course, a trick, but we had nothing to question them with. We had only accusations, suspicions, fears that things were not as they were described. If they told us that we could buy a second or third Chance in the lottery most of us took it, even if we didn't know how it worked, or if it worked the way they said it did.

We were used to not understanding. It had become a habit with the Americans who had left us with a technology we could neither control nor understand. So our failure to grasp the technicalities or even the principles of the Genetic Lottery in no way prevented us from embracing it enthusiastically. After all, we had never grasped the technicalities of the television sets the Americans sold us. Our curiosity about how things worked had atrophied to such an extent that few of us bothered with understanding such things as how the tides worked and why some trees lost their leaves in autumn. It was enough that someone somewhere understood these things. Thus we had no interest in the table of elements that make up all matter, nor in the names of the atomic sub-particles our very bodies were built from. Such was the way we were prepared, like South Sea Islanders, like yearning gnostics waiting to be pointed in the direction of the first tin shed called "God".

So now for two thousand inter-galactic dollars (IG$2,000) we could go in the Lottery and come out with a different age, a different body, a different voice and still carry our memories (allowing for a little leakage) more or less intact.

It proved the last straw. The total embrace of a cancerous philosophy of change. The populace became like mercury in each other's minds and arms. Institutions that had proved the very basis of our society (the family, the neighbourhood, marriage) cracked and split apart in the face of a new shrill current of desperate selfishness. The city itself stood like an external endorsement to this internal collapse and recalled the most exotic places (Calcutta, for instance) where the rich had once journeyed to experience the thrilling stink of poverty, the smell of danger, and the just-contained threat of violence born of envy.

Here also were the signs of fragmentation, of religious confusion, of sects decadent and strict. Wild-haired holymen in loincloths, palm-readers, seers, revolutionaries without followings (the Hups, the Namers, the L.A.K.). Gurus in helicopters flew through the air, whilst bandits roamed the countryside in search of travellers who were no longer intent on adventure and the beauty of nature, but were forced to travel by necessity and who moved in nervous groups, well-armed and thankful to be alive when they returned.

It was an edgy and distrustful group of people that made up our society, motivated by nothing but their self-preservation and their blind belief in their next Chance. To the Fastalogians they were nothing but cattle. Their sole function was to provide a highly favourable inter-galactic balance of payments.

It was through these streets that I strode, muttering, continually on the verge of either anger or tears. I was cut adrift, unconnected. My face in the mirror at morning was not the face that my mind had started living with. It was a battered, red, broken-nosed face, marked by great quizzical eyebrows, intense black eyes, and tangled wiry hair. I had been through the lottery and lost. I had got myself the body of an ageing street-fighter. It was a body built to contain furies. It suited me. The arrogant Gurus and the ugly Hups stepped aside when I stormed down their streets on my daily course between the boarding house where I lived to the Department of Parks where I was employed as a gardener. I didn't work much. I played cards with the others. The botanical gardens were slowly being choked by "Burning Glory", a prickly crimson flowering bush the Fastalogians had imported either by accident or design. It was our job to remove it. Instead, we used it as cover for our cheating card games. Behind its red blazing hedges we lied and fought and, on occasion, fornicated. We were not a pretty sight.

It was from here that I walked back to the boarding house with my beer under my arm, and it was on a Tuesday afternoon that I saw her, just beyond the gardens and a block down from the Chance Centre in Grove Street. She was sitting on the footpath with a body beside her, an old man, his hair white and wispy, his face brown and wrinkled like a walnut. He was dressed very formally in a three-piece grey suit and had an old-fashioned watch chain across the waistcoat. I assumed that the corpse was her grandfather. Since the puppet government had dropped its funeral assistance plan this was how poor people raised money for funerals. It was a common sight to see dead bodies in rented suits being displayed on the footpaths. So it was not the old man who attracted my attention but the young woman who sat beside him.

"Money," she said, "money for an old man to lie in peace."

I stopped willingly. She had her dark hair cut quite short and rather badly. Her eyebrows were full, but perfectly arched, her features were saved from being too regular by a mouth that was wider than average. She wore a khaki shirt, a navy blue jacket, filthy trousers and a small gold earring in her right ear.

"I've only got beer," I said, "I've spent all my money on beer."

She grinned a broad and beautiful grin which illuminated her face and made me echo it.

"I'd settle for a beer." And I was surprised to hear shyness.

I sat down on the footpath and we opened the six-pack. Am I being sentimental when I say I shared my beer without calculation? That I sought nothing? It seems unlikely for I had some grasping habits as you'll see soon enough. But I remember nothing of the sort, only that I liked the way she opened the beer bottle. Her hands were large, a bit messed-up. She hooked a broken-nailed finger into the ring-pull and had it off without even looking at what she was doing.

She took a big swallow, wiped her mouth with the back of her hand and said: "Shit, I needed that."

I muttered something about her grandfather, trying to make polite conversation. I was out of the habit.

She shrugged and put the cold bottle on her cheek. "I got him from the morgue."

I didn't understand.

"I bought him for three IGs." She grinned, tapping her head with her middle finger. "Best investment I've ever made."

It was this, more than anything, that got me. I admired cunning in those days, smart moves, cards off the bottom of the deck, anything that tricked the bastards — and "the bastards" were everyone who wasn't me.

So I laughed. A loud deep joyful laugh that made passers-by stare at me. I gave them the fingers-up and they looked away.

She sat on her hands, rocking back and forth on them as she spoke. She had a pleasantly nasal, idiosyncratic voice, slangy and relaxed. "They really go for white hair and tanned faces." She nodded towards a paint tin full of coins and notes. "It's pathetic isn't it? I wouldn't have gotten half this much for my real grandfather. He's too dark. Also, they don't like women much. Men do much better than women."

She had the slightly exaggerated toughness of the very young. I wondered if she'd taken a Chance. It didn't look like it.

We sat and drank the beer. It started to get dark. She lit a mosquito coil and we stayed there in the gloom till we drank the whole lot.

When the last bottle was gone, the small talk that had sustained us went away and left us in an uneasy area of silence. Now suspicion hit me with its fire-hot pinpricks. I had been conned for my beer. I would go home and lie awake without its benefits. It would be a hot sleepless night and I would curse myself for my gullibility. I, who was shrewd and untrickable, had been tricked.

But she stood and stretched and said, "Come on, now I've drunk your beer, I'll buy you a meal."

We walked away and left the body for whoever wanted it. I never saw the old man again.

The next day he was gone.

2.

I cannot explain what it was like to sit in a restaurant with a woman. I felt embarrassed, awkward, and so pleased that I couldn't put one foot straight in front of the other.

I fancy I was graciously old-fashioned.

I pulled out her chair for her, I remember, and saw the look she shot me, both pleased and alarmed. It was a shocked, fast flick of the eyes. Possibly she sensed the powerful fantasies that lonely men create, steel columns of passion appended with leather straps and tiny mirrors.

It was nearly a year since I'd talked to a woman, and that one stole my money and even managed to lift two blankets from my sleeping body. Twelve dull stupid drugged and drunken months had passed, dissolving from the dregs of one day into the sink of the next.

The restaurant was one of those Fasta Cafeterias that had sprung up, noisy, messy, with harsh lighting and long rows of bright white tables that were never ever filled. The service was bad and in the end we went to the kitchen where we helped ourselves from the long trays of food, Fastalogian salads with their dried intoxicating mushrooms, and that strange milky pap they are so fond of. She piled her plate high with everything and I envied the calm that allowed her such an appetite. On any other night I would have done the same, guzzling and gorging myself on my free meal.

Finally, tripping over each other, we returned to our table. She bought two more beers and I thanked her for that silently.

Here I was. With a woman. Like real people.

I smiled broadly at the thought. She caught me and was, I think, pleased to have something to hang on to. So we got hold of that smile and wrung it for all it was worth.

Being desperate, impatient, I told her the truth about the smile. The directness was pleasing to her. I watched how she leant into my words without fear or reservation, displaying none of the shiftiness that danced through most social intercourse in those days. But I was as calculating and cunning as only the very lonely learn how to be. Estimating her interest, I selected the things which would be most pleasing for her. I steered the course of what I told, telling her things about me which fascinated her most. She was pleased by my confessions. I gave her many. She was strong and young and confident. She couldn't see my deviousness and, no matter what I told her of loneliness, she couldn't taste the stale self-hating afternoons or suspect the callousness they engendered.

And I bathed in her beauty, delighting in the confidence it brought her, the certainty of small mannerisms, the chop of that beautiful rough-fingered hand when making a point. But also, this: the tentative question marks she hooked on to the ends of her most definite assertions. So I was impressed by her strength and charmed by her vulnerability all at once.

One could not have asked for more.

And this also I confessed to her, for it pleased her to be talked about and it gave me an intoxicating pleasure to be on such intimate terms.

And I confessed why I had confessed.

My conversation was mirrors within mirrors, onion skin behind onion skin. I revealed motives behind motives. I was amazing. I felt myself to be both saint and pirate, as beautiful and gnarled as an ancient olive. I talked with intensity. I devoured her, not like some poor beggar (which I was) but like a prince, a stylish master of the most elegant dissertations.

She ate ravenously, but in no way neglected to listen. She talked impulsively with her mouth full.

With mushrooms dropping from her mouth, she made a point. It made her beautiful, not ugly.

I have always enjoyed women who, whilst being conventionally feminine enough in their appearance, have exhibited certain behavioural traits more commonly associated with men. A bare-breasted woman working on a tractor is the fastest, crudest approximation I can provide. An image, incidentally, guaranteed to give me an aching erection, which it has, on many lonely nights.

But to come back to my new friend who rolled a cigarette with hands which might have been the hands of an apprentice bricklayer, hands which were connected to breasts which were connected to other parts doubtless female in gender, who had such grace and beauty in her form and manner and yet had had her hair shorn in such a manner as to deny her beauty.

She was tall, my height. Across the table I noted that her hands were as large as mine. They matched. The excitement was exquisite. I anticipated nothing, vibrating in the crystal of the moment.

We talked, finally, as everyone must, about the Lottery, for the Lottery was life in those days and all of us, or most of us, were saving for another Chance.

"I'm taking a Chance next week," she said.

"Good luck," I said. It was automatic. That's how life had got.

"You look like you haven't."

"Thank you," I said. It was a compliment, like saying that my shirt suited me. "But I've had four."

"You move nicely," she smiled. "I was watching you in the kitchen. You're not awkward at all."

"You move nicely too," I grinned. "I was watching you too. You're crazy to take a Chance, what do you want?"

"A people's body." She said it fast, briskly, and stared at me challengingly.

"A what?"

"A people's body." She picked up a knife, examined it and put it down.

It dawned on me. "Oh, you're a Hup."

Thinking back, I'm surprised I knew anything about the Hups. They were one of a hundred or more revolutionary crackpots. I didn't give a damn about politics and I thought every little group was more insane than the next.

And here, goddamn it, I was having dinner with a Hup, a rich crazy who thought the way to fight the revolution was to have a body as grotesque and ill-formed as my friends at the Parks and Gardens.

"My parents took the Chance last week."

"How did it go?"

"I didn't see them. They've gone to . . ." she hesitated ". . . to another place where they're needed." She had become quiet now, and serious, explaining that her parents had upper-class bodies like hers, that their ideas were not at home with their physiognomy (a word I had to ask her to explain), that they would form the revolutionary vanguard to lead the misshapen Lumpen Proletariat (another term I'd never heard before) to overthrow the Fastas and their puppets.

I had a desperate desire to change the subject, to plug my ears, to shut my eyes. I wouldn't have been any different if I'd discovered she was a mystic or a follower of Hiwi Kaj.

"Anyway," I said, "you've got a beautiful body."

"Why did you say that?"

I could have said that I'd spent enough of my life with her beloved Lumpen Proletariat to hold them in no great esteem, that the very reason I was enjoying her company so much was because she was so unlike them. But I didn't want to pursue it. I shrugged, grinned stupidly, and filled her glass with beer.

Her eyes flashed at my shrug. I don't know why people say "flashed", but I swear there was red in her eyes. She looked hurt, stung, and ready to attack.

She withdrew from me, leaning back in her chair and folding her arms. "What do you think is beautiful?"

Before I could answer she was leaning back into the table, but this time her voice was louder.

"What is more beautiful, a parrot or a crow?"

"A parrot, if you mean a rosella. But I don't know much about parrots."

"What's wrong with a crow?"

"A crow is black and awkward-looking. It's heavy. Its cry is unattractive."

"What makes its cry unattractive?"

I was sick of the game, and exhausted with such sudden mental exercise.

"It sounds forlorn," I offered.

"Do you think that it is the crow's intention, to sound forlorn? Perhaps you are merely ignorant and don't know how to listen to a crow."

"Certainly, I'm ignorant." It was true, of course, but the observation stung a little. I was very aware of my ignorance in those days. I felt it keenly.

"If you could kill a parrot or a crow which would you kill?"

"Why would I want to kill either of them?"

"But if you had to, for whatever reason."

"The crow, I suppose. Or possibly the parrot. Whichever was the smallest."

Her eyes were alight and fierce. She rolled a cigarette without looking at it. Her face suddenly looked extraordinarily beautiful, her eyes glistening with emotion, the colour high in her cheeks, a peculiar half-smile on her wide mouth.

"Which breasts are best?"

I laughed. "I don't know."

"Which legs?"

"I don't know. I like long legs."

"Like the film stars."

Like yours, I thought. "Yes."

"Is that really your idea of beautiful?"

She was angry with me now, had decided to call me enemy. I did not feel enemy and didn't want to be. My mind felt fat and flabby, unused, numb. I forgot my irritation with her ideas. I set all that aside. In the world of ideas I had no principles. An idea was of no worth to me, not worth fighting for. I would fight for a beer, a meal, a woman, but never an idea.

"I like grevilleas," I said greasily.

She looked blank. I thought as much! "Which are they?" I had her at a loss.

"They're small bushes. They grow in clay, in the harshest situations. Around rocks, on dry hillsides. If you come fishing with me, I'll show you. The leaves are more like spikes. They look dull and harsh. No one would think to look at them twice.

But in November," I smiled, "they have flowers like glorious red spiders. I think they're beautiful."

"But in October?"

"In October I know what they'll be like in November."

She smiled. She must have wanted to like me. I was disgusted with my argument. It had been cloying and saccharine even to me. I hadn't been quite sure what to say, but it seems I hit the nail on the head.

"Does it hurt?" she asked suddenly.

"What?"

"The Chance. Is it painful, or is it like they say?"

"It makes you vomit a lot, and feel ill, but it doesn't hurt. It's more a difficult time for your head."

She drained her beer and began to grin at me. "I was just thinking," she said.

"Thinking what?"

"I was thinking that if you have anything more to do with me it'll be a hard time for your head too."

I looked at her grinning face, disbelievingly.

I found out later that she hadn't been joking.

3.

To cut a long and predictable story short, we got on well together, if you'll allow for the odd lie on my part and what must have been more than a considerable suppression of commonsense on hers.

I left my outcast acquaintances behind to fight and steal, and occasionally murder each other in the boarding house. I returned there only to pick up my fishing rod. I took it round to her place at Pier Street swaggering like a sailor on leave. I was in a flamboyant, extravagant mood and left behind my other ratty possessions. They didn't fit my new situation.

Thus, to the joys of living with an eccentric and beautiful woman I added the even more novel experience of a home. Either one of these changes would have brought me some measure of contentment, but the combination of the two of them was almost too good to be true.

I was in no way prepared for them. I had been too long a grabber, a survivor.

So when I say that I became obsessed with hanging on to these things, using every shred of guile I had learned in my old life, do not judge me harshly. The world was not the way it is now. It was a bitter jungle of a place, worse, because even in the jungle there is co-operation, altruism, community.

Regarding the events that followed I feel neither pride nor shame. Regret, certainly, but regret is a useless emotion. I was ignorant, short-sighted, bigoted, but in my situation it is inconceivable that I could have been anything else.

But now let me describe for you Carla's home as I came to know it, not as I saw it at first, for then I only felt the warmth of old timbers and delighted in the dozens of small signs of domesticity everywhere about me: a toothbrush in a glass, dirty clothes overflowing from a blue cane laundry basket, a made bed, dishes draining in a sink, books, papers, letters from friends, all the trappings of a life I had long abandoned, many Chances ago.

The house had once been a warehouse, long before the time of the Americans. It was clad with unpainted boards that had turned a gentle silver, ageing with a grace that one rarely saw in those days.

One ascended the stairs from the Pier Street wharf itself. A wooden door. A large key. Inside: a floor of grooved boards, dark with age.

The walls showed their bones: timber joists and beams, roughly nailed in the old style, but solid as a rock.

High in the ceiling was a sleeping platform, below it a simple kitchen filled with minor miracles: a hot water tap, a stove, a refrigerator, saucepans, spices, even a recipe book or two.

The rest of the area was a sitting room, the pride of place being given to three beautiful antique arm-chairs in the Danish style, their carved arms showing that patina which only age can give.

Add a rusty coloured old rug, pile books high from the floor, pin Hup posters here and there, and you have it.

Or almost have it, because should you open the old high sliding door (pushing hard, because its roll-ers are stiff and rusty from the salty air) and the room is full of the sea, the once-great harbour, its waters rarely perturbed by craft, its shoreline dotted with rusting hulks of forgotten ships, great tankers from the oil age, tugs, and ferries which, even a year before, had maintained their services in the face of neglect and disinterest on all sides.

Two other doors led off the main room: one to a rickety toilet which hung out precariously over the water, the other to a bedroom, its walls stacked with files, books, loose papers, its great bed draped in mosquito netting, for there was no wiring for the customary sonic mosquito repellents and the mosquitoes carried Fasta Fever with the same dedicated enthusiasm that others of their family had once carried malaria.

The place revealed its secrets fast enough, but Carla, of course, did not divulge hers quite so readily. Frankly, it suited me. I was happy to see what I was shown and never worried about what was hidden away.

I mentioned nothing of Hups or revolution and she, for her part, seemed to have forgotten the matter. My assumption (arrogantly made) was that she would put off her Chance indefinitely. People rarely plunged into the rigours of the Lottery when they were happy with their life. I was delighted with mine, and I assumed she was with hers.

I had never known anyone like her. She sang beautifully and played the cello with what seemed to me to be real accomplishment. She came to the Park and Gardens and beat us all at poker. To see her walk across to our bed, moving with the easy gait of an Islander filled me with astonishment and wonder.

I couldn't believe my luck.

She had been born rich but chose to live poor, an idea that was beyond my experience or comprehension. She had read more books in the last year than I had in my life. And when my efforts to hide my ignorance finally gave way in tatters she took to my education with the same enthusiasm she brought to our bed.

Her methods were erratic, to say the least. For each new book she gave me revealed a hundred gaps in my knowledge that would have to be plugged with other books.

I was deluged with the whole artillery of Hup literature: long and difficult works like Gibson's *Class and Genetics*, Schumacher's *Comparative Physiognomy*, Hale's *Wolf Children*.

I didn't care what they were about. If they had been treatises on the history of Rome or the Fasta economic system I would have read them with as much enthusiasm and probably learnt just as little.

Sitting on the wharf I sang her "Rosie Allan's Outlaw Friend", the story of an ill-lettered cattle thief and his love for a young school mistress. My body was like an old guitar, fine and mellow with beautiful resonance.

The first star appeared.

"The first star," I said.

"It's a planet," she said.

"What's the difference?" I asked.

She produced a school book on the known solar system at breakfast the next morning.

"How in the hell do you know so little?" she said, eating the omelette I'd cooked her.

I stared at the extraordinary rings of Saturn, knowing I'd known some of these things long ago. They brought to mind classrooms on summer days, dust, the smell of oranges, lecture theatres full of formally dressed students with eager faces.

"I guess I just forgot," I said. "Maybe half my memory is walking around in other bodies. And how in the fuck is it that you don't know how to make a decent omelette?"

"I guess," she grinned, "that I just forgot."

She wandered off towards the kitchen with her

empty plate but got distracted by an old newspaper she found on the way. She put the plate on the floor and went on to the kitchen where she read the paper, leaning back against the sink.

"You have rich habits," I accused her.

She looked up, arching her eyebrows questioningly.

"You put things down for other people to pick up."

She flushed and spent five minutes picking up things and putting them in unexpected places.

She never mastered the business of tidying up and finally I was the one who became housekeeper.

When the landlord arrived one morning to collect the rent she introduced me as "my house-proud lover". I gave the bastard my street-fighter's sneer and he swallowed the smirk he was starting to grow on his weak little face.

I was the one who opened the doors to the harbour. I swept the floor, I tidied the books and washed the plates. I threw out the old newspapers and took down the posters for Hup meetings and demonstrations which had long since passed.

She came in from work after my first big clean-up and started pulling books out and throwing them on the floor.

"What in the fuck are you doing?"

"Where did you put them?"

"Put what?"

She pulled down a pile of old pamphlets and threw them on the floor as she looked between each one.

"What?"

"My posters, you bastard. How dare you."

I was nonplussed. My view of posters was purely practical. It had never occurred to me that they might have any function other than to advertise what they appeared to advertise. When the event was past the poster had no function.

Confused and angry at her behaviour, I retrieved the posters from the bin in the kitchen.

"You creased them."

"I'm sorry."

She started putting them up again.

"Why did you take them down? It's your house now, is it? Would you like to paint the walls, eh? Do you want to change the furniture too? Is there anything else that isn't to your liking?"

"Carla," I said, "I'm very sorry. I took them down because they were out-of-date."

"Out-of-date," she snorted. "You mean you think they're ugly."

I looked at the poster she was holding, a glorification of crooked forms and ugly faces.

"Well if you want to put it like that, yes, I think they're fucking ugly."

She glowered at me, self-righteous and prim. "You only say that because you're so conditioned that you can only admire looks like mine. How pathetic. That's why you like me, isn't it?"

Her face was red, the skin taut with rage.

"Isn't it?"

I'd thought this damn Hup thing had gone away, but here it was. The stupidity of it. It drove me insane. Her books became weapons in my hands. I threw them at her, hard, in a frenzy.

"Idiot. Dolt. You don't believe what you say. You're too young to know anything. You don't know what these damn people are like," I poked at the posters, "you're too young to know anything. You're a fool. You're playing with life." I hurled another book. "Playing with it."

She was young and nimble with a boxer's reflexes. She dodged the books easily enough and retaliated viciously, slamming a thick sociology text into the side of my head.

Staggering back to the window I was confronted with the vision of an old man's face, looking in.

I pulled up the window and transferred my abuse in that direction.

"Who in the fuck are you?"

A very nervous old man stood on a long ladder, teetering nervously above the street.

"I'm a painter."

"Well piss off."

He looked down into the street below as I grabbed the top rung of the ladder and gave it a little bit of a shake.

"Who is it?" Carla called.

"It's a painter."

"What's he doing?"

I looked outside. "He's painting the bloody place orange."

The painter, seeing me occupied with other matters, started to retreat down the ladder.

"Hey," I shook the ladder to make him stop.

"It's only a primer," he pleaded.

"It doesn't need any primer," I yelled, "those bloody boards will last a hundred years."

"You're yelling at the wrong person, fellah." The painter was at the bottom of the ladder now, and all the bolder because of it.

"If you touch that ladder again I'll have the civil police here." He backed into the street and shook his finger at me. "They'll do you, my friend, so just watch it."

I slammed the window shut and locked it for good measure. "You've got to talk to the landlord," I said, "before they ruin the place."

"Got to?"

"Please."

Her face became quiet and secretive. She started picking up books and pamphlets and stacking them against the wall with exaggerated care.

"Please Carla."

"You tell them," she shrugged. "I won't be here." She fetched the heavy sociology text from beneath the window and frowned over the bookshelves, looking for a place to put it.

"What in the hell does that mean?"

"It means I'm a Hup. I told you that before. I told you the first time I met you. I'm taking a Chance and you won't like what comes out. I told you before," she repeated, "you've known all along."

"Be buggered you're taking a Chance."

She shrugged. She refused to look at me. She started picking up books and carrying them to the kitchen, her movements uncharacteristically brisk.

"People only take a Chance when they're pissed off. Are you?"

She stood by the stove, the books cradled in her arms, tears streaming down her face.

Even as I held her, even as I stroked her hair, I began to plot to keep her in the body she was born in. It became my obsession.

4.

I came home the next night to find the outside of the house bright orange and the inside filled with a collection of people as romantically ugly as any I had ever seen. They betrayed their upper-class origins by dressing their crooked forms in such romantic styles that they were in danger of creating a new foppishness. Faults and infirmities were displayed with a pride that would have been alien to any but a Hup.

A dwarf reclined in a Danish-style armchair, an attenuated hand waving a cigarette. His overalls, obviously tailored, were very soft, an expensive material splattered with "original" paint. If he hadn't been smoking so languorously he might have passed for real.

Next to him, propped against the wall, was the one I later knew as Daniel. The grotesque pockmarks on his face proudly accentuated by the subtle use of make-up and, I swear to God, colour coordinated with a flamboyant pink scarf.

Then, a tall thin woman with the most pronounced curvature of the spine and a gaunt face dominated by a most extraordinary hooked nose. Her form was clad in the tightest garments and from it emanated the not unsubtle aroma of power and privilege.

If I had seen them anywhere else I would have found them laughable, not worthy of serious attention. Masters amusing themselves by dressing as servants. Returned tourists clad in beggars' rags. Educated fops doing a bad charade of my tough, grisly companions in the boarding house.

But I was not anywhere else. This was our home

and they had turned it into some spiderweb or nightmare where dog turds smell like French wine and roses stink of the charnel-house.

And there squatting in their midst, my most beautiful Carla, her eyes shining with enthusiasm and admiration whilst the hook-nosed lady waved her bony fingers.

I stayed by the door and Carla, smiling too eagerly, came to greet me and introduce me to her friends. I watched her dark eyes flick nervously from one face to the next, fearful of everybody's reaction to me, and mine to them.

I stood awkwardly behind the dwarf as he passed around his snapshots, photographs taken of him before his Chance.

"Not bad, eh?" he said, showing me a shot of a handsome man on the beach at Cannes. "I was a handsome fellow, eh?"

It was a joke, but I was confused about its meaning. I nodded, embarrassed. The photograph was creased with lines like the palm of an old man's hand.

I looked at the woman's curved back and the gaunt face, trying to find beauty there, imagining holding her in my arms.

She caught my eyes and smiled. "Well young man, what will you do while we have our little meeting?"

God knows what expression crossed my face, but it would have been a mere ripple on the surface of the feelings that boiled within me.

Carla was at my side in an instant, whispering in my ear that it was an important meeting and wouldn't take long. The hook-nosed woman, she said, had an unfortunate manner, was always upsetting everyone, but had, just the same, a heart of gold.

I took my time in leaving, fussing around the room looking for my beautiful light fishing rod with its perfectly preserved old Mitchell reel. I enjoyed the silence while I fossicked around behind books, under chairs, finally discovering it where I knew it was all the time.

In the kitchen, I slapped some bait together, mixing mince meat, flour and garlic, taking my time with this too, forcing them to indulge in awkward small talk about the price of printing and the guru in the electric cape, one of the city's recent contributions to a more picturesque life.

Outside the painters were washing their brushes, having covered half of the bright orange with a pale blue.

The sun was sinking below the broken columns of the Hinden Bridge as I cast into the harbour. I used no sinker, just a teardrop of mince meat, flour and garlic, an enticing meal for a bream.

The water shimmered, pearlescent. The bream attacked, sending sharp signals up the delicate light line. They fought like the fury and showed themselves in flashes of frantic silver. Luderick also swam below my feet, feeding on long ribbons of green weed. A small pink cloud drifted absent-mindedly through a series of metamorphoses. An old work boat passed, sitting low in the water like a dumpy brown duck, full of respectability and regular intent.

Yet I was anesthetized and felt none of what I saw.

For above my head in a garish building slashed with orange and blue I imagined the Hups concluding plans to take Carla away from me.

The water became black with a dark blue wave. The waving reflection of a yellow-lighted window floated at my feet and I heard the high-pitched wheedling laugh of a Fasta in the house above. It was the laugh of a Fasta doing business.

That night I caught ten bream. I killed only two. The others I returned to the melancholy window floating at my feet.

5.

The tissues lay beneath the bed. Dead white butterflies, wet with tears and sperm.

The mosquito net, like a giant parody of a wedding veil, hung over us, its fibres luminescent, shimmering with light from the open door.

Carla's head rested on my shoulder, her hair wet from both our tears.

"You could put it off," I whispered. "Another week."

"I can't. You know I can't. If I don't do it when it's booked I'll have to wait six months."

"Then wait . . ."

"I can't."

"We're good together."

"I know."

"It'll get better."

"I know."

"It won't last, if you do it."

"It might, if we try."

I damned the Hups in silence. I cursed them for their warped ideals. If only they could see how ridiculous they looked.

I stroked her brown arm, soothing her in advance of what I said. "It's not right. Your friends haven't become working class. They have a manner. They look disgusting."

She withdrew from me, sitting up to light a cigarette with an angry flourish.

"Ah, you see," she pointed the cigarette at me. "Disgusting. They look disgusting."

"They look like rich fops amusing themselves. They're not real. They look evil."

She slipped out from under the net and began searching through the tangled clothes on the floor, separating hers from mine. "I can't stand this," she said, "I can't stay here."

"You think it's so fucking great to look like the dwarf?" I screamed. "Would you fuck him? Would you wrap your legs around him? Would you?"

She stood outside the net, very still and very angry. "That's my business."

I was chilled. I hadn't meant it. I hadn't thought it possible. I was trying to make a point. I hadn't believed.

"Did you?" I hated the shrill tone that crept into my voice. I was a child, jealous, hurt.

I jumped out of the bed and started looking for my own clothes. She had my trousers in her hand. I tore them from her.

"I wish you'd just shut-up," I hissed, although she had said nothing. "And don't patronize me with your stupid smart-talk." I was shaking with rage.

She looked me straight in the eye before she punched me.

I laid one straight back.

"That's why I love you, damn you."

"Why?" she screamed, holding her hand over her face. "For God's sake, why?"

"Because we'll both have black eyes."

She started laughing just as I began to cry.

6.

I started to write a diary and then stopped. The only page in it says this:

"Saturday. This morning I know that I am in love. I spend the day thinking about her. When I see her in the street she is like a painting that is even better than you remembered. Today we wrestled. She told me she could wrestle me. Who would believe it? What a miracle she is. Ten days to go. I've got to work out something."

7.

Wednesday. Meeting day for the freaks.

On the way home I bought a small bag of mushrooms to calm me down a little bit. I walked to Pier Street the slow way, nibbling as I went.

I came through the door ready to face the whole menagerie but they weren't there, only the hook-nosed lady, arranged in tight brown rags and draped across a chair, her bowed legs dangling, one shoe swinging from her toe.

She smiled at me, revealing an uneven line of stained and broken teeth.

"Ah, the famous Lumpy."

"My name is Paul."

She swung her shoe a little too much. It fell to the floor, revealing her mutant toes in all their glory.

"Forgive me. Lumpy is a pet name?" She wiggled her toes. "Something private?"

I ignored her and went to the kitchen to make bait in readiness for my exile on the pier. The damn mince was frozen solid. Carla had tidied it up and put it in the freezer. I dropped it in hot water to thaw it.

"Your mince is frozen."

"Obviously."

She patted the chair next to her with a bony hand.

"Come and sit. We can talk."

"About what?" I disconnected the little Mitchell reel from the rod and started oiling it, first taking off the spool and rinsing the sand from it.

"About life," she waved her hand airily, taking in the room as if it were the entire solar system. "About . . . love. What . . . ever." Her speech had that curious unsure quality common in those who had taken too many Chances, the words spluttered and trickled from her mouth like water from a kinked and tangled garden hose. "You can't go until your mince . . . mince has thawed." She giggled. "You're stuck with me."

I smiled in spite of myself.

"I could always use weed and go after the luderick."

"But the tide is high and the weed will be . . .

impossible to get. Sit down." She patted the chair again.

I brought the reel with me and sat next to her slowly dismantling it and laying the parts on the low table. The mushrooms were beginning to work, coating a smooth creamy layer over the gritty irritations in my mind.

"You're upset," she said. I was surprised to hear concern in her voice. I supressed a desire to look up and see if her features had changed. Her form upset me as much as the soft rotting faces of the beggars who had been stupid enough to make love with the Fastas. So I screwed the little ratchet back in and wiped it twice with oil.

"You shouldn't be upset."

I said nothing, feeling warm and absent-minded, experiencing that slight ringing in the ears you get from eating mushrooms on an empty stomach. I put the spool back on and tightened the tension knob. I was running out of things to do that might give me an excuse not to look at her.

She was close to me. Had she been that close to me when I sat down? In the corner of my eye I could see her gaunt bowed leg, an inch or two from mine. My thick muscled forearm seemed to belong to a different planet, to have been bred for different purposes, to serve sane and sensible ends, to hold children on my knee, to build houses, to fetch and carry the ordinary things of life.

"You shouldn't be upset. You don't have to lose Carla. She loves you. You may find that it is not so bad . . . making love . . . with a Hup." She paused. "You've been eating mushrooms, haven't you?"

The hand patted my knee. "Maybe that's not such a bad thing."

What did she mean? I meant to ask, but forgot I was feeling the hand. I thought of rainbow trout in the clear waters at Dobson's Creek, their brains humming with creamy music while my magnified white hands rubbed their underbellies, tickling them gently before grabbing them, like stolen jewels, and lifting them triumphant in the sunlight. I smelt the heady smell of wild blackberries and the damp fecund odours of rotting wood and bracken.

"We don't forget how to make love when we change."

The late afternoon sun streamed through a high window. The room was golden. On Dobson's Creek there is a shallow run from a deep pool, difficult to work because of overhanging willows, caddis flies hover above the water in the evening light.

The hand on my knee was soft and caressing. Once, many Chances ago, I had my hair cut by a strange old man. He combed so slowly, cut so delicately, my head and my neck were suffused with pleasure. It was in a classroom. Outside someone hit a tennis ball against a brick wall. There were cicadas, I remember, and a water sprinkler threw beads of light onto glistening grass, freshly mown. He cut my hair shorter and shorter till my fingers tingled.

It has been said that the penis has no sense of right or wrong, that it acts with the brainless instinct of a venus fly-trap, but that is not true. It's too easy a reason for the stiffening cock that rose, stretching blindly towards the bony fingers.

"I could show," said the voice, "that it is something quite extraordinary ... not worse ... better

... better ... better by far, you have nothing to fear."

I knew, I knew exactly in the depth of my clouded mind, what was happening. I didn't resist it. I didn't want to resist it. My purpose was as hers. My reasons probably identical.

Softly, sonorously she recited:

"Which trees are beautiful?

All trees that grow.

Which bird is fairest?"

A zipper undone, my balls held gently, a finger stroked the length of my cock. My eyes shut, questions and queries banished to dusty places.

"The bird that flies.

Which face is fairest?

The faces of the friends of the people of the earth."

A hand, flat-palmed on my rough face, the muscles in my shoulders gently massaged, a finger circling the lips of my anal sphincter.

"Which forms are foul?

The forms of the owners.

The forms of the exploiters.

The forms of the friends of the Fastas."

Legs across my lap, she straddled me. "I will give you a taste ... just a taste ... you won't stop Carla ... you can't stop her."

She moved too fast, her legs gripped mine too hard, the hand on my cock was tugging towards her cunt too hard.

My open eyes stared into her face. The face so foul, so misshapen, broken, the skin marked with ruptured capillaries, the green eyes wide, askance, alight with premature triumph.

Drunk on wine I have fucked monstrously ugly whores. Deranged on drugs, blind, insensible, I have grunted like a dog above those whom I would as soon have slaughtered.

But this, no. No, no, no. For whatever reason, no. Even as I stood, shaking and trembling, she clung to me, smiling, not understanding. "Carla will be beautiful. You will do things you never did."

Her grip was strong. I fought through mosquito nets of mushroom haze, layer upon layer that ripped like dusty lace curtains, my arms flailing, my panic mounting. I had woken underwater, drowning.

I wrenched her hand from my shoulder and she shrieked with pain. I pulled her leg from my waist and she fell back on to the floor, grunting as the wind was knocked from her.

I stood above her, shaking, my heart beating wildly, the head of my cock protruding foolishly from my unzipped trousers, looking as pale and silly as a toadstool.

She struggled to her feet, rearranging her elegant rags and cursing. "You are an ignorant fool. You are a stupid, ignorant, reactionary fool. You have breathed the Fastas' lies for so long that your rotten body is soaked with them. You stink of lies . . . do you . . . know who I am?"

I stared at her, panting.

"I am Jane Larange."

For a second I couldn't remember who Jane Larange was, then it came to me: "The actress?" The once beautiful and famous.

I shook my head. "You silly bugger. What in God's name have you done to yourself."

She went to her handbag, looking for a cigarette.

"We will kill the Fastas," she said, smiling at me, "and we will kill their puppets and their leeches."

She stalked to the kitchen and lifted the mince meat from the sink. "Your mince is thawed."

The mince was pale and wet. It took more flour than usual to get it to the right consistency. She watched me, leaning against the sink, smoking her perfumed cigarette.

"Look at you, puddling around with stinking meat like a child playing with shit. You would rather play with shit than act like a responsible adult. When the adults come you will slink off and kill fish." She gave a grunt. "Poor Carla."

"Poor Carla." She made me laugh. "You try and fuck me and then you say 'poor Carla'!"

"You are not only ugly," she said, "you are also stupid. I did that for Carla. Do you imagine I like your stupid body or your silly mind? It was to make her feel better. It was arranged. It was her idea, my friend, not mine. Possibly a silly idea, but she is desperate and unhappy and what else is there to do? But," she smiled thinly, "I will report a great success, a great rapture. I'm sure you won't be silly enough to contradict me. The lie will make her happy for a little while at least."

I had known it. I had suspected it. Or if I hadn't known it, was trying a similar grotesque test myself. Oh, the lunacy of the times!

"Now take your nasty bait and go and kill fish. The others will be here soon and I don't want them to see your miserable face."

I picked up the rod and a plastic bucket.

She called to me from the kitchen. "And put your

worm back in your pants. It is singularly unattractive bait."

I said nothing and walked out the door with my cock sticking out of my fly. I found the dwarf standing on the landing. It gave him a laugh, at least.

8.

I told her the truth about my encounter with the famous Jane Larange. I was a fool. I had made a worm to gnaw at her with fear and doubt. It burrowed into the space behind her eyes and secreted a filmy curtain of uncertainty and pain.

She became subject to moods which I found impossible to predict.

"Let me take your photograph," she said.

"Alright."

"Stand over there. No come down to the pier."

We went down to the pier.

"Alright."

"Now, take one of me."

"Where's the button?"

"On the top."

I found the button and took her photograph.

"Do you love me? Now?"

"Yes damn you, of course I do."

She stared at me hard, tears in her eyes, then she wrenched the camera from my hand and hurled it into the water.

I watched it sink, thinking how beautifully clear the water was that day.

Carla ran up the steps to the house. I wasn't stupid enough to ask her what the matter was.

9.

She had woken in one more mood, her eyes pale and staring and there was nothing I could do to reach her. There were only five days to go and these moods were thieving our precious time, arriving with greater frequency and lasting for longer periods.

I made the breakfast, frying bread in the bacon fat in a childish attempt to cheer her up. I detested these malignant withdrawals. They made her as blind and selfish as a baby.

She sat at the table, staring out the window at the water. I washed the dishes. Then I swept the floor. I was angry. I polished the floor and still she didn't move. I made the bed and cleaned down the walls in the bedroom. I took out all the books and put them in alphabetical order according to author.

By lunchtime I was beside myself with rage.

She sat at the table.

I played a number of videotapes I knew she liked. She sat before the viewer like a blind deaf-mute. I took out a recipe book and began to prepare beef bourguignon with murder in my heart.

Then, some time about half past two in the afternoon, she turned and said "Hello."

The cloud had passed. She stood and stretched and came and held me from behind as I cooked the beef.

"I love you," she said.

"I love you," I said.

She kissed me on the ear.

"What's the matter?" My rage had evaporated, but I still had to ask the stupid question.

"You know." She turned away from me and went to open the doors over the harbour. "Let's not talk about it."

"Well," I said, "maybe we should."

"Why?" she said. "I'm going to do it so there's nothing to be said."

I sat across from her at the table. "You're not going to go away," I said quietly, "and you are not going to take a Chance."

She looked up sharply, staring directly into my eyes, and I think then she finally knew that I was serious. We sat staring at each other, entering an unreal country as frightening as any I have ever travelled in.

Later she said quietly, "You have gone mad."

There was a time, before this one, when I never wept. But now as I nodded tears came, coursing down my cheeks. We held each other miserably, whispering things that mad people say to one another.

10.

Orgasm curved above us and through us, carrying us into dark places where we spoke in tongues.

Carla, most beautiful of women, crying in my ear. "Tell me I'm beautiful."

Locked doors with broken hinges. Bank vaults blown asunder. Blasphemous papers floating on

110

warm winds, lying in the summer streets, flapping like wounded seagulls.

11.

In the morning the light caught her. She looked more beautiful than the Bonnards in Hale's *Critique of Bourgeois Art*, the orange sheet lying where she had kicked it, the fine hairs along her arm soft and golden in the early light.

Bonnard painted his wife for more than twenty years. Whilst her arse and tits sagged he painted her better and better. It made my eyes wet with sentimental tears to think of the old Mme Bonnard posing for the ageing M. Bonnard, standing in the bathroom or sitting on the toilet seat of their tiny flat.

I was affected by visions of constancy. In the busy lanes behind the central market I watched an old couple helping each other along the broken-down pavement. He, short and stocky with a country man's arms, now infirm and reduced to a walking stick. She, of similar height, overweight, carrying her shopping in an old-fashioned bag.

She walked beside him protectively, spying out broken cobblestones, steps, and the feet of beggars.

"You walk next to the wall," I heard her say, "I'll walk on the outside so no one kicks your stick again."

They swapped positions and set off once more, the old man jutting his chin, the old lady moving slowly on swollen legs, strangers to the mysteries of the Genetic Lottery and the glittering possibilities of a Chance.

When the sun, in time, caught Carla's beautiful face, she opened her eyes and smiled at me.

I felt so damned I wished to slap her face.

It was unbelievable that this should be taken from us. And even as I held her and kissed her sleep-soft lips, I was beginning, at last, to evolve a plan that would really keep her.

As I stroked her body, running one feathery finger down her shoulder, along her back, between her legs, across her thighs, I was designing the most intricate door, a door I could fit on the afternoon before her Chance-day, a door to keep her prisoner for a day at least. A door I could blame the landlord for, a door painted orange, a colour I could blame the painters for, a door to make her miss her appointment, a door that would snap shut with a normal click but would finally only yield to the strongest axe.

The idea, so clearly expressed, has all the tell-tale signs of total madness. Do not imagine I don't see that, or even that I didn't know it then. Emperors have built such monuments on grander scales and entered history with the grand expressions of their selfishness and arrogance.

So allow me to say this about my door: I am, even now, startled at the far-flung originality of the design and the obsessive craftsmanship I finally applied to its construction. Further: to this day I can think of no simpler method by which I might have kept her.

12.

I approached the door with infinite cunning. I took time off from work, telling Carla I had been temporarily suspended for insolence, something she found easy enough to believe.

On the first day I built a new door frame, thicker and heavier than the existing one and fixed it to the wall struts with fifty long brass screws. When I had finished I painted it with orange primer and rehung the old door.

"What's all this?" she asked.

"Those bloody painters are crazy," I said.

"But that's a new frame. Did the painters do that?"

"There was a carpenter, too," I said. "I wish you'd tell the landlord to stop it."

"I bought some beer," she said, "let's get drunk."

Neither of us wanted to talk about the door, but while we drank I watched it with satisfaction. The orange was a beautiful colour. It cheered me up no end.

13.

The dwarf crept up on me and found me working on the plans for the door, sneaking up on his obscene little feet.

"Ah-huh."

I tried to hide it, this most complicated idea which was to lock you in, which on that very afternoon I would begin making in a makeshift workshop I had set up under the house. This gorgeous door of iron-hard old timber with its four concealed locks, their keyholes and knobs buried deep in the door itself.

"Ah," said the dwarf who had been a handsome fellow, resting his ugly little hand affectionately on my elbow. "Ah, this is some door."

"It's for a friend," I said, silently cursing my carelessness. I should have worked under the house.

"More like an enemy," he observed. "With a door like that you could lock someone up in fine style, eh?"

I didn't answer. The dwarf was no fool but neither was he as crazy as I was. My secret was protected by my madness.

"Did it occur to you," the dwarf said, "that there might be a problem getting someone to walk through a doorway guarded by a door like this? A good trap should be enticing, or, at least neutral, if you get my meaning."

"It is not for a jail," I said, "or a trap, either."

"You really should see someone," he said, sitting sadly on the low table.

"What do you mean, 'someone'?"

"Someone," he said, "who you could see. To talk to about your problems. A counsellor, a shrink, someone . . ." He looked at me and smiled, lighting a stinking Fasta cigarette. "It's a beautiful door, just the same."

"Go and fuck yourself," I said, folding the plans. My fishing rod was in the corner.

"After the revolution," the dwarf said calmly, "there will be no locks. Children will grow up not understanding what a lock is. To see a lock it will be necessary to go to a museum."

"Would you mind passing me my fishing rod. It's behind you."

He obliged, making a small bow as he handed it over. "You should consider joining us," he said, "then you would not have this problem you have with Carla. There are bigger problems you could address your anger to. Your situation now is that you are wasting energy being angry at the wrong things."

"Go and fuck yourself," I smiled.

He shook his head. "Ah, so this is the level of debate we have come to. Go and fuck yourself, go and fuck yourself." He repeated my insult again and again, turning it over curiously in his mind.

I left him with it and went down to talk to the bream on the pier. When I saw him leave I went down below the house and spent the rest of the day cutting the timber for the door. Later I made dovetail joints in the old method before reinforcing them with steel plates for good measure.

14.

The door lay beneath us, a monument to my duplicity and fear.

In a room above, clad by books, stroked slowly by Haydn, I presented this angry argument to her while she watched my face with wide wet eyes. "Don't imagine that you will forget all this. Don't imagine it will all go away. For whatever comfort you find with your friends, whatever conscience you pacify, whatever guilt you assuage, you will always look back on this with regret and know that it was unnecessary to destroy it. You will curse the schoolgirl morality that sent you to a Chance Centre and in your dreams you will find your way back to me and lie by my side and come fishing with me on the pier and everyone you meet you will compare and find lacking in some minor aspect."

I knew exactly how to frighten her. But the fear could not change her mind.

To my argument she replied angrily: "You understand nothing."

To which I replied: "You don't yet understand what you will understand in the end."

After she had finished crying we fucked slowly and I thought of Mme Bonnard sitting on the edge of the bath, all aglow like a jewel.

15.

She denied me a last night. She cheated me of it. She lied about the date of her Chance and left a day before she had said. I awoke to find only a note, carefully printed in a handwriting that seemed too young for the words it formed. Shivering, naked, I read it.

Dear Lumpy,
   You would have gone crazy. I know you. We couldn't part like that. I've seen the hate in your eyes but what I will remember is love in them after a beautiful fuck.
   I've got to be with Mum and Dad. When I see beggars in the street I think it's them. Can't you imagine how that feels? They have turned me into a Hup well and proper.
   You don't always give me credit for my ideas. You

call me illogical, idealist, fool. I think you think they all mean the same thing. They don't. I have no illusions (and I don't just mean the business about being sick that you mentioned). Now when I walk down the street people smile at me easily. If I want help it comes easily. It is possible for me to do things like borrow money from strangers. I feel loved and protected. This is the privilege of my body which I must renounce. There is no choice. But it would be a mistake for you to imagine that I haven't thought properly about what I am doing. I am terrified and cannot change my mind.

There is no one I have known who I have ever loved a thousandth as much as you. You would make a perfect Hup. You do not judge, you are objective, compassionate. For a while I thought we could convert you, but c'est la vie. You are a tender lover and I am crying now, thinking how I will miss you. I am not brave enough to risk seeing you in whatever body the comrades can extract from the Fastas. I know your feelings on these things. It would be too much to risk. I couldn't bear the rejection.

I love you, I understand you,

Carla

I crumpled it up. I smoothed it out. I kept saying "Fuck" repeating the word meaninglessly, stupidly, with anger one moment, pain the next. I dressed and ran out to the street. The bus was just pulling away. I ran through the early morning streets to the Chance Centre, hoping she hadn't gone to another district to confuse me. The cold autumn air rasped my lungs, and my heart pounded wildly. I grinned to myself thinking it would be funny for me to die of a heart attack. Now I can't think why it seemed funny.

16.

Even though it was early the Chance Centre was busy. The main concourse was crowded with people waiting for relatives, staring at the video display terminals for news of their friends' emergence. The smell of trauma was in the air, reminiscent of stale orange peel and piss. Poor people in carpet slippers with their trousers too short sat hopefully in front of murals depicting Leonardo's classic proportions. Fasta technicians in grubby white coats wheeled patients in and out of the concourse in a sequence as aimless and purposeless as the shuffling of a deck of cards. I could find Carla's name on none of the terminals.

I waited the morning. Nothing happened. The cards were shuffled. The coffee machine broke down. In the afternoon I went out and bought a six-pack of beer and a bottle of Milocaine capsules.

17.

In the dark, in the night, something woke me. My tongue furry, my eyes like gravel, my head still dulled from the dope and drink, half-conscious I half saw the woman sitting in the chair by the bed.

A fat woman, weeping.

I watched her like television. A blue glow from the neon lights in the street showed the coarse, folded surface of her face, her poor lank greying hair, deep creases in her arms and fingers like the folds in babies' skin, and the great drapery of chin and neck was reminiscent of drought-resistant cattle from India.

It was not a fair time, not a fair test. I am better than that. It was the wrong time. Undrugged, ungrogged, I would have done better. It is unreasonable that such a test should come in such a way. But in the deep grey selfish folds of my mean little brain I decided that I had not woken up, that I would not wake up. I groaned, feigning sleep and turned over.

Carla stayed by my bed till morning, weeping softly while I lay with my eyes closed, sometimes sleeping, sometimes listening.

In the full light of morning she was gone and had, with bitter reproach, left behind merely one thing: a pair of her large grey knickers, wet with the juices of her unacceptable desire. I placed them in the rubbish bin and went out to buy some more beer.

18.

I was sitting by the number five pier finishing off the last of the beer. I didn't feel bad. I'd felt a damn sight worse. The sun was out and the light dancing on the water produced a light dizzy feeling in my beer-sodden head. Two bream lay in the bucket, enough for my dinner, and I was sitting there pondering the question of Carla's flat: whether I should get out or whether I was meant to get out or whether I could afford to stay on. They were not difficult questions but I was managing to turn them into major events. Any moment I'd be off to snort a couple more caps of Milocaine and lie down in the sun.

I was not handling this well.

"Two fish, eh?"

I looked up. It was the fucking dwarf. There was nothing to say to him.

He sat down beside me, his grotesque little legs hanging over the side of the pier. His silence suggested a sympathy I did not wish to accept from him.

"What do you want, ugly?"

"It's nice to hear that you've finally relaxed, mm? Good to see that you're not pretending any more." He smiled. He seemed not in the least malicious. "I have brought the gift."

"A silly custom. I'm surprised you follow it." It was customary for people who took the Chance to give their friends pieces of clothing from their old bodies, clothing that they expected wouldn't fit the new. It had established itself as a pressure-cooked folk custom, like brides throwing corsages and children putting first teeth under their pillows.

The dwarf held out a small brown-paper parcel.

I unwrapped the parcel while he watched. It contained a pair of small white lady's knickers. They felt as cold and vibrant as echoes across vast canyons: quavering questions, cries, and thin misunderstandings.

I shook the dwarf by his tiny hand.

The fish jumped forlornly in the bucket.

19.

So long ago. So much past. Furies, rages, beer and sleeping pills. They say that the dwarf was horribly tortured during the revolution, that his hands were literally sawn from his arms by the Fastas. The hunchback lady now adorns the 50 IG postage stamps, in celebration of her now famous role at the crucial battle of Haytown.

And Carla, I don't know. They say there was a fat lady who was one of the fiercest fighters, who attacked and killed without mercy, who slaughtered with a rage that was exceptional even in such a bloody time.

But I, I'm a crazy old man, alone with his books and his beer and his dog. I have been a clerk and a pedlar and a seller of cars. I have been ignorant, and a scholar of note. Pock-marked and ugly I have wandered the streets and slept in the parks. I have been bankrupt and handsome and a splendid conman. I have been a river of poisonous silver mercury, without form or substance, yet I carry with me this one pain, this one yearning, that I love you, my lady, with all my heart. And on evenings when the water is calm and the birds dive amongst the white-bait, my eyes swell with tears as I think of you sitting on a chair beside me, weeping in a darkened room.

Fragrance of Roses

I have looked for the village in an atlas and cannot find it. It is a poor town, made from the same grey granite as the mountain it clings to. The cobbled streets are of the same grey stone, often wet with rain, occasionally covered with a heavy blanket of snow.

There are twenty-five houses in the village and the old man lived at the very last one on the high side, above the school. The house was as bleak and unremarkable as any other house in the village. But behind it was the most intricately wrought glasshouse, as delicate and weblike as the glasshouse in Kew Gardens in London.

In this house the old man grew roses. It is probable that the glasshouse was warmer than his own mean bedroom and his bleak kitchen. If the ashes in his stove were often white and cold, the furnace for the glasshouse never died through the winter. And in the very worst months he would move his mattress into the glasshouse and spend his nights there.

He spoke Spanish very badly and often irritated the storekeeper with his requests. The people in the village had never had a foreigner in their midst before and after twenty-five years he was seen as more of a pest than a novelty.

His mail was often needlessly delayed by the post

office clerk, an idle and malicious game which gave less pleasure than teasing the old peasant woman who waited for letters from her son. The clerk tormented the old man quietly and determinedly, placing his parcels in full view on the shelf and insisting they were not for him.

The old man accepted this quietly, and called at the post office persistently, day after day, waiting patiently at the counter rubbing his small dry hands together and breathing into them to make them warm. He never complained. He never explained that the books were about the production of hybrid roses, and it would have made no difference if he had.

When his books were finally made available he walked painfully back to his house, a small grey figure who looked fragile and pitiable in this village where everything seemed so cold and massive and unsympathetic.

Earlier he had donated a large clock for the small village school. The gift had been received with embarrassment. A year later the clock stopped. The opinion in the village was that the clock had been of inferior quality.

So its hands were still showing eighteen minutes past seven when two more foreigners arrived in the village fifteen years afterwards.

They asked questions at the post office and the clerk gladly told them everything he knew about the old man with the glasshouse. He even gave them two parcels he had been keeping for over a month.

That night the old man left the village with the

other two foreigners who were members of the Israeli security service.

Later the town was to learn that the small, quiet foreigner had been none other than the former commandant of Auschwitz.

The locals will now tell you that when they visited the old man's glasshouse they discovered the most beautiful rose that anyone could ever dream of. It was twice the size of a man's fist and was almost black in colour, with just the faintest hint of red in its velvety petals.

When I visited the town in the spring of 1974, the rose, or one of its descendants, was still there, carefully nurtured by the townspeople and shown with pride to visitors.

The locals insist that you can smell the mass graves of Auschwitz in the glasshouse, and that the heavy, sweet odour of death emanates from this one black rose.

They have named it "the Auschwitz Rose" and have printed a cheap colour postcard to celebrate their peculiar good fortune.

The Puzzling Nature of Blue

PART 1

Vincent is crying again. Bloody Vincent. Here I am, a woman of thirty-five, and I still can't handle a fool like Vincent. He's like a yellow dog, one of those curs who hangs around your back door for scraps and you feed him once, you show him a little affection, and he stays there. He's yours. You're his. Bloody Vincent, crying by the fire, and spilling his drink again.

It began as stupidly as you'd expect a thing like that to begin. There was no way in which it could have begun intelligently. Vincent put an ad in the *Review*: Home and companionship wanted for ex-drunken Irish poet shortly to be released from Long Bay. Apply V. Day Box 57320.

I did it. I answered it. And now Vincent is crying by the fire and spilling his drink and all I can say is, "Get the Wettex."

He nods his head determinedly through his tears, struggles to get up, and falls over. He knocks his head on table. I find it impossible to believe that he hasn't choreographed the whole sequence but I'm the one who gets up and fetches the Wettex. I use it to wipe up the blood on his head. God save me.

Yesterday I kicked him out. So he began to tear down the brick wall he'd started to build for me.

125

Then he gave up and started crying. The crying nauseated me. But I couldn't kick him out. It was the fifth time I couldn't kick him out.

I'm beginning to wonder if I'm not emotionally dependent on the drama he provides me. What other reason is there for keeping him here? Perhaps it's as simple as pity. I know how bad he is. Anyone who knew him well wouldn't let him in the door. I have fantasies about Vincent sleeping with the winos in the park. I refuse to have that on my head.

"How many people answered your ad?" I asked.

"Only you."

Thus he makes even his successes sound pitiful.

Tonight I have made a resolution, to exploit Vincent to the same extent that he has exploited me. He has a story or two to tell. He is not a poet. He was never in Long Bay. But he has a story or two. One of those interests me. I intend to wring this story from Vincent as I wring this Wettex, marked with his poor weak blood, amongst the dirty dishes in the kitchen sink.

Before I go any further though, in my own defence, I intend to make a list of Vincent's crimes against me, for my revenge will not be inconsiderable and I have the resources to inflict serious injuries upon him.

Vincent's first crime was to lie to me about having been in Long Bay, to ask for sympathy on false grounds, to say he was a poet when he wasn't, to say he was a reformed alcoholic when he was a soak.

Vincent's second crime was to inflict his love on me when I had no wish for it. He used his dole money to send me flowers and stole my own money to buy himself drink. He stole my books and (I suppose) sold them. He gave my records to a man in the pub, so he says, and if that's what he says then the real thing is worse.

Vincent's third crime was to tell Paul that I loved him (Vincent) and that I was trying to mother him, and because I was mothering him he couldn't write any more.

Vincent's fourth crime was to perform small acts that would make me indebted to him in some way. Each time I was touched and charmed by these acts. Each time he demanded some extraordinary payment for his troubles. The wall he is propped against now is an example. He built this wall because he thought I couldn't. I was pleased. It seemed a selfless act and perhaps I saw it as some sort of repayment for my care of him. But building the wall somehow, in Vincent's mind, was related to him sleeping with me. When I said "no" he began to tear down the wall and call me a cock-teaser. The connection between the wall and my bed may seem extreme but it was perfectly logical to Vincent who has always known that there is a price for everything.

Vincent's fifth crime was his remorse for all his other crimes. His remorse was more cloying, more clinging, more suffocating, more pitiful than any of his other actions and it was, he knew, the final imprisoning act. He knows that no matter how hardened I might become to everything else that the display of remorse always works. He knows that I suspect it is false remorse, but he also knows that I am not really sure and that I'll always give him the benefit of the doubt.

Vincent is crying again. I'd chuck him out but he's got nowhere else to go and I've got nothing else to trouble me.

I can't guarantee the minor details of what follows. I've put it together from what Vincent has told me and checked it against what he's told others. Often he's contradicted himself. Often he's got the dates wrong. Sometimes he tells me that it was he who suggested Upward Island, sometimes he tells me that the chairman mumbled something about it and no one else heard it.

So what happens here, in this reconstruction, is based on what I know of the terrible Vincent, not what I know of the first board meeting he ever went to, a brand new director who was, even then, involved with the anti-war movement.

The first board meeting Vincent ever went to took place when the Upward Island Republic was still plain Upward Island, a little dot on the map to the north of Australia. I guess Vincent was much the same as he is now, not as pitiful, not as far gone, less of a professional Irishman, but still as burdened with the guilt that he carries around so proudly to this day. It occurs to me that he was, even then, looking for things to be guilty about.

Allow for my cynicism about him. Vincent was never, no matter what I say, a fool. I have heard him spoken of as a first-rate economist. He had worked in senior positions for two banks and as a policy adviser to the Labor Party. In addition, if he's to be believed, he was a full board member of Farrow (Australasia) at thirty-five. It is difficult to imagine an American company giving a position to someone like Vincent, no matter how clever. But Farrow were English and it is remotely possible that they didn't know about his association with the anti-war movement, his tendency to drink too much, and his unstable home life.

In those days he had no beard. He wore tailored suits from Eugenio Medecini and ate each day at a special table at the Florentino. He may have seemed a little too smooth, a trifle insincere, but that is probably to underestimate his not inconsiderable talent for charm.

Which brings us back at last to the time of the first board meeting.

Vincent was nervous. He had been flattered and thrilled to be appointed to the board. He was also in the habit of saying that he had compromised his principles by accepting it. In the month that elapsed between his appointment and the first meeting his alternate waves of elation and guilt gave way to more general anxiety.

He was worried, as usual, that he wasn't good enough, that he would make a fool of himself by saying the wrong thing, that he wouldn't say anything, that he would be expected to perform little rituals the nature of which he would be unfamiliar with.

The night before he went out on a terrible drunk with his ex-wife and her new lover, during which he became first grandiose and then pathetic. They took him home and put him to bed. The next morning he woke with the painful clarity he experienced in those days from a hangover, a clarity he claimed helped him write better.

He shaved without cutting himself and dressed in the fawn gaberdine suit which he has often described to me in loving detail. I know little about the finer details of the construction of men's suits, so I can't replay the suit to you stitch for stitch the way Vincent, slumped on the floor in his stained old yellow T-shirt and filthy jeans, has done for me. I sometimes think that the loss of that suit has been one of the great tragedies of Vincent's life, greater than the loss of his wife Jenny to Frank, greater than the loss of his fictitious manuscripts which he claims he left on a Pioneer bus between Coffs Harbour and Lismore.

But on the day of his first board meeting the suit was still his and he dressed meticulously, tying a big knot in the Pierre Cardin tie that Jenny and Frank had given him to celebrate his appointment. His head was calm and clear and he ignored the Enthal asthma inhaler which lay on his dresser and caught a cab to the office.

Whenever Vincent talks about the meeting his attitude to the events is ambivalent and he alternates between pride and self-hatred as he relates it. He has pride in his mental techniques and hatred for the results of those techniques.

"As a businessman," he is fond of saying, "I was a poet, but as a poet, I was a fucking whore." He explains the creative process to me in insulting detail, with the puzzled pride of someone explaining colour to the blind. He is eager that business be seen as a creative act. He quotes Koestler (who I know he has never read) on the creative process and talks about the joining of unlikely parts together to create a previously unknown whole.

There were a number of minor matters on the early part of the agenda, the last of which was a letter from the manager of the works at Upward Island. Upward was a vestige of an earlier empire when the company had been heavily involved in sugar, pearling, and other colonial enterprises. Now it was more an embarrassment than a source of profit and no one knew what to do with it. No one in the company was directly responsible for affairs there which is why such a trivial matter was now being referred to the full board for a decision.

The letter from the manager complained about pilferage from the company stores. He apologized profusely for the trouble he was causing but stressed at the same time the importance of his complaint. The natives had less and less respect for the company and were now stealing not only rum (which was traditional and accepted) but many other things for which they could have no conceivable use. For instance a whole case of 25 amp. fuses had disappeared and their absence had put the company Land Rover out of action. The manager was now forced to travel around the island by mule, a sight which caused him much embarrassment and the natives much amusement.

Vincent, cool and professional in his new suit, searched his mind for some dramatically simple answer to this problem, but he came up with nothing. When the chairman asked him his opinion, he felt embarrassed to say that he could think of nothing.

As usual with matters concerning Upward Island,

the matter was delegated to the chairman's secretary who would, it was expected, send the manager a beautifully typed and completely useless letter.

With the matter of Upward Island thus disposed of, the next item on the agenda was considered. This was a problem which caused the board some serious anxiety and was to do with two million dollars worth of Eupholon which was at this moment on the seas and heading for Australia.

You may or may not be aware of the nature of Eupholon. There was some coverage in the international press when the American Food and Drug Administration committee ordered its withdrawal from the U.S. market and most western governments followed suit. During the late sixties Eupholon had been prescribed as a central nervous system stimulant not unrelated to amphetamines. However prolonged use of the drug produced a number of nasty side effects, the most dramatic of these being a violent blue colour in the extremities of the body. Normally the fingers and hands were first affected, but cases of feet, noses and ears were also mentioned in the reports.

Farrow International was thus left with an inventory of millions of dollars worth of Eupholon which it had little hope of selling but which it also refused to destroy. The Birmingham head office lived in the fond hope that the Food and Drug Administration's earlier decision would be reversed. However the drug was still legally available in Australia, and the U.K. office, in an attempt to minimize its losses, had planned a big push on the Australian market. The two million dollar shipment at present on the water was to be sold in the first six months.

Unfortunately the Australian government had banned the drug soon after the ship entered the Pacific. And now the Australian board was meeting to decide what to do with such a large quantity of such an undesirable drug.

The international directive was to warehouse it and wait. But warehouse space in Melbourne and Sydney was at a premium and the cost of hiring space for what might be an indefinite period gave the board members worried faces and expensive frowns.

It was then that Vincent asked his question about Upward Island which, at first, seemed so irrelevant that nobody bothered to answer him. His question had been about harbour facilities.

The chairman reminded him that the Upward Island matter had been settled but Vincent insisted on an answer and was told that Upward Island had an excellent harbour.

He then asked about the company store.

He was told that the company store was very large indeed.

Could it accommodate the Eupholon?

Yes, it could.

Could the ship be diverted to Upward?

Yes, it could.

Vincent must have smirked. He would have felt it childish to smile, and his repressed smiles look like nasty little smirks. So I can see the board members looking with wonder at his face, not knowing whether to be pleased with his suggestion or irritated by the smirk.

Vincent had solved the problem but he was not content to leave it at that and, in a demonstration of his creative genius, went on to spell out the ramifications of this plan.

The problem of pilferage on Upward Island would be simply cured. When the Eupholon arrived it would certainly be subject to pilferage. This in itself didn't matter and would hardly occasion huge losses, but perhaps this pilfering could be used to stop other pilfering.

Assuming the islanders maintained their habits (the manager, in a crude attempt at humour, had euphemistically detailed the effects on several men who had stolen a carton of laxatives) then whoever stole the Eupholon would quickly become visible. Their hands would turn blue. They would not only become visible to the authorities but would provide a living demonstration of the powers of the company to mark those who transgressed its laws.

Thus Vincent explained, the two problems could be solved at once. Pilferage on Upward Island would be prevented effectively and the Eupholon could be warehoused at no extra cost to the company.

It seems likely that no one gave a damn about the pilferage problem, but Vincent was so obviously thrilled with the neatness of his solution and they were so grateful for a place to put the Eupholon that they were in no mood to nit-pick or to criticize the more far-fetched aspects of the scheme.

As soon as his plan was formally adopted and a cable sent to Birmingham with a request to re-route the ship, Vincent was immediately stricken with terrible remorse. He had fallen, once more, victim to his own terrible brilliance. He had helped a colonial power (Farrow) wreak havoc and injury on an innocent people (the Upward Islanders) and he had been proud to do it.

The thought of those islanders walking around with blue hands suddenly seemed obscene and terrible to him and he immediately sent a memo to the managing director wherein he requested that an armed guard be placed on the warehouse at all times and that the man be given instructions to shoot anyone attempting to enter the warehouse without proper reason. He was confident that one wounding (unfortunate though that might be) would act as an effective deterrent and prevent the realization of the nightmare he had created. He investigated the award rates for armed guards and included in his memo a breakdown of all costs involved in the scheme. The amounts were so minor that the matter was approved without comment, although it seems likely that Vincent was pushing the Upward Island idea to the point where it would become a private joke amongst his fellow directors.

Satisfied with all this Vincent went off to a meeting of the Vietnam Moratorium Committee where, dressed in faded jeans and a blue workshirt, he was among those who supported a call for physical confrontation with the police. Excepting the few who suspected he was an agent provocateur, those who saw him speak were impressed by the emotion of his appeal and the fact that there were tears in his eyes when he spoke about the Vietnamese people.

It would be wrong to think that the tears were false or his appeal cynical. Vincent was continually in a state of conflict between his heartfelt principles and his need to be well thought of by people.

I don't think that there's any need to say any more about Vincent's life at this time. The shipment duly arrived at Upward Island and was stored as expected. Considerable quantities of Eupholon were stolen. Several islanders were shot dead by over-zealous guards, many were wounded.

It is thought that the Gilbert and Sullivan revolution which took place on Upward Island last week may well have been directly attributable to these shootings. Vincent himself chooses to believe this, which is no reason for believing that it isn't true. Certainly it was a painless revolution and the small island, against the advice but not the wishes of the Australian government, was granted its independence. The company was expelled and its stocks of Eupholon confiscated. This caused Farrow International no pains at all as by this time it had become obvious, even to Birmingham, that Eupholon would never be acceptable to the market again.

Reports of the revolution have noted the blue hands of certain members of the revolution, but these have been generally described in the press as "war-paint".

It is on account of those blue hands that Vincent is sitting in my room and weeping.

In the year that has elapsed since the first board meeting he has slowly and gracelessly slid down hill. He became more and more outspoken in his anti-war activities until such time as these activities became an embarrassment to the company and he was fired on the direct instruction of Birmingham. It is perhaps unfortunate that at the same time the members of the Moratorium Committee discovered that he was actually a director of Farrow (whose French subsidiary was actively involved in the production of chemical warfare agents) and expelled him for his moral duplicity.

With these two emotional props removed Vincent went to pieces. He departed for Queensland to write but only got as far as Lismore where he was looked after briefly by communards.

His memory of events after this time is either unclear or so embarrassing to him that he is not prepared to reveal any significant details. He still insists that it all came to a climax two months ago with him being interned in Long Bay for assaulting a policeman at a demonstration, but I know this is untrue. It is possible he would have liked the idea of going to Long Bay, but he never has.

Now I can let you into a secret.

This is something I've been hoping might happen as I've worked. Had it not happened, this little account of Vincent's involvement with Upward Island would still have been of some real interest. However, recent events mean that I may be able to pursue the matter in a more purposeful way.

Vincent assaulted me last night. He came home with some people I'd never seen before, demanded I feed them, abused me when I refused, and punched me in the mouth when they left.

I'm afraid that I am now angry with him. I can no longer be dispassionate. The tiny part of me that observed Vincent with god-like pity has gone. I talked of revenge before. I was speaking of some minor bitching revenge of exploiting his story for my own gain. Now, however, I have a broken tooth which will have to be capped. It'll cost me two hundred dollars. My warfare with Vincent has come into the open.

I have told him to go and I will not change my mind. He knows it. At this moment his bags are packed but he is staying to finish dismantling the brick wall, a job he does with sullen thoroughness. He watches me typing over the top of it, a self-satisfied smirk on his face. I'd love to know what he thought he was doing with that brick wall. I'm sure it represents all kinds of incredible things for him. There is mortar dust over the dishes in the kitchen and all the furniture. There is mortar dust over the typewriter and between my teeth.

Well, Vincent my friend, the paper I work for is committed to sending me to Upward Island to look at this quaint little revolution. And now I've got a little background information from you, I'll use it and broaden it in the best way I can. I shall publicize you, Vincent, both here and on Upward Island. I'm sure the leaders of Upward Island will be most interested to know who is responsible for their blue hands. I'm not sure if you're legally responsible but I'm sure you should be.

PART 2

I have led you on with promises of a spectacular revenge, and now I will tell you that there shall be no revenge. Instead, I hope, a more substantial meal awaits you.

In four days on Upward Island I have seen three months' planning come undone. Am I so shallow, so easily swayed? Am I like an adolescent girl, jumping from love to hatred with every change in the weather?

Whatever my mental balance, there is more than a little explaining to do. Vincent is sitting on my bed in the Rainbow Motel, Upward Island. The fan turns overhead. The cockroaches stroll casually across the concrete floor. In the corner, above the basin, a little lizard lies, occasionally making small bird noises.

Vincent informs me that he is a chee-chuk.

He leans back against the pillow and I observe for the twentieth time what I never saw until this week: what lovely legs he has: long, slim straight legs as deeply tanned as rich students on long holidays. He looks so clean, so healthy. His beard is gone and there is no longer anything to veil his fine sensitive chiselled features with those beautiful sad grey eyes. Vincent, did I tell you that even when I was most angry with you I loved your eyes? They are less of an enigma to me now.

We have not arrived easily at this still, calm moment in this little room. We have travelled via suspicion and rage. I have watched him, on other days, as he earnestly helped me prepare my article, providing me with facts I hadn't known about his past, and easing my way into knowledge of his present. He has acted as my guide and denied me nothing and I watched carefully for his sleight of hand as he prepared the scaffolding for his own execution.

But there have been no tricks. Neither has there been remorse, tears, demands, or violence.

Instead I have come to envy him his calm, his

contentment, his ability to sit still and keep his silence.

Vincent left for Upward Island on the day I threw him out. He had been planning it from the time he met me. He paid for the fare with money from my stolen books and records and a number of even less savoury transactions. I can imagine him arriving: bedraggled, dirty, full of guilt and speed in equal proportions, going from one bar to the next in search of someone who would forgive him the sin he hadn't the courage to confess. He had no money, no plan, and existed in drunken agony at the bottom of the big black pit he had dug for himself. He had come, classically, with remorse, but the remorse would not go away and with each day he fell further and further into the grips of despair. He couldn't leave. It was impossible to stay.

It was finally Solly Ling, the new president himself, who picked him up off the floor and took him home. Taking him for a derelict (which he was) Solly set about drying him out. He found him clothes and gave him food and then, sternly, put him to work.

Vincent had never done sustained physical labour in his life. But now he was forced to work on the building of the Upward Island school. There was no alternative. He dug stump holes until his hands were raw and bleeding. He carried bricks until his arms only existed as a nagging pain in his brain. He poured concrete.

He spoke little and never complained. There was a logic in it. It was a penance. He accepted it.

Solly had cleared out an old shed in his backyard and there Vincent, wide-eyed and sleepless, listened with terror to toads and rats and flying foxes and other nocturnal mysteries slither and flap and eat and dig around the hut.

Vincent and Solly ate together, mostly in silence, for Vincent was terrified of revealing anything of his past. But Solly was a patient man and a curious one. He sensed Vincent's education and with one question one day and another the next he finally learned that Vincent was a lawyer and an economist, that he had worked for big companies including several banks. At that time the island council was making heavy weather of the constitution and one night Solly broached the subject with Vincent and he watched with pleasure as Vincent took the thing apart and put it together in a neat, simple and logical way. The next day Vincent met the council. He was patient and self-effacing. Solly watched him and saw a sensitive diplomat, a man who listened to every speaker and was able to see the value of a sensible objection, but who could also politely point out the disadvantages of a less sensible one.

It was a touchy business. The council could have rejected him, found him patronizing, or too clever by half. But none of these things happened. Vincent's guilt had made his nerve ends as raw as his blistered hands and he felt their feelings with a peculiar intensity. He acted as a servant, never once imposing his own will.

His service to the council, however, was but a drop of water on the fires of his guilt. He sat in the old Waterside Workers Union shed where the council meetings were held and all he could see were the blue hands of the councillors. Surrounded by the evidence of his crime there was no room for escape.

He drafted three new prawning contracts and volunteered for the unpleasant job of cleaning the mortar off the old bricks for the school. He painted Solly's house for him and went on to start the vegetable garden.

These acts were in no way intended to curry favour or gain friendship (in fact they were some sort of substitute for wrath) but they succeeded in spite of that. The islanders took to him: not only was he educated but he was also prepared to work at the nastiest jobs side by side with them, he could tell funny stories, he didn't flirt with their wives, and he'd negotiated the best damn prawn contracts they'd ever had.

It is doubtful if Vincent noticed this. He was not accustomed to being liked and would have never expected it on Upward Island.

Given his skills, it's natural enough that he should have been co-opted as an assistant to the council. But that he should be elected formally to the council after only two months is an indication of the popularity he had begun to enjoy. Again, it is doubtful if he saw it.

On the night after his election to the council he sat on the verandah with Solly and looked out at the approaching night, a night that was still foreign to him and full of things he neither liked nor understood.

Solly was a big man. The stomach that bulged beneath his white singlet betrayed his love of beer, just as the muscular forearms attested to his years as a waterside worker. The great muscled calves that protruded from his rolled-up trousers were the legs of a young man, but the creased black face and the curly greying hair betrayed his age. It was a face that could show, almost simultaneously, the dignity of a judge and the bright-eyed recklessness of a born larrikin.

He sat on the verandah of his high-stilted house, one big blue hand around a beer bottle, the other around a glass which he filled and passed to Vincent. The hand which took the glass was now calloused and tough. The arm, never thick, was now wiry and hard, tatooed with knicks and scratches and dusty with mortar. A flea made its way through the hairs and dust on the arm. Vincent saw it and knocked it off. It wasn't worth killing them. There were too many.

As the darkness finally shrouded the garden a great clamour began in the hen house.

"Bloody python," said Solly.

"I'll go." Vincent stood up. He didn't want to go. He hadn't gone yet, but it was about time he went.

"I'll go." Solly picked up a shotgun and walked off into the dark. Vincent sipped his beer and knew that next time he'd have to go.

There was a shot and Solly came back holding the remains of a python in one hand and a dead chicken in the other.

"Too late," he grinned, "snake got him first."

He sat down, leaving the dead bird on the floor, and the snake draped across the railing.

"Now you're on the council," he said, "we're going to have to do something to get your hands in shape."

"Ah, they're alright. The blisters have all gone." Vincent wondered what blisters had to do with the council.

"I wasn't talking about blisters, Mr Economics. I was discussing the matter of your hands." Solly chuckled. His white teeth flashed in the light from the kitchen window. "You're going to have to take some medicine."

Vincent was used to being teased. He had faced poisonous grasshoppers, threatened cyclones and dozens of other tricks they liked to play on him. He didn't know what this was about, but he'd find out soon enough.

"What medicine is that, Sol?"

"Why," laughed Solly, "little pills, of course. You need a few little pills now you're on the council. We can't have you sitting on the council with the wrong coloured hands."

Vincent couldn't believe what he was hearing. They'd never discussed the blue hands. His mind had been full of it. Not a day had gone by when the blue hands hadn't caused him pain. But he had avoided mentioning them for fear of touching so nasty a wound.

"Eupholon?" He said it. The word.

"For a smart boy you're very slow. Sure, that's what they call it."

Vincent's scalp prickled. He had said the name. How did he know the name? They knew about him. It was a trap. Now it would be the time for justice to be done. They would force him to take the poison he'd given them.

There was a silence.

"Solly, you know where I worked before?"

"Sure, you was the great Economics man."

"I mean what company."

"Sure, you worked for Mr Farrow." Solly's voice

was calm, but Vincent's ears were ringing in the silence between the words.

"How you know that, Solly?"

"Oh, you got a lady friend who reckons you're a bad fella. She wrote us a letter. Three pages. Boy, what you do to her, eh?" He laughed again. "She's a very angry lady, that one."

"Anita."

"I forget her name," he waved an arm, dismissing it. "Some name like that."

In the corner of his eye, Vincent saw the headless python twitch.

"That why you want me to take the pills?"

"Christ no." Solly roared with laughter, a great whooping laugh that slid from a wheezing treble to deepest bass. "Christ no, you crazy bastard." He stood up and came and sat by Vincent on the step, hugging him. "You crazy Economics bastard, no." He wiped his eyes with a large blue hand. "Oh shit. You are what they call a one-off model. You know what that means?"

"What?" Vincent was numb, almost beyond speech.

"It means you are fucking unique. I love you."

Vincent was very confused. He slapped at a few mosquitoes and tried to puzzle it out. Every shred of fact that his life was based on seemed as insubstantial as fairy floss. "You don't care I sent the pills here?"

"Care!" the laughter came again. "To put it properly to you, we are fucking delighted you sent the pills here. Everything is fine. Why should we be mad with you?"

"The blue hands . . ."

"You are not only crazy," said Solly affectionately. "You are also nine-tenths blind. Don't you notice anything about the blue hands?"

"What do you mean?"

"I mean you're bloody blind. All the best men got blue hands. All the bravest men. We're bloody proud of these hands. You got blue hands on Upward, Vincent, you got respect. How come you can live here so long and not notice that? We had to beat that damn guard to get these hands, Vincent. When the time came to kick out Farrow, everyone knows who's got the guts to do it, because we're the only ones that's got the hands."

"So I've got to have blue hands, to be on the council?"

"You got it. You got perfect understanding."

"OK," Vincent grinned. He felt as light as air. He poured himself another beer. He wanted to get drunk and sing songs. He didn't dwell on the idea of the blue hands. That was nothing. All he said was, "Where do I get the pills?"

Solly scratched his head. "Well, I suppose there must be some up at the warehouse. You better go up and take a look."

Vincent started laughing then, laughing with pure joy and relief. The more he thought about it, the funnier it was and the more he laughed. And Solly, sitting beside him, laughed too.

I imagine the pair of them hooting and cackling into the dark tropical night, a dead chicken at their feet, a headless python twitching on the railing. Not surprisingly, they were laughing about different things.

Late the next morning Vincent set off to walk to the warehouse. He felt marvellous. In the kitchen he cut himself some sandwiches and on the dusty road he found a long stick. He walked the three-mile track with a light heart, delighting in the long seas of golden grass, finding beauty in the muddy mangrove shoreline and its heat-hazed horizon.

Vincent in white shorts with his cut lunch and walking stick like a tourist off to visit Greek ruins.

The warehouse shone silver in the harsh midday sun. There was something written on the side. As he came up the last steep slope he finally made it out: someone had painted a blue hand on the longest side of the building and added, for good measure: WARNING — DEATH. He wondered vaguely if this had been the manager's work. How gloriously ineffective it had been. What total misunderstanding had been displayed.

He was still a hundred yards from the warehouse when he saw a man, dressed in white shorts like himself, standing at the front of the building.

The man called.

Vincent waved casually and continued on, wondering who it was. The man was white. He had seen no white people until now.

As he walked up the hill, being careful not to slip on the shale which made up the embankment, the man disappeared for a second and then came back with what looked like a rifle. Vincent's first thought was: a snake, he's seen a snake. He grasped his stick firmly and walked ahead, his eyes on the ground in front.

So he didn't see the man lift the rifle to his shoulder and fire.

The bullet hit the ground a yard ahead of him and ricocheted dangerously off the rocks.

Vincent stopped and yelled. The man was a lunatic. The bloody thing had nearly got him. Even as he shouted he saw him raise the rifle again.

This time he felt the wind of the bullet next to his cheek.

He didn't stay to argue any longer, he turned to run, fell, dropped the sandwiches and stick and slithered belly down over shale for a good twenty feet. When he stood up it was to run.

From the next hill he saw the man with the gun walk down the hill, pick up the sandwiches and slowly saunter back to the warehouse.

Imagine Vincent, cut, bruised, covered in sweat, his eyes wide with outrage and anger as he strode into the Royal Hotel and found Solly at the bar.

"Solly, there's some crazy bastard at the warehouse. He shot at me. With a fucking rifle."

"No," said Solly, his eyes wide.

"Yes," said Vincent. "The bugger could have killed me."

They bought drinks for Vincent that night and he finally learned that the guards he had once employed for Farrow were now employed by the council to continue their valuable work. Those with blue hands did not want them devalued.

And Vincent, nursing his bruises at the bar, tried to smile at the joke. It was not going to be as easy to get his blue hands as he'd thought.

Faced with the terrifying prospect of death or wounding, he began to consider the possibility of blue hands more carefully. Whilst they would give him some prestige on Upward Island, they would make him grotesque anywhere else, of interest only to doctors and laughing schoolchildren on buses. He saw himself in big cities on summer days, wearing white gloves like Mickey Mouse. He saw the embarrassed eyes of people he knew and, he says, my own triumphant face as I revelled in the irony of it: Dr Strangelove with radiation poisoning.

If there had been anywhere left to run to, he would have gone. If there was a job he could have taken, he would have taken it. Even without this, he would have gone, if he'd had the money.

But he had no money. No chance of a job. And he was forced to consider what he would do.

And as he thought about it, lying on his bed, drinking with Solly, nailing down the roof on the schoolhouse, he came to realize that not only couldn't he leave, he didn't want to. He came to see that he was liked, respected, even loved. For the first time in his life he considered the possibility of happiness. It was a strange thing for him to look at, and he examined it with wonder.

What was so wrong with Upward Island?

He couldn't think of anything.

Did he miss the city? Not particularly. Did he miss friends? He didn't have any. Did he miss success? He had failed. Strangely, he had become somebody: he was Vince, he worked down at the school, he cleaned bricks, he did the prawn contracts.

On the morning of the second day after the shooting he came to the realization that he had no option but to stay. And if he was to stay he had no option but to get his hands the right colour. He looked the prospect of the warehouse in the eye and was filled with terror at what he saw.

Vincent was frightened of snakes, lizards, bats, spiders, scorpions, large ants, and noises in the night he didn't understand. He used what daylight he could and crept to the point in the track where the warehouse was just visible, then he sat on a rock and waited for darkness.

His face and hands were blackened. His shirt sleeves were long. In his pocket he carried the torch Solly had given him. As the sun set a crow flew across the sky, uttering a cry so forlorn that it struck a chill in Vincent's heart.

The sky turned from melodramatic red, to grey, and slowly to darkness. He edged painfully up the path convinced he would put his hand on a snake. A rustle in the grass kept him immobile for two minutes. He stared into the darkness with his hair bristling. A toad jumped across his boot and he slipped backwards in fright. He pressed on, crawling. His hand grasped a nettle. A sharp rock pierced his trousers and tore his skin. Tiny pieces of gravel inflicted a hundred minor tortures on his naked hands. A flying fox, its wings as loud as death itself, flew over him on its way to a wild guava bush.

Yet there were few noises loud enough to distract him from his beating heart. It felt as if his head was full of beating blood.

Slowly, very slowly, he edged his way to the

warehouse. Once it had been nothing more than a word in a memo, but now it gleamed horribly under a bright moon, the colourless words on its side clearly visible and exactly calculated in their effect

The guards were well paid and took three shifts. They were established in very good houses, were given three months' holiday a year and were encouraged to bring their families to Upward. They were stable, serious men, and if they mixed little in the society, they were certainly vital to it.

Tonight it was Van Dogen. They had teased Vincent about this, saying Van Dogen was the best shot of them all.

He could hear Van Dogen above him, walking up and down on the gravel. Once his face flared white from the darkness as he lit a cigarette. Vincent watched the tiny red speck of cigarette as it swung around the building like a deadly firefly.

Now, he made his way slowly to where there was no red dot, to the back of the warehouse where the water tank stood. For here, he knew, was the way to the roof. Onto the wooden stand, then to the tank, a slow dangerous arm lift to the roof. Now he moved on borrowed sandshoes across the vast expanse of metal roof, a loud footstep disguised by the noises caused by the contraction of the metal in the cool night air.

The third skylight from the end awaited him as promised. He climbed through slowly and his dangling feet found the rafter. Slowly, quietly, he closed the skylight and giddily, fearfully, lowered himself from the rafter.

He let go, hoping the superphosphate sacks were

still below. It was further than he thought. He fell onto the hard bags with a frightened grunt.

In an instant there was a key in the door and the guard stood flashing a strong torch. Vincent rolled quietly from the bags. As he lay on top of two metal U-bolts he wanted to cry. He wanted to stand up and say: "Here I am."

Van Dogen couldn't shoot him. Not in cold blood. The whole thing was impossible. It was he, Vincent, who had constructed Van Dogen's original salary. He had invented Van Dogen. He had arranged aeroplanes to fly him through the sky. He had arranged for a gun. He had told Van Dogen to shoot.

Van Dogen walked the aisles of the vast warehouse. It took everything in Vincent to stop himself standing up. "Here I am. I'm a friend." He was like a man who jumps from a tall building because he is frightened of falling from it.

Van Dogen was faceless. A lethal shadow behind a bright light, the formless creature of the very brain that was now sending panic signals to every part of a prickling body.

But Van Dogen noticed nothing. It was simply part of his nightly routine and he left after a couple of minutes.

Vincent lay still for a long time, caught in the sticky webs of his nightmare. When he moved it was because a mouse ran across his shoulder and down his back. He shuddered and jumped back onto the superphosphate. Then although he felt himself already condemned, he moved to the crates of Eupholon. He blinked the torch on for half a second, then off. Another lightning flash. He found them. He took the hateful bottles and filled his shirt pockets and his trouser pockets with them. He didn't know how much to take. He took everything he could fit in.

And now he faced the side door. It was one of four doors. One was the right choice. Two were dangerous. One was deadly. He stood behind the side door and waited. He could hear nothing. No footstep, no breathing, nothing. Slowly, silently, he slid back the latch and waited. Still nothing.

He opened the door and ran. He had been told not to run. He ran straight into Van Dogen who had been standing in front of it.

Vincent shrieked with fear. The shriek came from him without warning, high and piercing, as horrible as a banshee wail. Van Dogen fell. Vincent fell. The track lay ahead. Vincent was berserk. He kicked Van Dogen's head and threw his rifle against the wall where it went off with a thunderclap.

Half falling, half running, Vincent was on the track down the hill. He tripped, fell, stood and ran. As he tripped the third time he heard a shot and felt a shock in his leg. But he could still run. He felt no pain. In his pockets the broken Eupholon bottles gently sliced his unfeeling skin.

When he woke he was in bed. There was a bandage on his leg and another on his chest. But the first thing he noticed were the three Eupholon bottles standing beside his bed. Beside them, the contents of the five other broken bottles were piled in a little saucer.

The little yellow capsules seemed as precious and beautiful as gold itself. He lay on his bed, laughing.

He balanced the little saucer on his stomach and smiled at the capsules. He took one, not bothering with water. He looked through the open door of the shed to where Solly was digging in the vegetable garden. He took another, impatient for the moment when he would have hands as beautiful as those that now grasped the garden spade.

My revenge lies about me in tatters. Shredded sheets of confusion drift through the air. My story written, but not a story I intended or one my editor will accept.

But I know, if I know anything, that he changed, and I now like him as much as I once despised him.

If I said I was a child, an adolescent, do not take me too literally. Whatever questions you ask of me I have asked myself. We might start with the simplest: has he conned me by helping me prepare my case against him?

It is a possibility. I can't reject it.

Am I reacting to the esteem in which he is held here? When I despised him he was a public joke. Now he is liked. Is this why I like him?

A possibility. I grasp it. It does not sting unduly.

Do I like him because he no longer demands my affection? Do I wish to conquer him now that he has less need of me?

Possibly. But so what?

Do I lack any solid system of values? Is this why I

now find blue hands beautiful where once I called them grotesque?

Certainly I have changed. But there must be a functional basis for aesthetics. Blue hands on Upward Island are not blue hands anywhere else.

But then, what of this function? What of the regard blue hands are held in? Should prestige be granted only to the brave? Does physical bravery not suggest a certain lack of imagination? Is it a good qualification for those who will rule?

I don't know.

Is bravery seen to be a masculine virtue? Where are the women with blue hands?

There are none, as yet.

Then am I like a crippled female applauding male acts of bravado?

No, I am not.

I know only that he walks slowly and talks calmly, is funny without being attention-seeking, accepts praise modestly and is now lying on my bed smiling at me.

I don't move. There is no hurry. But in a moment, sooner or later, I will go over to him and then I will, slowly, carefully, unzip his shorts and there I will see his beautiful blue penis thrusting its aquamarine head upwards towards me. It will be silky, the most curious silkiness imaginable.

I will kneel and take it in my mouth.

If I moan, you will not hear me. What I say, you will never know.

Questions, your questions, will rise like bubbles from deeper water, but I will disregard them, pass them, sinking lower to where there are no questions, nothing but a shimmering searing electric blue.

Ultra-Violet Light

My mother is growing plants under ultra-violet light nowadays. She has this plan, so let me recount how it happened from the beginning.

She was at the doctor's in Geelong. And there they were: plants growing in a glass-fronted chest under ultra-violet light. In the waiting room.

Naturally this satisfied her: the very sight of it. She is amused by novelties: foaming soap pads, oriental games with indecipherable characters, bird baths with unusual characteristics, plans for tourism involving apples.

And here, in Geelong, she encounters the ultra-violet light and manages to worm from the doctor himself the story of how it all works.

Well, her liver was fine.

She returned home and called up the cabinet-maker and got him to construct a fine chest just like the doctor's, had the ultra-violet lights fitted, and didn't give a damn that they all thought she was crazy. The plants were from Africa, with great red and green leaves. God knows how they developed this exotic taste for ultra-violet food. I have visions of African jungles with incandescent tubes hanging from trees like crystalline fruit in a Space Adventure, my mother plucking them carefully, wiring them to a battery in case they go flat, or bad, or whatever happens to them when they're plucked.

"It is the new thing," my mother has declared many times.

The cabinet was made, the plants procured, and she has now set up the whole kit and kaboodle in the shop window so that the entire town can see her new hobby.

She revealed her plan to me. "People will come and ask me about it and I'll explain it. Then they'll have to phone up Mr Dickens (the cabinetmaker) and he'll get all the work, making new cabinets."

Oh, the mysteries of my mother, capitalism, entrepreneurs, and ultra-violet light.

I understand nothing but am dazzled, continually, by all these new inventions.

When the revolution comes we can all look back on my mother and see how people live these days.

Kristu-Du

The man who brings water shall be blessed.
He carrieth fat to the cattle,
ears to the corn.
The sound of such water can be likened
to the laughter of children.

(Traditional Deffala Song)

1.

While the architect's wife carefully folded a pair
of white slacks, five men were hanged. As she
hunted through the drawer for her cosmetics and
packed them neatly, one by one, in a small leather
carrying case, an old man died of dehydration and
starvation beside a dusty road. As she slipped the
case shut and fiddled inexpertly with its lock, teams
of imported builders laboured on the great domed
building in the middle of the cruel rock-filled
valley.

The architect sat on the edge of the neatly made
bed and watched his wife. He was a slim tall man in
his late forties. He had fine blue eyes, unusually
large eyelids, and a high forehead made even higher
by the receding crop of curling grey hair. His mouth
was perhaps his best feature, containing as it did the
continual promise of a smile. But now the promise
was not honoured. His eyes were red-rimmed and
tired. His long fingered hands were clasped on his
lap and he watched his wife make her final pre-

parations for her departure. She was leaving him and returning to Europe.

Now she was packed she sat on the bed beside him. They had entered those white corridors where there is neither shadow nor feeling.

He wished to say many things to her but he had said them all already. He said them badly and she had not listened in any case.

He wished to say: the building I have designed will last a thousand years and will endure beyond the tyrant who rules this place.

He would have added: you are only leaving because you saw a soldier shoot a dog, not because of anything else.

But all these things had been covered time and time again and she was returning to the civilization of Europe and he was to remain to build his master-piece, the great dome of the desert, Kristu-Du, the meeting house of the tribes.

He picked up her two cases from the bed and took them out to the Land Rover. When he returned she was standing in the living room look-ing at an old book of his work. As he walked in she put it down on the coffee table.

Neither of them said anything.

On their way out she placed her front door key on top of the refrigerator. Then, hesitating, she opened her handbag and took out a small bottle of pills. These she placed beside the keys.

They were sleeping pills, difficult to come by.

The noise of the Land Rover always made con-versation difficult, but now it made the lack of it somehow more bearable. Gravel rattled against the aluminium floor, the engine and the transmission were loud and unrelenting, rock samples in the back jumped and crashed on the tray with every bump. He saw now, as he had seen when he first arrived three years ago, the terrible bleakness of the town, a bleakness that did not even have the redeeming virtue of being exotic. The buildings constructed by the now departed Russians all looked like grey hospitals. They stood at the grand height of four storeys, towering over a collection of ugly shops and houses of white concrete blocks. In the unpaved streets stunted palm trees died from lack of water. He saw the terrible poverty of the people as they squatted on the footpath or walked aimlessly in groups along the broken streets. Tall Itos, Berehvas with pierced ears, Deffalas with the yellow eyes of desert people. It was nobody's home, everyone's exile. A city planned where no one had ever wished to live.

Only the soldiers seemed well-fed. They lounged everywhere, these tall warriors of the president's own tribe, clustering in doorways or patrolling in groups of two or three, machine-guns slung over their shoulders.

He saw the big white colonial building which he now recognized as a place to be feared, the detention centre, and behind it in the high-walled garden of the palace, a tasteless mock-Spanish edifice built on the president's instruction to a photograph torn from a badly printed American newspaper.

From here the president ruled with a skilful and unique blend of violence and magic. The magic, of course, was not magic at all, but rather an array of technological tricks which were impressive to a primitive and unlettered people. Oongala was a giant of a man, half-educated, barely literate, but he understood his people all too well. Those who were too educated or enraged to be impressed by magic could be handled with simple violence, torture and murder. With the rest he reinforced his claim to be the Great Magician of tribal myth by utilizing a continual array of new tricks.

The great canal which would have brought water to the drought-stricken land had been abandoned when he came to power. The railway which would have joined its disparate peoples lay unfinished with two stations built and the rails lying on the parched soil like pick-up sticks abandoned by a bored child. This was not the technology Oongala preferred.

The man who was known throughout the world as a comic-strip dictator, a clown, a buffoon and a mass murderer, chose to travel across his land in a hovercraft, to drop out of the sky in a white helicopter, or simply to star in one more badly made motion picture which he wrote, directed, produced and starred in. These films were the staple diet of his starving populace. They cheered him as he jumped thirty feet from ground to roof top to battle and destroy armed villains. They watched open-mouthed as he defeated bands of machine-gunning renegades. Bullets could not harm him, gravity hold him, or the engines of war overpower him.

And now they were treated to the works of the man whom Gerrard had privately named Mr Meat, the ex arms dealer Wallis who was now making a fortune from constructing holograms in the bigger villages. The work had barely begun but if the reaction to the one in the capital was any indication, it was a popular piece of magic. Inside a concrete building that had all the charm of a public urinal the faithful could see a three-dimensional image of their dictator levitating above the desk in his big office.

Now, as the Land Rover left the town and rattled down the track towards the airport, Gerrard looked across at his wife. She caught his eye for a moment and then looked hurriedly away, she who had once encouraged him with his plans, bolstered him in the face of failure and criticism, who had stood by him fiercely when his controversial works had been disbanded by one municipal authority because of cost, another because of a provincial sense of what was beautiful. And now, here, when a great building was nearing completion, she was leaving him, washing her hands of him, joining the ranks of the old associates who had publicly criticized his role in working for the glorification of a mass murderer.

The hypocrites, he thought now, they sit in their exquisite offices while their own governments torture and kill, and because there isn't a scandalized headline in the newspapers they pretend these things don't go on. They are so clean, so pure, and I am so terrible. They want me to say: no, I shall abandon this project, the greatest domed structure in the world. I should walk away from it and leave it unfinished or to be ruined by incompetent fools. Would they? Would his fine pure friends have walked away from such a triumph simply because a government had changed? A building seven times as big as St Peters in Rome? He smiled thinly.

The airport was almost empty. He checked-in his wife's baggage whilst she looked in the duty-free shop. When he came back he saw that she had bought perfume. He said nothing and gave her the ticket.

"There is no point in you waiting," she said.

He looked at her: eyes that had once looked at him with love, now dull and lustreless, lips that had covered his body in soft passionate kisses, now thin and full of tension.

"I wanted to say. . ." he began.

"What?" she interrupted nervously, on the defensive, worried that he would ask anything of her, make any claim.

He had wanted to say that he would miss her dreadfully, that he would think of her continually, that he would endure his loneliness in the hope that the separation would not be permanent.

But instead, he merely smiled a wry smile and said, "I just wanted to say goodbye."

"Goodbye," she said. She kept her hands clutched around her perfume and handbag. She did not lean towards him. "Goodbye," she said again.

"Goodbye," he said then turned on his heel.

She watched him walk away, casually throwing his keys up and down in his hand. It was the walk of a person who might have been on his way to an expensive lunch. She never forgave him for it.

2.
There were many who would have described Gerrard Haflinger as a solitary man. It is true that conversation did not come easily to him and he had a peculiar mixture of shyness and arrogance in his

character that normally made him appear more than a little aloof. His dealings with governments, municipal authorities and the Medicis of modern business had always been made more difficult by his inability to unbend, to be anything other than the bristling defendant of the purity of his vision. But solitary he was not.

In an interview in a popular European magazine he had once been asked what was most precious to him in life and he had answered, without hesitation, that it was to be with true friends. And what was a true friend? A true friend, he had answered, was someone you could stand naked before, who would never judge you, whom you could share your darkest secrets with, and so on.

By this definition Gerrard Haflinger had no more friends. He had been judged and found guilty not only by the three men he respected and loved most, but also by his wife.

Gerrard Haflinger no longer remembered the interview but if he had he would have reflected that he had not answered truthfully: his work was the most precious thing in his life. For this, this one project, he had been prepared to give up everything else. Possibly if his other work had proceeded properly, if the theatre complex had not been bungled, if the state library had ever gone ahead, he might have abandoned the Kristu-Du on the day Oongala took power and parliamentary democracy was abolished, or, if not then, at least in the following months when it became clear to everyone what sort of a leader Oongala would be.

But he was forty-six years old and the Kristu-Du was all that stood between him and the terrifying abyss of the total and complete failure of his life's ambition. To abandon the domed building would be to throw away everything he had ever worked for and join the faceless ranks of those clever men and women who had seen their dreams crash and splinter through lack of drive, charm, talent, or, as Gerrard saw this issue, courage.

His refusal to abandon his project had brought him to sit in this white sparse living room by himself. He felt like a man who comes to stand on the edge of a desert which stretches as far as the eye can see. He felt the cold wind already stinging him and was sorry that he had come to stand here. Yet he felt also, in the midst of the jumbled emotions of fear, loneliness, and self-pity, a certain tingling of excitement that he did not know what to do with.

He walked to the bedroom and stared at the neatly made bed. The sight gave him a sharp and sudden pain and he turned quickly. In the kitchen he opened the refrigerator door and stood for some time staring into it. He was shutting its door when his eye lighted on the key and the bottle of sleeping tablets. He put the key in his pocket and walked to the sink, carefully reading the instructions on the label of the pills. He poured a glass of boiled water and returned to the living room where he made himself comfortable on the big black Italian couch. He took the two pills and waited for them to work.

It was seven o'clock at night.

3.
It was just after eight o'clock in the morning and

the air was still crisp and cold when he arrived at the small pass which opened onto Hi-Dahlian (the Valley of the Spirits). As he drove to the rise he waited impatiently, as he always did, for the moment when the poor dusty drought-stricken landscape would suddenly cease and there before him would lie the harsh boulder-strewn valley filled with dazzlingly white round rocks, a great basin of egg-smooth boulders that stretched to the mountains on every side. And there, in the middle, would stand his Kristu-Du, its soaring walls as smooth and white as the rocks themselves, its copper dome gleaming golden in the morning sun.

The Land Rover lumbered onto the pass, and there it was. He stopped, as he always stopped, and looked at it with pride and satisfaction. For now there was no doubting the greatness of the work, its perfect scale, its harmonious integration into the spectacular landscape. It was a glistening rock in a sea of shining pebbles, of them and yet apart from them. Only as one came very close did one appreciate the immense size of the building: 1,000 feet high, 850 feet in diameter, seven times the size of St Peters. In its glowing eggshell interior there was room for 100,000 tribesmen.

It had been designed to the brief of Oongala's first victim, the late president, as a unifying symbol for the eight tribes, sited in the holiest place, a neutral ground where a new democracy would start to spread its fragile wings. Gerrard, in the early days when the plan had been selected, had spoken of its function with a fierce obsessive poetry, likening it to a vast machine which would take an active role in the birth of the new democracy. It was not a symbol, he said. It was not a building. It was one of those rare pieces of architecture which would act on the future as well as exist in the present.

In those innocent days the plans provided for an extensive water system, with supplies for the watering of horses, mules and camels. There was to have been a small lake around which shade trees were to be planted, pleasant camping for those who had journeyed so far. But there was, of course, no water now. Oongala had stopped work on the great canal and the drought, the terrible drought, continued to kill the people and their livestock and to raise the very earth itself so that on some days the sun was blotted out by an endless ocean of flying dust.

As he drove down into the valley Gerrard looked at what he saw with a selective eye. He did not see the section of roof that was still missing. He eliminated the giant blue and red cranes, the bird's-nest ugliness of scaffolding, the twisted piles of abandoned reinforcing mesh, the glistening corrugated-iron offices and the workers' ammenity blocks. He saw trees which would one day be planted and fountains that would burst spectacularly from fissured rock. But most of all he adjusted his vision to ignore the grey and white clusterings of figures that gathered around the west entrance of the building like swarms of virulent organisms which would destroy their host. Yet in this he was not wholly successful, so that as he entered the plain itself, winding along the carefully planned road between the giant rocks, lines of tension formed across his face and two small vertical lines appeared on his forehead, just to the left of his nose.

The road was planned to be a continuous series of surprises, of opened vistas and closed canyons, of startling glimpses of the building, and veiled promises of what was to come. Now, at the last moment, he came round the rock he had named "Old Man Rock" and he was at the edge of the site itself and the great building towered above him in all its breathtaking beauty. And now he could eliminate things no more and the lines on his forehead deepened as the white and grey clusterings of figures revealed themselves to be a meeting of one hundred and fifty skilled European workers.

A strike.

He drove past them slowly, aware of the turned eyes but unable to acknowledge them in any natural way. He parked outside his office and went in to wait.

He sat on his swivel chair and played with some paperclips, his apprehension showing in the way he took them, one by one, and twisted them and bent them until they grew hot and snapped with fatigue. It was here that he was bad, here that he ruined things. It was here that his associates succeeded and he failed. For they were charming and persuasive men who could sway hard-headed businessmen in their own language, and overcome the problems of site disputes with their negotiators' skills and hard-headed bargaining.

He no longer talked to the men who were building his dream. Even his assistants found him distant and cold. And he had so badly offended the engineers that they would barely speak to him. It was not as he wished it. He would have dearly loved to have taken them to town, to have bought them beers, to have gone whoring with them, to have shared the easy relaxed talk he had overheard between them. But there was something stiff in him, something that would not bend.

So he waited in his office for the deputation, breaking paperclips and throwing them into the rubbish bin.

4.

He disapproved of bribes and so gave this one badly. Rather than speeding his interview with the minister it produced the opposite effect. The minister's secretary, a uniformed sergeant from the 101, was now punishing him for such a tasteless and inelegant performance.

He had now waited an hour, his agitation becoming more and more pronounced. He crossed his long legs and then uncrossed them. He stared at a yellowed five-year-old copy of *Punch* and could find nothing funny in it. He stared at the bleak anteroom with a practised eye, observing a thousand defects in workmanship and finish, noting a wall that was not quite vertical, automatically relocating a window so that it was lower, wider, and placed on a wall where it might have collected some of the chilly winter sunshine.

He stood and examined the tasteless paintings on the walls.

He sat and looked at his fingernails, wondering if it was true that the long curved shells indicated a propensity to lung disease as he has once been told.

As to how he would persuade the minister to

make extra funds available to meet the men's demands, he had no idea. If he had been Mr Meat he would not have bothered with the minister, he would have gone straight to Oongala, played polo with him and spent a night at the billiard table. He would have laughed at the dictator's jokes and told even cruder ones of his own. But he was not Mr Meat and his grey formal reserve made the dictator uneasy, as if he were being secretly laughed at. Oongala would no longer see him.

What the men wanted was fair and reasonable. It was quite correct. But the correctness did not help. Everything in him wanted to say: "Give the money, find it, do anything, but let the work proceed." But that, of course, was not an argument.

Finally the secretary had had enough of the agitated movements of his prisoner. He phoned through to the minister and told Gerrard he could go in.

Gerrard smiled at the secretary, thanking him.

The secretary stared at him, the merest flicker of a smile crossing his stony face.

5.

The minister sat behind his large desk doing the *Times* crossword. He was, for this country, an unusually short man. He had a sensitive face and particularly nervous hands, which seemed to flutter through a conversation like lost butterflies. On occasions they had discussed Proust and the minster had talked dreamily of days at Oxford and invited the Haflingers to visit socially, an invitation that

Gerrard, had he been a trifle more calculating, would have realized was an important one to accept. Yet he had managed to neither accept nor decline and had left the minister with the feeling, correct as it happened, that Gerrard found his company unstimulating. The minister was a man of sensitive feelings and weak character, a failing that had kept him alive while stronger men had long since disappeared into jail.

"Good morning, Gerrard. What would you make of this — Ah! A cross pug leaps across funereal stone? It is eleven letters," he smiled apologetically, "beginning with S."

"I don't know."

"Neither do I." He folded the delicate rice-paper pages of the airmail edition and plugged in a small electric jug which sat on the low filing cabinet beside him. "Coffee?"

"That would be pleasant, thank you." Gerrard was trying to be pleasant, to unbend, to relax, to be patient enough to discuss all ten volumes of *Recherche du Temps Perdu* if it was necessary. He sat in the low visitor's chair and they both waited for the jug to boil.

"How is Mrs Haflinger?"

"Gone, I'm afraid."

The eyebrows raised and the tongue clucking sympathetically. "Our country is not to everybody's taste," he picked up *The Times,* weighed it, and let it fall to the desk, "as I read every day."

"Unfortunately it isn't." Gerrard attempted to match the sad ironical smile on the other's face.

"Black with two?"

"Thank you." Gerrard watched as the minister

fussed over the coffee and thought how much he hated the metallic taste of Nescafe.

"Excuse me," said the minister, "I seem to have spilled some into the saucer. Now what is the problem? I take it the visit isn't social." And he allowed the merest glint of malice to enter his voice.

"I have a strike."

"And the particular matter of the dispute? Ah," he smiled, "if only our industrial relations laws were in a more advanced stage. But," the smile again, "I'm sure you understand that as well as I."

"There is no particular matter. It is a question of conditions generally. The shortage of water, the absence of power in their quarters, the quarters themselves." Gerrard thought of the old army barracks where his men were quartered: squalid rows of huts with no partitions and a complete lack of privacy for even the most basic matters.

The minister nodded sympathetically: "Oh, I know, I know. The latrines, I imagine, are also a problem. One cannot blame them. I would be upset myself."

"There is a list." Gerrard was beginning to hope. Against his best sense he hoped that this man might actually have the guts to do something. He gave the minister the list of the men's complaints. It contained ten points.

"What do they ask?"

"Either the matters be upgraded or they be paid at a special penalty rate."

"And," the minister blew into the steaming coffee, "if that is not possible, and I mean 'if'?"

"They will leave, en masse."

"Oh dear."

"Yes."

"And you think they will carry out the threat?"

In his blind anxiety it had never occurred to Gerrard that they wouldn't, but he said simply: "They will carry it out."

"Oh dear."

"Quite," said Gerrard. "What shall we do, what can we do?"

"For me," the minister held his pale palms upwards, "my hands are tied. I myself can do nothing." The hands came together in an attitude of prayer and the index fingers plucked nervously at the pendulous lower lip. "My department's funds are already overcommitted. It would take the president himself to approve a special allowance."

"And the president," Gerrard smiled thinly, "is not likely to be sympathetic."

"As you know," the minister clasped his hands across his breast and leant back dolefully in his big squeaking chair, "as you know the president is of the view that they are being paid far too much as it is. It was only after my most earnest plea . . ."

"For which I am most grateful." The minister was lying. Gerrard lied in return. He had never spoken in these terms to the minister before. He was finding it repulsive. He felt vaguely ill. "But if there were anything . . ."

The minister snapped forward in his chair and leaned across the table. "I will speak to him," he said with the air of a man who has made a reckless decision. "I will go to him this morning. The president is most anxious that the project be finished quickly. He feels that in the absence of rain," and here he allowed the merest trace of treasonable sarcasm to enter his voice, "the people are in need of a boost in morale. He is relying on the Kristu-Du. He will be most eager to end the dispute."

"Which means?"

"It means," the minister winked slyly, "that I will speak on your behalf and that finally you need not worry. Your building will go ahead without serious delay. You have my word for it. You will not be unhappy with the result." And the wink came again. Gerrard, who wondered if he had seen the first wink, had no doubts about the second.

"And the men?" he asked.

"The men," said the minister, "will not leave, I promise you."

Gerrard stood, unsure of what he had done. He looked at the minister's face and wondered if it was capable of winking. "You will be in touch?" he said.

"Most definitely. And perhaps, when this little crisis is over, you might like to join my family for a luncheon. Next Sunday perhaps — the eleventh."

"Thank you. That would be delightful."

The minister held out his small hand. It clung to Gerrard's hand spreading a damp film of secret fear around it.

6.

When the Land Rover entered the site on the following morning he understood immediately the agreement he had made with the minister. As he turned off the engine he finally admitted that he had known all along. He had understood exactly and precisely what would happen but he had not allowed himself to look at it. The minister's wink had produced a tightening in his stomach. The sweat he had felt in the handshake had been as much his as the minister's. Their fears had met and smudged together between their two hands.

As he walked between the big khaki trucks of Oongala's army he felt shame and triumph, elation and despair. They mixed themselves together in the terrible porridge his emotions had become.

All around him the work continued, watched by the keen arrogant eyes of Oongala's elite force: the notorious 101s.

The English doctor had seen the Land Rover approach and now he watched angrily as the tall man in the grey safari suit walked towards him. His walk did not belong here, amongst these harsh rocks and calloused hands. It was a city walk, the walk of a man who strolls boulevards and sips vermouth in side-walk cafes. The doctor detested the walk. "Like an evil little spider," he thought, "who will soon proclaim his innocence."

Now the tall man stopped. Now he ran. He sprinted towards the doctor, jumping across a pile of piping. The doctor grimaced and transferred his attention to the young Danish worker who lay on the ground before him. The injection had at last eased the pain. Soon he'd be able to shift him to town. He heard rather than saw Gerrard squat beside him. He said nothing and busied himself repacking the syringe with exaggerated care. He picked up the two ampoules from the dusty ground, tossed them in his hand, and with a sudden expression of rage threw them against the wall of the building.

"What's up?"

The architect smelt of expensive shampoo. The doctor couldn't bear to look at him. He took the young man's pulse and was surprised to find his own hand shaking. "I would have thought it was obvious."

"What may be obvious to you is not obvious to me. Kindly tell me what has happened." There was a tremor in the architect's voice, and the doctor, looking up, was astonished to see despair in the other's eyes. "Kindly tell me what has happened."

"He was shot by your friends here. He told them he was a free man and didn't have to work. He made quite a speech. It is a shame you missed it," he smiled nastily, "all about freedom and democracy."

Gerrard looked down at the young man on the ground. He was no more than twenty. Someone had placed a shirt under his naked back. His left calf was heavily bandaged, but his clear blue eyes showed no trace of pain. It was a romantic face, Gerrard reflected, with its sparse blonde beard, its tousled hair and those luminous eyes. As Gerrard watched he saw, on the young man's face, the beginning of a smile. He knelt, bending hungrily towards the smile, hoping to kill his own pain with it. He saw the lips move. He bent further, reaching towards words. So he was only six inches from the young face when the lips parted and a hot stream of spittle issued from them with hateful speed, hitting Gerrard on the left cheek. He stood, as if stung, and turned on his heel towards the office. Then, changing his mind, he returned to his Land Rover.

As he left the site in a cloud of dust the Kristu-Du continued its inexorable progress as inch by inch, pound by pound it moved towards its majestic finale.

7.

For two days Gerrard Haflinger remained in his house without going out. Each hour he stayed away from the site made it harder for him to return to it. The thought of a return was hateful to him. The thought of not returning was impossible to contemplate.

Dirty clothes lay on the living room floor beside the sleeves of twenty recordings, not one of which had given any solace. The empty bottle of sleeping pills lay in the kitchen, its white plastic cap on the dining table.

It was night and the black windows reflected his unshaven face as he stared out into the empty street.

He sat down at the desk in the living room and began to type a letter, but he stopped every few characters, cocking his head and listening. He had become nervous, fearful of intruders, although he could not have explained who these intruders might be or why they would wish to enter his house.

He loosened the tension of the typewriter roller so that the paper could be removed silently from it, flattened the sheet, and began to write by hand.

As he wrote the letter to his son the only noises he heard were the loud scratching of the pen and the regular click of a digital clock.

The difficulty with both of us is that we were

raised to believe that we were somehow special. In my case this has resulted in my coming to this: to build a grand building for a murderer because it is the only path left to me to realize my sense of 'specialness' (an ugly inelegant word but it is late at night and I can think of no other). You, for your part, could find nothing in the world that corresponded with your sense of who you were, or rather who we had taught you you were. I now understand as I never did before how very painful and disappointing this must have been for you.

Yet tonight, sitting in an empty room and thinking about you in America and your mother in Paris, I envy you the good luck or misfortune in avoiding the trap we laid so lovingly for you.

For now I recognize this sense of specialness as the curse and conceit that it is and I would rather be without it.

Yesterday I was responsible for a man being wounded. The same man spat in my face when I bent to speak to him. And it is this thing, a small thing when compared with the great charges that have been laid against me, that has brought me to toy (flirt is a better word) with the idea of abandoning the project totally. My mind is not made up either way, but I have come to the position of recognizing the possibility. The final straw for your mother was the sight of a dog being machine-gunned by a drunk soldier. I thought that ridiculous, a piece of dishonest sentimentality. But now I understand that too. It is not the wounding of the man that brings me to my present state, but the fact that he spat in my face.

It is too late for me to be forgiven by my self-righteous colleagues (architects are surely the most hypocritical group on earth) but possibly not too late for me to forgive myself.

When we last heard from you you were just starting the vegetable shop. Please write and tell me if the venture has proven successful.

What is your life like?

Love, father.

When he had finished the letter he folded it hastily, placed it inside an envelope, and, having consulted a small notebook, addressed it. Then he sat with his head in his hands while the digital clock clicked through four minutes. His thoughts were slippery, elusive, tangled strands of wet white spaghetti which he could neither grasp nor leave alone.

He stood up then and went to the bathroom where he looked for pills in the little cabinet above the basin. There were none, but he found instead a small bottle of nail polish which he considered with interest.

He shut the door.

First he washed his arm with soapy water. Then he methodically worked up some shaving cream into a thick, creamy lather. Sitting on the small stool in front of the mirror he brushed the lather into the dense black hair along his left arm. When he was done, he took a safety razor and, very carefully, shaved the arm until it was perfectly smooth.

He washed his arm and examined it in the mirror: a slender tanned arm with long delicate fingers.

Seeing hair on the knuckles he also lathered these and, being careful not to knick himself, shaved them.

Now he picked up the nail polish and applied it carefully. It took him three attempts to get it right.

When the nail polish had dried he undressed completely, folding his white trousers carefully and placing them on the carpeted floor in the passage outside.

He shut the door again and sat on the basin and

watched in the mirror as the red fingernailed hand of a beautiful woman crept across his stomach and took his penis, stroking it slowly.

"I've missed you," said the voice, a quiet, shy tentative voice that seemed afraid of derision or rejection, and then, gathering confidence: "I love you, my darling."

In the street outside a man laughed.

At the detention centre a young shopkeeper was being given the merest touch of an electric cattle prod.

At the Merlin Hotel, Wallis, alias Mr Meat, the man who sold holograms, picked up his telephone and dialled Gerrard's number.

When the number finally rang Gerrard Haflinger grabbed a bathrobe and ran to answer it. He stood in the living room accepting a dinner invitation, semen dripping down his stomach like spittle.

8.

In a minute or two Mr Meat would change Gerrard's mind entirely about the whole question of his involvement with the building. He would do it quite unintentionally. In a minute or two he would give Gerrard his scenario. In fact it was one of four such scenarios that he considered to be possible, but he would insist on the veracity of this one because it was the one most likely, in his calculation, to frighten Gerrard, to undo a little of his arrogance and moral superiority.

Mr Meat thought Gerrard was a pompous pain in the arse, but he was bored and lonely and wished to fill in one last night before he escaped this dung hole of a country and went back to more predictable and respectable work selling armaments.

So he was not aware that the ascetic man who sat opposite him in the deserted dining room of the Merlin Hotel was more than a little unhinged with guilt and despair, that he was on the point of renouncing his life's work, and entering the cold empty landscape he had always feared.

But first they had to sit through this circus that was going on at the bar, all because Haflinger had ordered a Campari and the waiters didn't know what in the hell a Campari was, even though it was sitting on the shelf in the bar, practically biting their silly snub noses.

"You're going to have to help them," Wallis said, "or we'll never get a bloody drink."

The architect turned in his seat to look at the embarrassed conference of white-coated waiters. "Oh," he said, "they'll work it out."

Wallis sighed. "You're about to get a Drambuie."

Gerrard began to get up but sat down again as the Drambuie was returned to the shelf.

"Oh Christ, I can't stand it." Mr Meat pushed his chair back and Gerrard watched him as he strode across to the bar, this big beefy-faced man with the arrogant aggressive walk of a military policeman. He saw the waiters' mortified faces. He saw the big impatient hand haul the Campari from the shelf, snatch a glass, and pour an unmeasured quantity into it. He couldn't bear to watch anymore and looked instead at the bleak empty tables of the dining room, too depressed to be amused by the fake Doric columns.

Wallis brought back Campari, soda and a beer for himself. "Now you know why I stick to beer," he said, "they can't fuck it up." He raised his glass, holding it with peculiar daintiness with thumb and middle finger, "Here's to the drought."

"You've made them embarrassed."

"So they should be. Christ, it's their job to know a Campari from a Drambuie. They bloody should be embarrassed."

"Still . . ."

Wallis leant his bulk into the table, the beakish nose thrusting from the great florid face, his big index finger poking in the direction of the Campari. "Listen, old son, you're too sensitive. People in our line of work can't afford to be so sensitive. Skol." He drank again.

"Our occupations are hardly similar."

"Oh come on, tell me what the difference is?" Wallis smiled. He was starting to enjoy himself.

"I think there's a difference," Gerrard attempted a smile. It didn't work out very well. "There is a difference between an important work of architecture and what you yourself describe as magic." None of this exactly reflected Gerrard's viewpoint but he had no intention of discussing anything so serious with Wallis.

"It's all magic here, old son, so don't look so superior. As a matter of fact I'll lay you a thousand U.S. dollars that it'll be your magic that brings Oongala undone. There is a limit to magic when people are starving. The holograms might be a big hit here, but they're not very popular in the villages. In fact I'd say they were very counter-productive. I would say that Oongala is not a popular man with the tribes at the moment. I'd give him three months at the most. When will your great work," he pronounced "Great Work" slowly and sarcastically, "be completed?"

"Four, five months."

"Then it'll be four or five months before Oongala gets kicked out and things get very nasty for you. Look I can tell you exactly what'll happen. And listen to me, because this is something I bloody well know about. I am an expert, old boy, in knowing when to leave a country. You can't survive in my business without knowing that."

Gerrard looked at the great red face with fascination. "Go on."

But they were interrupted by the approach of a waiter and Wallis fell suddenly silent. They ordered the Merlin's safest and most predictable dishes: pea soup followed by vegetable omelette. Wallis, in spite of his avowed dedication to beer, ordered Veuve Clicquot.

The food arrived too quickly and the champagne too slowly.

As he alternated sips of pea soup with Veuve Clicquot, Wallis continued: "Let me give you the exact scenario, as a little present, eh? Oongala will not know how unpopular he is. There is not a man left who is brave enough to tell him. However, he will know that things are not exactly rosy. People are dying. They are upset because there is no water and by now they all know about the canal and they know Oongala stopped it to spend money on your building. They're angry about that, but Oongala can't know how angry otherwise he'd drop your building like a hot cake and get stuck into the canal.

However, he does know he needs a very powerful piece of magic and your building is about the only trick he has left up his sleeve. But," Wallis smiled, delighting in the drama of his scenario, "but to impress everyone with the dear old Kristu-Du he'll have to bring them to see it, eh? He will bloody well be forced to have the famous gathering of the tribes." He laughed a strange dry cackle. "How about that, eh, isn't that neat?"

"It was exactly what Daihusia asked me to design it for."

"Sure," Wallis brushed that aside like the misunderstanding of a rather dull pupil. "But Daihusia was smart enough to have never built it."

Gerrard laughed indulgently. "You're very cynical."

Wallis's black eyebrows shot up and his small eyes narrowed and became dark and challenging. "You don't believe me? You're living in a dream world. It was a stunt. You, of all people, should have known that. It was a symbol. It was useful to Daihusia as an idea, but he was clever enough to know that the canal was more useful to him as a fact, and he couldn't afford to have both. If he'd given them water he would have ruled until he was a hundred, a fact our present fellow doesn't seem to have cottoned on to."

"You really think so?"

"I know so. Dear fellow, you wouldn't be building your great masterpiece if Daihusia was in power. Or, if you were, you'd still be buggering around with the foundations and not having money for anything else."

"Go on with your scenario."

Wallis looked at him sharply, aware of a new interest in the architect: the contempt had gone from his eyes and been replaced by a deep, quiet interest. "My scenario," he said, "is that in order to control the tribes, Oongala is going to do what Daihusia would never have done: he is going to have to bring them here to see the Kristu-Du. And when he does that, when god knows how many thousands arrive to see this spectacle, they will be coming as very angry people. They will be angry enough to forget their differences. They may be superstitious and primitive, but they are not stupid."

"The army, surely . . ."

Wallis waved his hand disdainfully tidying up minor objections before he came to deliver his coup de grace. "Apart from his beloved 101s, the rest of them are all tribally mixed. They're not going to shoot their own people. The army, old son, will not be worth a pinch of shit." And he brought thumb and index finger together as if offering Gerrard a pinch of it there and then. As he did so he noted the strange excited light in the architect's eyes. He interpreted it, incorrectly, as fear. "When the day comes," he said softly, "they will not love you." And he drew his index finger across his throat.

He leaned back and waited for this to sink in.

"Oh," Gerrard smiled, "I'm staying if that's what you mean."

The smile irritated Wallis beyond belief. "Look," he put his champagne glass down on the table and rivetted Gerrard with his dark eyes. "Look, Mr Architect, you better listen to me. I know what I'm talking about. I've seen this sort of thing before. I have had conversations, almost identical conversations, with people like you before. You will be no different from the bastards who run the detention centre. No one who has helped Oongala will be safe. They won't indulge in fine discussion about the history of architecture. If you stay, you're as good as dead."

"How do I know that what you say is true?"

Quietly, smugly, Wallis took out his wallet. From it he removed an airline ticket. He threw it across to Gerrard who opened it and read it.

"Tomorrow," Wallis said.

"But you haven't finished."

"I've finished everything I'm going to do."

"Then you really think it's true."

"I know it." He retrieved the ticket and returned it to the wallet.

Gerrard returned to his cold half-eaten omelette with a new enthusiasm. His mind was kindled again with the fierce hard poetry of his obsession: a structure whose very existence would create the society for which it was designed.

Wallis saw him smiling to himself and felt an almost uncontrollable desire to punch him in the face.

9.

Three months later the letter to his son lay forgotten in the top drawer of his desk, documentation of a temporary aberration, a momentary loss of faith.

In the spare white-walled house not an item was

out of place, not a match, a piece of fluff, a suggestion of lint, an unwashed plate or a carelessly dropped magazine disturbed its pristine tidiness. The records were stacked neatly, the edge of each sleeve flush with the shelf, arranged in faultless alphabetical order.

The dirty clothes in the laundry basket were folded as fastidiously as the dresses in a bride's suitcase.

Gerrard, sitting at the desk, continued work on the fourth draft of an ever lengthening article which he planned for world release. It had many titles. The current one was "A Machine Built for Freedom". The title, of course, referred to the Kristu-Du. The treatise itself was gradually becoming less coherent and more obscure, as it attributed almost mystical power to the great domed building. What had begun as a simple analogy with a machine had long since ceased to be that. The building was a machine, an immense benevolent force capable of overthrowing tyrannies and welding tribes into nations.

Now he was speeding through a long and difficult section on the architecture of termites in relationship to their social structure. The handwriting became faster and faster as the pen jabbed at the paper and stretched small words into almost straight lines. There was little time, a week at most, and the more he wrote the more he thought of that he should include. For now, today, it seemed that his faith had been well-placed: the scenario was going through its first movement. As the site had at last been tidied, as most of the workers had left, the rumours had begun about a gathering of the tribes, and now today it had been publicly proclaimed. Gerrard read the morning newspaper with the tense elation of a man who is three good shots away from winning a golf tournament. He knew he was not there yet. Not yet. Not yet.

But the gamble would pay off, it must pay off. It had not been an easy time and his faith in the scenario had been by no means constant, but a cautious inquiry here, a journey there, a piece of gossip from the minister, little odds and ends had confirmed the probability of the events the departed Wallis had predicted.

If three months ago he had been despised at the site, he had become openly hated. If he had once been distant, he had since become rude. If once he had been insensitive, he had become ruthless. He was anesthetized, a man running over hot coals towards salvation. The second shooting barely touched him, the reported beatings had become technical difficulties to overcome. A list had been compiled by the staff and the workers containing serious allegations about him. Even as he wrote his treatise this list was being released to the world press. Had he known, he would have considered it part of the gamble. As he introduced Pericles into the termite society, he was afire with faith.

This time next week the Kristu-Du would have produced a new society. He prayed feverishly that it wouldn't rain.

10.
It was happening.

It was said that Oongala skulked in his palace afraid. It was said openly in the streets.

Already the tribes had been gathered for four days. They camped around the Kristu-Du in their hundred thousands and inside it as well. Oongala's army brought them water in trucks, and delivered food daily. Goats were slaughtered and fires lit.

The minister was no longer to be found in his office and Gerrard found only a chicken clicking down the tiled corridors of the state offices.

Tanks were in evidence in the town and helicopters hovered anxiously.

Gerrard remained in his house, waiting for the call that would tell him Oongala was on his way to the site. One visit to the site had convinced the architect that he had nothing to fear about the accuracy of Wallis's scenario. The mood amongst the tribes was distinctly hostile. Soldiers of the army were spat on and dared not retaliate. Gerrard himself, an unknown white man, was bustled and shouted at. The hatred thrilled him. Each curse brought him closer to the realization of his dream. He saw Itos talking to Berehvas, Joflas to Lebuya, and in the midst of such violent concorde he felt an excitement of almost sexual dimensions.

Finally, on the fifth day, Oongala emerged from the palace, an uncertain parody of a triumphant smile on his huge cruel face. Gerrard, receiving his long-awaited phone call, followed the entourage in his Land Rover.

It was not a sensible thing to do, to associate himself publicly with the ruling party, but he followed it like a child following a circus parade.

The tribes waited sullenly, united beside and beneath the awesome dome.

In the four days Gerrard had been away from the site many words had been spoken. As tribe spoke with tribe, brother with brother, as they fired each other with their common anger, their breath rose high inside the great copper dome. So many people, each one breathing, speaking, some shouting, singing, and from each the breath rose and was held and contained by the copper cupola.

By the third day the roof of the dome was no longer visible to those who sat one thousand feet below on the tiered steps. A fine mist, like a fog, hung there, a curious contradiction to the cold cloudless day outside.

By the fourth day the mist had turned to a definite cloud. And Gerrard, had he seen this, would have immediately understood the enormity of the mistake he had made. For the copper dome was acting as an enormous condenser and the breath of the people swirled in strange clouds inside the dome, regarded with fear and apprehension by the tribes.

Oongala entered the valley at precisely four o'clock on the fifth day, just as the weak sun disappeared behind the mountains and a sharp chill descended on the valley.

He drove through the crowd to the door, waving and smiling. Their mood was uncertain, and if there was a little cheering there was also much silence. Oongala entered the Kristu-Du in full military uniform, one large man going to meet death with more courage than many would have thought him capable of.

Gerrard Haflinger strode jauntily towards the building in a crisp white suit, not yet aware that he had built a machine that would keep these primitive people in Oongala's murderous grip for another forty-three years.

For at this instant the great clouds inside the cupola could hold the water no more and rain fell inside the Kristu-Du, drenching the drought-stricken people in a heavy continuous drizzle.

Gerrard Haflinger had designed a prison, but he did not know this yet and for the eighty seconds that it took him to force his way through the hysterical crowd he still remained, more or less, sane.

He Found Her in Late Summer

1.

He found her in the later summer when the river ran two inches deep across glistening gravel beds and lay resting in black pools in which big old trout lay quietly in the cool water away from the heat of the sun. Occasionally a young rainbow might break the surface in the middle of the day, but the old fish did no such thing, either being too well fed and sleepy or, as the fisherman would believe, too old and wise to venture out at such a time.

Silky oaks grew along the banks and blackberries, dense and tangled, their fruit long gone into Dermott's pies, claimed by birds, or simply rotted into the soil, vigorously reclaimed the well-trodden path which wound beside fallen logs, large rocks, and through fecund gullies where tree ferns sent out tender new fronds as soft and vulnerable as the underbellies of exotic moths.

In one such gully a fallen tree had revealed a cave inside a rocky bank. It was by no means an ideal cave. A spring ran continually along its floor. Great fistfuls of red clay fell frequently and in the heat of the day mosquitoes sheltered there in their swarming thousands.

Three stalks of bracken outside its dirty mouth had been broken and the sign of this intrusion made him lower his hessian bag of hissing crayfish and quietly peer inside.

It was there he found her, wild and mud-caked, her hair tangled, her fair skin scratched and festered and spotted with infected insect bites. She was no more than twenty years old.

For a long time they regarded each other quietly. He squatted on his heels and slapped at the mosquitoes that settled on his long, wiry brown legs. She, her eyes swollen, fed them without complaint.

He rolled down the sleeves of his plaid shirt and adjusted his worn grey hat. He pulled up his odd grey socks and shifted his weight.

She tugged at her dress.

At last he held out his hand in the way that one holds out a hand to a shy child, a gentle invitation that may be accepted or rejected.

Only when the hand was lowered did she hold hers out. It was small and white, a city hand with the last vestiges of red nail polish still in evidence. He took the hand and pulled her gently to her feet, but before a moment had passed she had collapsed limply onto the muddy floor.

Dermott adjusted his hat.

"I'm going to have to pick you up," he said. It was, in a way, a question, and he waited for a moment before doing as he'd said. Then, in one grunting movement, he put her on his shoulders. He picked up the bag of crayfish and set off down the river, wading carefully, choosing this way home to save his passenger from the blackberry thorns which guarded the path along the banks.

Neither spoke to the other, but occasionally the girl clenched his shoulder tightly when they came to a rapid or when a snake, sleeping lightly on a hot rock, slipped silkily into the water as they approached.

Dermott carried his burden with pleasure yet he did not dwell on the reason for her presence in the cave nor attempt to invent theories for her being so many hundred miles from a town. For all of these things would be dealt with later and to speculate on them would have seemed to him a waste of time.

As he waded the river and skirted the shallow edges of the pools he enjoyed his familiarity with it, and remembered the time twenty years ago when it was as strange to him as it must be to his silent guest. Then, with the old inspector, he had done his apprenticeship as his mother had wished him to, read books, learned to identify two hundred different dragonflies, studied the life cycle of the trout, and most particularly the habits of the old black crayfish which were to be his alone to collect. It was an intensive education for such a simple job, and he often reflected in later years that it may not have been, in an official sense, compulsory, but rather a private whim of the old inspector who had loved this river with a fierce protectiveness.

The examination had been a casual affair, a day trek in late spring from where the old Chinese diggings lay in soft mossy neglect to the big falls five miles up river, yet at the end of it he had successfully identified some two hundred trees, thirty insects, three snakes, and described to the old inspector's satisfaction the ancient history of the rocks in the high cliffs that towered above them.

It was only much later, after a child had died, a

wife had left and floods had carried away most of his past, that he realized exactly what the old man had given him: riches more precious than he could ever have dreamed of. He had been taught to know the river with the quiet confident joy of a lover who knows every inch of his beloved's skin, every hair, every look, whether it denoted the extremes of rage and passion or the quieter more subtle moods that lie between.

Which is not to suggest that he was never lonely or that the isolation did not oppress him at times, but there were few days in which he did not extract some joy from life, whether the joys be as light as the clear web of a dragonfly or as turbulent as the sun on the fast water below Three Day Falls.

The winters were the hardest times, for the river was brown and swollen then and crayfish were not to be had. Then he occupied himself with a little tin mining and with building in stone. His house, as the years progressed, developed a unique and eccentric character, its grey walls jutting out from the hill-side, dropping down, spiralling up. And if few walls were quite vertical, few steps exactly level, it caused him no concern. Winter after winter he added more rooms, not from any need for extra space, but simply because he enjoyed doing it. Had ten visitors descended on him there would have been a room for each one, but there were few visitors and the rooms gave shelter to spiders and the occasional snake which feasted on mice before departing.

Once a gypsy had stayed during a period of illness and repaid his host with a moth-eaten rug of Asiatic origin. Other items of furniture were also gifts. An armchair with its stuffing hanging out had been left by a dour fisheries inspector who had carried it eighty miles on top of his Land Rover, knowing no other way to express his affection for this man on the river with his long silences and simple ways.

Books also were in evidence, and there was an odd assortment. Amongst them was a book on the nature of vampires, the complete works of Dickens, a manual for a motor car that now lay rusting in a ravine, and a science fiction novel entitled *Venus in a Half-Shell.* He had not, as yet, read any of them although he occasionally picked one up and looked at it, thinking that one day he would feast on the knowledge contained within. It would never have occurred to him that the contents of these books might reflect different levels of truth or reality.

"Nearly home," he said. They had left the river and passed through the high bracken of Stockman's Flat. He trudged in squelching boots along the rutted jeep track that led to the house. He was hot now, and tired. "Soon be there," he said, and in a moment he had carried her through the thick walls of his house and gently lowered her down into the old armchair.

She huddled into the armchair while he filled a big saucepan with water and opened the draught on the stained yellow wood stove.

"Now," he said, "we'll fix you up."

From the armchair the girl heard the words and was not frightened.

2.

There was about him a sense of pain long past, a

196

slight limp of the emotions. His grey eyes had the bitter sweet quality of a man who has grasped sorrow and carries it with him, neither indignant at its weight nor ignorant of its value. So if his long body was hard and sinewy, if his hair was cut brutally short, there was also a ministering gentleness that the girl saw easily and understood.

He brought warm water in a big bowl to her chair and with it two towels that might once, long ago, have been white.

"Now," he said, "one of us is going to wash you."

He had large drooping eyelids and a shy smile. He shifted awkwardly from one water-logged boot to the other. When she didn't move he put the towels on the arm of the chair and the bowl of water on the flagstone floor. "Don't worry about getting water on the floor," he said.

She heard him squelch out of the room and, in a moment, imagined she heard a floor being swept elsewhere in the house. Outside the odd collection of windows she could see the tops of trees and below, somewhere, she heard the sound of the river.

She picked up a grey towel and went to sleep.

3.

The tin roof was supported by the trunks of felled trees. The stone walls were painted white, veiled here and there by the webs of spiders and dotted with the bodies of dead flies. In one corner was a bed made from rough logs, its lumpy mattress supported by three thicknesses of hessian. A tree brushed its flowers against the window and left its red petals, as fine and delicate as spider legs, caught in the webs that adorned the glass.

She lay naked on the bed and let him wash her.

Only when he came in embarrassed indecision to the vulva did she gently push his hand away.

When the washing was over he took a pair of tweezers, strangely precise and surgical, and removed what thorns and splinters he found in her fair skin. He bathed her cuts in very hot water, clearing away the yellow centres of red infections, and dressed each one with a black ointment from a small white jar which bore the legend, "For Man or Beast".

He denied himself any pleasure he might have felt in touching her naked body, for that would have seemed wrong to him. When the wounds were all dressed he gave her an old-fashioned collarless shirt to wear for a nightdress and tucked her into bed. Only then did he allow himself the indulgence of thinking her pretty, seeing behind the cuts and swellings, the puffed eyelids, the tangled fair hair, a woman he might well have wished to invent.

She went to sleep almost immediately, her forehead marked with a frown.

He tiptoed noisily from the room and busied himself tidying up the kitchen in a haphazard fashion. But even while he worried over such problems as where to put a blackened saucepan his face broke continually into a grin. "Well," he said, "wonders will never cease."

When dinner came he presented her with two rainbow trout and a bowl of potatoes.

4.

It would be two days before she decided to talk and he passed these much as he would normally have, collecting the crayfish both morning and afternoon, gardening before lunch, fishing before dinner. Yet now he carried with him a new treasure, a warm white egg which he stored in some quiet dry part of his mind and as he worked his way down the rows of tomato plants, removing the small green grubs with his fingers, he smiled more often than he would have done otherwise.

When a shadow passed over the tangled garden and he looked up to admire the soft drift of a small white cloud, he did not look less long than he would have normally but there was another thing which danced around his joy, an aura of a brighter, different colour.

Yet he was, through force of habit, frugal with his emotions, and he did not dwell on the arrival of the girl. In fact the new entry into his life often slipped his mind completely or was squeezed out by his concentration on the job at hand. But then, without warning, it would pop up again and then he would smile. "Fancy that," he'd say. Or: "Well I never."

The girl seemed to prefer staying in the house, sometimes reading, often sleeping with one of Dermott's neglected books clutched to her chest. The swellings were subsiding, revealing a rather dreamy face with a wide, sad mouth and slightly sleepy blue eyes. A haze of melancholy surrounded her. When she walked it was with the quiet distraction of a sleep-walker. When she sat, her slow eyes followed Dermott's progress as he moved to and fro across the room, carrying hot water from the fire to the grimy porcelain sink, washing a couple of dishes, or one knife or two forks, stewing peaches from the tree in the garden, brewing a herb tea with a slightly bitter flavour, sweeping the big flagstone floor while he spread dirt from his hob-nailed boots behind him, cleaning four bright-eyed trout, feeding the tame magpie that wandered in and out through the sunlit patch in the back door.

He whistled a lot. They were old-fashioned optimistic songs, written before she was born.

When, finally, she spoke, it was to talk about the sweeping.

"You're bringing more dirt in than you're sweeping out."

He did not look surprised that she had spoken but he noted the softness of her voice and hoarded it away with delight. He considered the floor, scratching his bristly head and rubbing his hand over his newly shaven chin. "You're quite correct," he said. He sat on the long wooden bench beneath the windows and began to take off his boots, intending to continue the job in stockinged feet.

"Here," she said, "give it to me."

He gave her the broom. A woman's touch, he smiled, never having heard of women's liberation.

5.

That night at dinner she told him her story, leaning intently over the table and talking very softly.

It was beyond his experience, involving drugs,

men who had abused her, manipulated her, and finally wished to kill her. He was too overwhelmed by it to really absorb it. He sat at the table absently cleaning a dirty fork with the table cloth. "Fancy that," he would say. Or: "You're better off now." And again: "You're better off without them, that's all."

From the frequency of these comments she judged that he wished her to be quiet, but really they were produced by his feeling of inadequacy in the face of such a strange story. He was like a peasant faced with a foreigner who speaks with a strange accent, too overcome to recognize the language as his own.

What he did absorb was that Anna had been treated badly by the world and was, in some way, wounded because of it.

"You'll get better here," he said, "You've come to the right place."

He smiled at her, a little shyly, she thought. For a brief instant she felt as safe and comfortable as she had ever been in her life and then fear and suspicion, her old friends, claimed her once more. Her skin prickled and the wind in the trees outside sounded forlorn and lonely.

She sat beside the kerosene lamp surrounded by shadows. That the light shone through her curling fair hair, that Dermott was almost unbearably happy, she was completely unaware.

6.

Weeks passed and the first chill of autumn lay

along the river. Dermott slowly realized that Anna's recovery would not be as fast as he had imagined, for her lips remained sad and the sleepy eyes remained lustreless and defeated.

He brought things for her to marvel at: a stone, a dried-out frog, a beetle with a jewel-like shell, but she did not welcome the interruptions and did not try to hide her lack of interest so he stood there with the jewel in his hand feeling rather stupid.

He tried to interest her in the river, to give to her the pleasure the old inspector had given him, but she stood timidly on the bank wearing a dress she had made from an old sheet, staring anxiously at the ground around her small flat feet.

He stood in the water wearing only baggy khaki shorts and a battered pair of tennis shoes. She thought he looked like an old war photo.

"Nothing's going to bite you," he said, "You can stand in the water."

"No," she shook her head.

"I'll teach you how to catch crays."

"No."

"That's a silky oak."

She didn't even look where he pointed. "You go. I'll stay here."

He looked up at the sky with his hands on his hips. "If I go now I'll be away for two hours."

"You go," she insisted. The sheet dress made her look as sad as a little girl at bedtime.

"You'll be lonely. I'll be thinking that you're lonely," he explained, "so it won't be no fun. Won't you be lonely?"

She didn't say no. She said, "You go."

And he went, finally, taking that unsaid no with

him, aware that his absence was causing her pain.
He was distracted and cast badly. When a swarm of
caddis flies hatched over a still dark pool he did not
stay to cast there but pushed on home with the
catch he had: two small rainbows. He had killed
them without speaking to them.

He found her trying to split firewood, frowning
and breathing hard.

"You're holding the axe wrong," he said, not un-
kindly.

"Well how should I hold it then?"

She stood back with her hands on her hips. He
showed her how to do it, trying to ignore the anger
that buzzed around her.

"That's what I was doing," she said.

He retired to tend the garden and she thought he
was angry with her for intruding into his territory.
She did not know that his mother had been what
they called "a woman stockman" who was famous
for her toughness and self-reliance. When she saw
him watching her she thought it was with dis-
approval. He was keeping an anxious eye on her,
worried that she was about to chop a toe off.

7.

"Come with me."

"No, you go."

That is how it went, how it continued to go. A
little litany.

"Come, I'll teach you."

"I'm happy here."

"When I get back you'll be unhappy."

Over and over, a pebble being washed to and fro in a rocky hole.

"I can't enjoy myself when you're unhappy."

"I'm fine."

And so on, until when he waded off downstream he carried her unhappiness with him and a foggy film lay between him and the river.

The pattern of his days altered and he in no way regretted the change. Like water taking the easiest course down a hillside, he moved towards those things which seemed most likely to minimise her pain. He helped her on projects which she deemed to be important, the most pressing of which seemed to be the long grass which grew around the back of the house. They denuded the wild vegetable garden of its dominant weed. He had never cared before and had let it grow beside the tomatoes, between the broad leaves of the pumpkin, and left it where it would shade the late lettuce.

As he worked beside her it did not occur to him that he was, in fact, less happy than he had been, that his worry about her happiness had become the dominant factor of his life, clouding his days and nagging at him in the night like a sore tooth. Yet even if it had occurred to him, the way she extended her hand to him one evening and brought him silently to her bed with a soft smile on her lips, would have seemed to him a joy more complex and delightful than any of those he had so easily abandoned.

He worked now solely to bring her happiness. And if he spent many days in shared melancholy with her there were also rewards of no small magnitude: a smile, like a silver spirit breaking the water, the warmth of her warm white body beside him each morning.

He gave himself totally to her restoration and in so doing became enslaved by her. Had he been less of an optimist he would have abandoned the project as hopeless.

And the treatment was difficult, for she was naked and vulnerable, not only to him, to the world, but to all manner of diseases which arrived, each in their turn, to lay her low. In moments of new-found bitterness he reflected that these diseases were invited in and made welcome, evidence of the world's cruelty to her, but these thoughts, alien to his nature and shocking for even being thought, were banished and put away where he could not see them.

She lay in his bed pale with fever. He picked lad's love, thyme, garlic and comfrey and ministered to her with anxious concern.

"There," he said, "that should make you better."

"Do you love me, Dermott?" she asked, holding his dry dusty hand in her damp one. They made a little mud between them.

He was surprised to hear the word. It had not been in his mind, and he had to think for a while about love and the different things he understood by it.

"Yes," he said at last, "I do."

He felt then that he could carry her wounded soul from one end of the earth to the other. He was bursting with love.

8.

As he spent more and more time dwelling with her unhappiness he came to convince himself that he was the source of much of her pain. It was by far the most optimistic explanation, for he could do nothing to alter her past even if he had been able to understand it. So he came to develop a self-critical cast of mind, finding fault with himself for being stubborn, silent, set in his ways, preferring to do a thing the way he always had rather than the way she wished.

Eager to provide her with companionship he spent less and less time on the river, collecting the crays just once, early in the morning while she slept. In this way he lost many but this no longer seemed so important.

When she picked up a book to read in the afternoons he did likewise, hoping to learn things that he might share with her. He felt himself unlettered and ignorant. When he read he followed the lines of words with his broken-nailed finger and sometimes he caught her watching his lips moving and he felt ashamed. He discovered things to wonder at in every line and he often put his book down to consider the things he had found out. He would have liked to ask Anna many things about what he read but he imagined that she found his questions naive and irritating and did not like to be interrupted. So he passed over words he did not understand and marvelled in confused isolation at the mysteries he found within each page.

The True Nature of Vampires had been written long ago by a certain A. A. Dickson, a man having no great distinction in the world of the occult, whose only real claim to public attention had been involved with extracting twenty thousand pounds from lonely old women. Needless to say none of this was mentioned in the book.

Dermott, sitting uncomfortably on a hard wooden bench looked like a farmer at a stock sale. He learned that vampirism does not necessarily involve the sucking of blood from the victim (although this often is the case) but rather the withdrawal of vital energy, leaving the victim listless, without drive, prey to grey periods of intense boredom.

On page ten he read, "The case of Thomas Deason, a farmer in New Hampshire provides a classic example. In the spring of 1882 he befriended a young woman who claimed to have been beaten and abandoned by her husband. Deason, known to be of an amiable disposition, took the woman into his home as a housekeeper. Soon the groom and farm workers noticed a change in Deason: he became listless and they remarked on the 'grey pallor of his skin'. The groom, who was a student of such matters, immediately suspected vampirism and using rituals similar to those described in the Dion Fortune episode, drove the woman from the house. It was, however, too late to save Deason who had already become a Vampire himself. He was apprehended in a tavern in 1883 and brought to trial. After his conviction and execution there was still trouble in the area and it was only after a stake was driven through the heart of his exhumed corpse in 1884 that things returned to normal in the area."

One night, when making love, Anna bit him passionately on the neck. He leapt from her with a cry and stood shivering beside the bed in the darkness.

Suspicion and fear entered him like worms, and a slow anger began to spread through him like a poison, nurtured and encouraged each day by further doses of A. A. Dickson's musty book. His mind was filled with stories involving marble slabs, bodies that did not decompose, pistol wounds and dark figures fleeing across moonlit lawns.

His eyes took on a haunted quality and he was forever starting and jumping when she entered the room. As he moved deeper and deeper into the book his acknowledgment of his own unhappiness became unreserved. He felt that he had been tricked. He saw that Anna had taken from him his joy in the river, turned the tasks he had enjoyed into chores to be endured.

He began to withdraw from her, spending more and more time by himself on the river, his mind turning in circles, unable to think what to do. He moved into another bed and no longer slept with her. She did not ask him why. This was certain proof to him that she already knew.

Yet his listlessness, his boredom, his terrible lethargy did not decrease, but rather intensified.

When the jeep arrived to pick up the crayfish its driver was staggered to see the haunted look in Dermott's eyes and when he went back to town he told his superiors that there was some funny business with a woman down at Enoch's Point. The superiors, not having seen the look in Dermott's eyes, smiled and clucked their tongues and said to each other: "That Dermott, the sly old bugger."

9.

He had nightmares and cried in his sleep. He dreamed he had made a silver stake and driven it through her heart. He dreamed that she cried and begged him not to, that he wept too, but that he did it anyway driven by steel wings of fear. He shrieked aloud in his sleep and caused the subject of his dreams to lie in silent terror in her bed, staring into the blackness with wide open eyes.

He thought of running away, of leaving the river and finding a new life somewhere else, and this is almost certainly what he would have done had he not, returning from a brooding afternoon beside the river, discovered the following note: "Dear Dermott, I am leaving because you do not like me anymore and I know that I am making you unhappy. I love you. Thank you for looking after me when I was sick. I hate to see you unhappy and I know it is me that is doing it." It was signed: "With all the love in my heart, Anna."

The words cut through him like a knife, slicing away the grey webs he had spun around himself. In that moment he recognized only the truth of what she wrote and he knew he had been duped, not by her, but by a book.

It was evening when he found her, sitting on the bank of a small creek some three miles up the jeep track. He said nothing, but held out his hand. They walked back to the river in darkness.

He did not doubt that she was a vampire, but he had seen something that A.A. Dickson with his marble tombs and wooden stakes had never seen: that a vampire feels pain, loneliness and love. If vampires fed on other people, he reflected, that was the nature of life: that one creature drew nourishment and strength from another.

When he took her to his bed and embraced her soft white body he was without fear, a strong animal with a heavy udder.

Exotic Pleasures

1.

Lilly Danko had a funny face, but the actual point where one said "this is a funny face" rather than "this is a pretty face" was difficult to establish. Certainly there were little creases around the eyes and small smile lines beside the mouth, yet they had not always been there and she had always had a funny face. It was a long face with a long chin and perhaps it was the slight protuberance of her lower lip that was the key to it, yet it was not pronounced and could be easily overlooked and to make a fuss about it would be to ignore the sparkle in her pale blue eyes. Yet all of this is missing the point about faces which are not static things, a blue this, a long that, a collection of little items like clues in a crossword puzzle. For Lillian Danko had a rubber face which squinted its eyes, pursed its lips, wrinkled its nose and expressed, with rare freedom, the humours of its owner.

At the age of eight she had written in a school composition that she wished, when fully grown, to take the profession of clown. And although she had long since forgotten this incident and the cold winter's afternoon on which she had written it, she would not now, at the age of thirty, sitting in a boiling old Chevrolet at the Kennecott Interstellar Space Terminal, have found anything to disown.

Here she was, knitting baby clothes in a beaten-up car while Mort, dressed up in a suit like a travelling salesman, walked the unseen corridors inside the terminal in search of a job as a miner on one of the company's planets, asteroids or moons. She was not likely to share any jokes on the subject with Mort who was stretched as tight as a guitar string about to break. And she wished, as she had found herself wishing more and more lately, that her father had been alive to share the idiocies of the world with.

She would have astonished him with the news, made him laugh and made him furious all at once. Here, she would have said, we have the romance of space and pointed to the burnt ugly hulk of an interstellar cargo ship lowering itself on to the earth like a dirty old hen going down on its nest. Space had yielded no monsters, no martians, no exotic threats or blessings. The ship roaring bad-temperedly on the platform would contain nothing more beautiful than iron ingots, ball bearings, and a few embittered workers who were lucky enough to have finished their stint in the untidy backyards of space.

It wasn't funny unless you made it funny and Lilly, four months pregnant, with twenty dollars in her purse, a car that needed two hundred dollars and a husband who was fighting against three million unemployed to get a job, had no real choice but to make it funny.

"C'est la bloody guerre," she said holding up her knitting and reflecting that two hundred miles of dusty roads had not done a lot for the whiteness of the garment.

Fuck it, she thought, it'll have to do.

When the face appeared in the open window by her shoulder she got such a fright she couldn't remember whether she'd said "fuck" out loud or just thought it.

"I beg your pardon," she said to the bombed-out face that grinned crookedly through the window.

"Pardon for what?" He was young and there was something crazy about him. His black eyes looked as sleepy as his voice sounded. He was neglected and overgrown with wild curling black hair falling over his eyes and a bristling beard that was just catching up to an earlier moustache.

"I thought I may have said something."

"If you said something," he said, "I didn't hear it. I am definitely at least half deaf in one ear."

"I probably didn't say it then," she said carefully, wondering if he was going to rob her or if he was just crazy. "Are you looking for a lift?"

"Not me." He stood back from the windows so she could see his white overalls with their big Kennecott insignia. He was tall and thin like a renegade basketball player. "This," he gestured laconically to include the whole area of car park, administration building, docking platforms and dry parched earth, "This is my home. So," he paused for a moment as if what he had said had made him inexplicably sad, "so I don't need a lift, thank you."

"Any jobs in there?"

"Let's say there are an awful lot of people in there waiting to be told no."

Lilly nodded. "Yeah, well . . ."

"You want to see something?"

"Well that depends what is is."

He walked smoothly back to a little white cleaner's trolley he had left marooned a few yards from the car and trundled it back whistling like one who carries rare gifts.

"If anyone comes," he whispered, "you're asking me directions, OK?"

"OK."

"This," he reached a large hand into the white cart, "is really something special."

He was not exaggerating. For what he now pushed through the window and onto her lap was the most beautiful bird that Lilly Danko had ever dreamed might be possible, more exquisite and delightful than a bird of paradise, a flamingo, or any of the rare and beautiful species she had ever gazed at in picture books. It was not a large bird, about the size of a very big pigeon, but with a long supple neck and a sleek handsome head from which emerged a strong beak that looked just like mother of pearl. Yet such was the spendour of the bird that she hardly noticed the opaline beauty of the beak, or the remarkable eyes which seemed to have all the colours of the rainbow tucked into a matrix of soft brown. It was the bird's colouring that elicited from her an involuntary cry. For the feathers that ran from its smooth head to its graceful tail were of every blue possibly imaginable. Proud Prussian blue at the head then, beneath a necklace of emerald green, ultramarine and sapphire which gave way to dramatic tail feathers of peacock blue. Its powerful chest revealed viridian hidden like precious jewels in an aquamarine sea.

When she felt the first pulse of pure pleasure she imagined that it came from the colours themselves and later when she tried to explain this first feeling to Mort she would use the word "swoon", savouring the round smooth strangeness of the word.

"Don't it feel nice when you touch it?"

"Oh, yes."

And even as she answered she realized that it was not the colours that gave such pleasure, but that the feeling was associated with stroking the bird itself. "It's like having your back rubbed."

"Better."

"Yes," she said, "better. It gets you right at the base of the neck."

"It gets you just about everywhere." And something about the way he said it made her realize that he wasn't showing her this bird out of idle interest, but that he was going to offer it for sale. It was an exotic, of course, and had probably been smuggled in by some poor miner looking for an extra buck. If the crew-cut Protestants who had begun the push into space with such obsessive caution had seen the laxness of the space companies with quarantine matters they would have shrieked with horror. But NASA has wilted away and no terrible catastrophe had hit the earth. There were exotic shrubs which needed to be fed extra-terrestrial trace elements to keep them alive, a few dozen strange new weeds of no particular distinction, and a poor small lizardish creature raised for its hallucinogenic skin.

But there had been nothing as strange and beautiful as this and she calculated its value in thousands of dollars. When she was invited to make an offer she reluctantly handed it back, or tried to, because as she held it up to the man he simply backed away.

"You've got to make an offer. You can't not make an offer."

She put the bird, so placid she thought it must be drugged, back on her lap and stroked sadly. "OK, I'll be the bunny. How much do you want?"

He held up two hands.

"Ten dollars?"

"Is that cheap or is it cheap."

"It's cheap, but I can't."

"You should have made an offer."

"I can't," she said hopelessly, thinking of Mort and what he would say. God knows the world pressed in on him heavily enough. Yet the thrilling thought that she could own such a marvel, that she need never hand it back, crept into her mind and lodged there, snug and comfortable as a child sleeping beneath a soft blanket.

"I can only offer five," she said, thinking that she couldn't offer five at all.

"Done."

"Oh, shit."

"You don't want it?"

"Oh yes, I want it," she said dryly, "you know I want it." She put the bird down on the seat, where it sat waiting for nothing more than to be picked up again, and took five of their precious dollars from her handbag. "Well," she said, handing over the money, "I guess we can always eat it." Then, seeing the shocked look on the wild young face: "Just joking."

"If you don't want it . . ."

"I want it, I want it. What does it eat? Breakfast cereal and warm milk?"

"I've got feed for it, so don't sweat."

"And the feed is extra, right?"

"My dear Dolores," he said, "where this bird comes from, the stuff it eats grows on trees. If you'd be nice enough to open the boot I'll give you a bag of it and our transaction, as they say, will be finito."

She opened the boot and he wheeled round his cleaner's trolley and hoisted a polythene sack into the car.

"What do I do when it's eaten all this?"

But he was already gliding across the car park towards the administration building. "Well *then*," he giggled over his shoulder, "you're going to have to *eat* it."

The giggling carried across the hot tarmac and got lost in the heat haze.

Lillian went back to the car and was still stroking the bird when Mort came back.

Through pale veils of pleasure she saw him walking back across the blistering car park and she knew, before he arrived at the car, exactly what his eyes would look like. She had seen those eyes more and more recently, like doors to comfortable and familiar rooms that suddenly open to reveal lift wells full of broken cables. She should have taken him in her arms then and held him, stroked his neck until the lights came back on in those poor defeated eyes, eyes which had once looked at the world with innocent certainty, which had sought nothing more than the contentment of being a good gardener, calm eyes without fear and ambition. She should have taken him in her arms, but she had the bird and she sat there, stroking it stupidly, like someone who won't leave a hot shower until the water goes cold.

He came and sat behind the wheel, not looking at her.

"Take off your coat, honey," she said gently, putting a hand on his. "Come on, take it off."

It was then that he saw the bird.

"What's that?"

Her left hand was still stroking it. She ran a finger down its opaline bill, across its exquisitely smooth head and down its glowing blue back. "It's a bird. Stroke it." She tugged his hand, a hand which each day had become smoother and softer, towards the bird, and the bird, as if understanding, craned its supple neck towards him. "It'll make you feel better."

But Mort put both hands on the steering wheel and she saw his knuckles whiten. She was frightened then. He was a dark well she had only thought of as calm and still, but that was in the easy confidence of employment, in times without threat. Now, when she said what she had to say, something would happen.

"Mort, I'm sorry. I paid five dollars for it. I'm sorry Mort."

He opened the door and walked slowly around the car. She watched him. He didn't look at her. He walked around the car a second time and she saw his face colouring. Then he started kicking it. He moved slowly, methodically, kicking it every couple of feet as if he wished to leave no part of its dull chalky body unpunished. When he had finished he came and sat down again, resting his head against the wheel.

Lilly got out of the car and walked to the driver's side.

"Come on bugalugs," she said, "move over. I'm driving."

She slid behind the wheel, thinking that in another month she wouldn't be able to fit behind it, and when he moved over she passed him the bird. By the time they had left the terminal he was stroking it. His face had relaxed and resumed its normal quiet innocence and she remembered the days they had worked together as gardeners on the Firestone Estate as if this were some lost Paradise from which they had been inexplicably expelled by a stern fascist god.

"Let's stay in a motel," she said. "Let's have a hot shower and a good meal and get drunk and have a nice fuck in a big bed."

"And be broke in the morning," he said, but smiled.

"One morning we'll be broke. We might as well have fun doing it."

Mort stroked the bird slowly, dreamily.

"Do you like our bird?" she asked.

He smiled. "You're a crazy person, Lilly."

"Do you still love me?"

"Yes," he said, "and I like the bird. Let's have champagne and piss off without paying."

"Champagne it is."

As it turned out, the motel they chose didn't have champagne, but it had an architecture well suited to their plans. Its yellow painted doors faced the highway and when they backed the car into the space in front of the room there was nothing in their way to prevent a fast getaway.

2.

Lillian lay on the bed stroking the bird which sat comfortably between her breasts and her swollen belly. The bottle of wine which stood amongst the debris of a meal on the table beside her was very nearly empty.

Mort, his hair wet, sat naked in a chair staring at the television. She envied him his looseness, his easy sexual satisfaction.

"Why don't you put it down," he said.

"In a minute."

"Come and rub my back."

"You're a greedy bugger, Morto."

"You want to be careful with that bird. It probably should have injections or something. You shouldn't fuck around with exotics when you're pregnant."

"You're the only exotic I fuck around with." She looked at him and thought for the millionth time how pretty he was with his smooth skin and his hard muscles and that beautiful guileless face. "Let's get another bottle." The drunk Mort was more like the old Mort.

Without waiting for an answer she reached over and picked up the phone. She ordered the wine, put the bird in the bathroom with a saucer of seed, threw Mort a pair of trousers and picked up her own dress from where she had dropped it.

It was the manager himself who brought the wine. He wasn't content to hand it through the door. "I'll just pick up the trays," he said and Lilly noted that he already had his foot in the door, like an obnoxious encyclopedia salesman.

He was a short, slim man, handsome in an over-

ripe way, with a mole near his eye and waving dark
hair. Lilly didn't like him. She didn't like his highly
shined shoes or his neatly pressed flannel trousers.
She didn't like the way he looked at the wet towel
lying on the floor and the rumpled disordered bed
freshly stained from love making.

She sat on the bed while he busied himself with
the trays. When she saw he was actually counting
the knives and forks she started mimicking him
behind his back.

When he announced that a saucer was missing
she nearly burst out laughing, as if anyone would
pinch one of his stupid tasteless saucers.

"It's in the bathroom," she said and was wondering if she should add, "where it belongs" when the
man took the opportunity to inspect the bathroom.

When he came back he was holding the bird in
one hand and the saucer of seed in the other. Lilly
took the bird from him and watched him drop the
seeds into the rubbish bin.

"There is a house rule against pets. It's quite
clearly displayed."

"It's not a pet," she said.

"I can't have people bringing pets here."

She saw Mort put his head in his hands as he anticipated one more setback, one more razor-nick
defeat.

She took the saucer from the manager's mani-
cured hand. "Just stroke it," she said, "it has special
properties," and smiled inwardly to hear herself use
a word like "properties", a left over from her wasted
education.

The manager looked at her with supercilious eyes
and was about to give her back the bird when she

firmly took hold of his free hand (which she was astonished to find damp with anxiety) and rubbed it down the bird's back. When she took her hand away he continued to stroke it mechanically, the threatened light of authority still shining in his eyes.

"Go on," she encouraged, "it feels nice."

In spite of a private conviction that he was being made a fool of, the manager stroked the bird, at first tentatively and then more surely. The bird, as if understanding the importance of the occasion, brushed its cheek against the manager's and then for a minute or two very little moved in the room but the manager's hand.

Lights from the highway flowed across the wall.

On the television a mute reporter held a microphone towards a weeping man.

Twice Lilly saw the manager trying to give the bird back and twice she saw him fail.

"Feels nice, doesn't it?"

The manager nodded his head and looked embarrassed. She could see that pleasure had made his eyes as gooey as marshmallow.

"Now," she said briskly, holding out her hands for the bird, "I'll put it in the car so we won't be breaking the rules."

"No." He was like a two-year-old with a teddy bear.

"You'll exhaust it," Lilly said, "and we need it for tomorrow. It's our business. That's what I mean about it not being a pet."

"Your business?" the manager asked, and in truth every person in the room was trying to think how this beautiful bird might be anyone's "business".

"It's a Pleasure Bird," Lilly said, lighting a cigarette although she had given them up three months ago. It gave her time to think. "We charge a dollar a minute for people to stroke it."

"You people in show business?"

"Sure am." Lilly exhaled luxuriously and sat down on the bed.

"Dollar a minute, eh. Good work if you can get it." He was being nice now and she allowed herself the luxury of not despising him for it.

"You think that's too expensive?" She held out her arms for the bird. "We've charged more and no one's ever complained."

The manager stepped back from the extended arms, cooing over the bird like a mother keeping its baby from harm.

Lilly started talking. Ideas came to her so fast that she hardly knew how the sentence would end when she started it. "You can have it for half an hour." She watched the manager glow. "In return for the price for this room and the food."

"Done."

"And wine, of course."

"Done."

"For an extra five dollars in cash you can take it to the office so we won't disturb you. We'll get it when time's up."

"Done."

"What's the time Mort?"

Mort picked up his wristwatch from the top of the mute television. "Nine twenty-three."

"OK, it is now nine twenty-three." She opened the door and ushered the manager out into the night. "I'll pick it up from you at exactly nine fifty-three."

When she shut the door she was grinning so broadly her face hurt. She hugged Mort and said, "I'm a genius. Tell me I'm a genius."

"You're a genius," he said, "but you were crazy to let him take it away."

"Why for Chrissakes?"

"He mightn't give it back."

"Oh fuck, Mort. Stop it."

"I'm sorry, it was just a thought."

"Be positive."

"I am positive."

"Well pour me a glass of wine and tell me I'm beautiful."

The manager had taken the corkscrew and they had to shove the cork in with a pencil.

As it turned out they made an extra twenty dollars cash that night. It was 10.13 before they persuaded the manager to relinquish the bird. They stood in his office holding the wristwatch while the man bought minute after minute of extra time from his petty cash. The phone rang and wasn't answered.

As they left his office, the bird ruffled its feathers and shat on the concrete.

3.

Mort didn't want to look at the empty wine bottle or the plan he had agreed to so easily the night before. When Lillian got up he curled himself into a ball and pretended he was still asleep. Lilly knew he wasn't asleep and knew why he was pretending.

"Come on, Mort, don't be chicken shit."

Mort moaned.

"Come on Mort honey or we won't get a stall." She rattled a coffee cup near his ear. "Do you want to get rich or do you want to stay poor? Here's your coffee, baby. It's getting cold."

When Mort finally emerged, tousle-headed and soft as a child's toy, he was in no way prepared for what he saw. Lilly was wearing white overalls and clown's make-up. There were stars round her eyes and padding in her bum.

"Oh Christ, Lilly, please."

"Please what? Drink your coffee."

"Oh shit, please don't. We don't have to do that."

"You heard what I told the man. We're in show business."

"Take it off, please. I don't mind the business with the bird, but we don't have to do all this."

"Drink your coffee and I'll take Charley-boy out for a shit."

When he drove to the markets it was in strained silence. The clown held the bird. The straight man was at the wheel. When the car finally lost its muffler neither of them said anything.

4.

The markets had sprung up to meet the needs of the new poor and were supplied and operated by an increasingly sophisticated collection of small-time crooks. The police, by mutual agreement, rarely entered their enclosures and business was thus conducted with some decorum, whether it was the purchase of stolen clothing or illicit drugs (the notorious Lizard Dust was sold here and it was only the poor who tolerated the violent illnesses that preceded its more pleasant effects). Here you could buy spare parts for rubber thongs, fruit, vegetables, motor cars of questionable origin, poisonous hot dogs and bilious-coloured drinks.

The market they drove to was a vast concrete-paved car park which, at nine o'clock in the morning, was already unpleasantly hot. A blustery wind carried clouds of dust through the stalls, rattled the canvas roofs, and lodged a fine speck of dust in Mort's eye. So it was Lillian who joined the queue for temporary stalls while Mort adjourned, more in embarrassment than pain, to minister to his eye in the men's toilets.

The stall number was 128. It was nothing more than a wooden trestle table with a number painted on the top. Canvas awnings were a luxury they could not yet afford.

Mort stood behind the stall in his suit and tie, red-eyed and sulky. The bird stood stoically on the table. Lilly, resplendent in overalls and clown's face, waddled to and fro in front, a balloon of swollen belly and padded bum.

"It won't work."

"Of course it'll work," she said. But her stomach was a mass of nerves and the baby, probably nervous of the life she had in store for it, kicked irritably inside her. "Don't look like that," she hissed. "I can't do it when you're looking at me like that."

"Do what?"

And she started to do it. She felt a fool. She did badly what she had dreamed would be easy. Her voice sounded high and when she tried to lower it, it came out worse. What she said was hardly impressive and rarely funny. But she began to lumber amongst the crowds clapping her hands and making a fuss.

"See the Pleasure Bird at Stall 128," she yelled. "First three customers get a minute of pleasure for free. Oh yes, oh yes, oh yes. One dollar, one minute. They say it's better than sex. One dollar, one minute and the first three customers get it free."

A crowd of ragged children followed her. She did a cake walk. She danced a waltz with a black man in a pink suit. She fell over a guy-rope and made it look intentional. She attracted a small crowd by the simple device of placing a match box on the ground and making a big show of jumping over it, bowing and smiling when the jump was done. The matchbox jump was the most successful stunt of all and she gave the laughing crowd the news about stall 128 and the Pleasure Bird.

By the time she'd got lost in an alley of used car parts and been threatened by a woman who was trying to sell bruised apples she was exhausted. She had blisters on her feet from Mort's sandshoes which were four sizes too big and a cut on her hand from the fall over the guy-rope. She limped back to the stall to find an enormous crowd huddled around an old woman who was dreamily stroking the bird. Mort stood beside her with his watch in his hand. The crowd was strangely silent and the woman crooning to the bird seemed vulnerable and rather sad.

"Ten minutes," said Mort.

The woman reluctantly handed the bird back and, from a pocket of her voluminous black dress, produced a half-unravelled blue sock from which she counted out, in notes and coins, ten dollars.

As Mort handed the bird to the next person in the queue, the quiet solemnity of the recipient's face reminded Lilly of a face in her childhood taking communion in a small country church. He was an Italian, a labourer with a blue singlet and dusty boots and he had only had the bird for thirty seconds when he cradled it in one arm and dragged a bundle of notes from his pockets which he placed on the table in a crumpled heap.

"Tell me when time's up," he said, and sat on the trestle table, hunched over the bird, lost in his own private world, impervious to the mutterings of the impatient crowd.

After that they limited the time to three minutes.

They could have worked the market all day but Mort, rather than sharing Lilly's ever increasing sense of triumph, became more and more upset with her costume.

"Take it off. You don't need it now."

"No."

"Please."

"Don't be silly Mort. It's part of the act."

"You look a fool. I can't stand people laughing at you."

They hissed at each other until one o'clock when Mort, his face red and sullen, suddenly dumped the bird in Lilly's lap and walked away.

At two o'clock she closed the stall and limped painfully back to the car. The bird shat once or twice on the way back, but apart from that seemed none the worse for its handling. Mort didn't seem to have fared so well. He was sitting woodenly inside the boiling car and when she asked him how much he'd taken he simply handed her the money.

She counted two hundred and thirty dollars in notes and didn't bother with the silver.

5.

The balcony of their room looked across the wide graceful river which was now silvery and cool in the late light. A rowing eight moved with svelte precision through a canopy of willows and the two black swans descended from the sky above the distant city and Lilly, watching them, imagined the pleasant coolness of the water on their hot bodies.

Her make-up was gone now and she wore a loose white cheesecloth dress. The ice clinked in her gin and tonic and even the small chink of the glass as it touched the metal filigree table sounded cool and luxurious to her ears. She put her blistered feet up on the railing and stroked the bird gently, letting the pleasure saturate her body.

"Mort."

"Yes."

"You feel OK now?"

He leant across and put his arm on her shoulder. His face was sunburnt and there was a strange red V mark on his chest. He nodded. "Put the bird inside."

"In a minute."

He took his hand back and filled his glass.

Lillian was feeling triumphant. She had a fair idea of the worms that were eating at Mort and she was surprised and a little guilty to discover that she didn't care excessively. She felt cool and rich and amazingly free. After a few minutes she picked up the bird and put it in front of the bathroom mirror where, she discovered, for all its unearthly qualities, it behaved just like a budgerigar.

She went back to the balcony and stood behind Mort, rubbing his broad back and loosening the tense muscles in his neck.

"Tell me I was terrific," she said. "Please say I was great."

Mort hesitated and she felt the muscles under her fingers knot again. "Let's not talk about it now."

She smiled just the same, remembering checking into this hotel, Mort dressed in his salesman's suit, she in her clown's make-up, the bird quietly hidden in a plastic shopping bag.

"Lillian," she said, "you were terrific."

The river was almost black now and, when two birds cut across it towards a certain tree, it was too dark to see the stunning colours by which she might have identified them.

6.

Their days were lined with freeways and paved with concrete. They limped south with a boiling radiator and an un-muffled engine. They worked markets, factory gates and even, on one occasion, a forgotten country school where the children let down their tyres to stop them leaving.

Mort no longer complained about the clown, yet his resentment and embarrassment grew like a cancer inside him and he seldom thought of anything else. He had long since stopped touching the Pleasure Bird and the full force of his animosity was beamed towards its small colourful eyes which seemed to contain a universe of malignant intentions.

"God, Jesus, it likes freeways." Lillian held the bird in the air, displaying its ruffled feathers, a signal that it was going to shit.

Mort didn't appear to hear.

"Well stop the car. You're the one who's always worried about where it shits."

Slowly, irritatingly slowly, Mort pulled the car into the white emergency lane and the bird hopped out, shat quickly and effectively, and hopped back in.

"This bird seems intent on spreading shit from one end of Highway 31 to the other."

Mort pulled back onto the road.

"It's really crazy for doing it on nice clean roads. Do you notice that, Morty?"

"Why don't you put it down for a while. You're getting like a bloody junkie."

Lilly said nothing. Her clown's face showed no emotions but those she had painted on it, and in truth she did not allow herself to think anything of Mort's jealousies. She stroked her index finger slowly down the bird's sensuous back and the slow waves of pleasure blotted out anything else that might have worried her. Even the police siren, when it sounded outside the window, did not startle her. It reached her distantly, having no more importance than a telephone ringing in someone else's dream.

She watched the police car park in front of them and watched the policeman walk back towards their car, pink book in his hand. She heard him talk to Mort about the muffler and saw them both walk around the car looking at the tyres. Even when the policeman stood beside her window and spoke to her she did not think that the words were really addressed to her.

"What sort of bird is that?"

It was only when the question was repeated that she managed to drag her mind to the surface and stare blinking into the strangely young face.

"It's a Pleasure Bird," she smiled, "here." And she passed the passive bird into the big white hands.

"Sure does give a lot of pleasure."

"Sure does."

The bird was passed back and the pink notebook opened.

"Now," he said, "how about we start by you telling me where you got this."

"Why?"

"Because it's an exotic."

"No. It's from New Guinea."

"Look madam, you've chosen the wrong fellow to lay that on. This bird comes from Kennecott 21. I was there two years."

"Fancy that," said Lilly, "we were told it was from New Guinea."

The notebook closed. "I'll have to take it."

Lilly was struck by the early rumbles of panic. "You can't take it. It's how we earn our living."

But the policeman was already leaning over into

the car, his hands ready to engulf the plump jewel-like body.

Then he was suddenly lurching back from the car window with his hands to one eye. Blood streamed down across his knuckles. The bird was pecking at the fingers which covered the other eye. The noise was terrible. She saw Mort running around the car and he was beside her starting the engine, and the bird, as if nothing had happened, was back sitting on her lap.

"Don't go," she said. "Mort. Don't."

But Mort was white with panic and as he accelerated onto the highway Lilly turned helplessly to watch as the policeman staggered blindly onto the road where a giant container truck ran over the top of him.

Even as she watched she stroked the bird in her lap so she had the strange experience of seeing a man killed, of feeling guilt, horror and immeasurable pleasure all at once. The floodgates lifted. Seven colours poured into her brain and mixed into a warm sickly brown mud of emotion.

They turned east down a dusty road which led through the rusting gates of neglected farms. Grass grew through the centre of the road and swished silkily beneath the floor. Lillian began to remove her make-up. Mort, pale and shaken, hissed inaudible curses at the dusty windscreen.

7.

Yet their life did not stop, but limped tiredly on through a series of markets and motel rooms and if their dreams were now marred by guilt and echoes, neither mentioned it to the other.

They bought a small radio and listened to the news, but nothing was ever said about the policeman and Lilly was shocked to find herself hoping that his head had been crushed, obliterating the evidence of the attack.

Mort drew away from her more and more, as if the crime had been hers and hers alone. When he spoke, his sentences were as cold and utilitarian as three-inch nails.

He took to calling the bird "the little murderer". There was something chilling in the way that dreamy childlike face moved its soft lips and said such things as: "Have you fed the little murderer?"

He was filled with anger and resentment and fear which had so many sources he himself didn't know where the rivers of his pain began, from which wells they drew, from which fissures they seeped.

He watched Lillian perform at the markets, saw the bird shit on every hard surface that came its way, and he watched it narrowly, warily, and on more than one occasion thought he saw the bird watching him. Once, removing the bird from bedroom to bathroom for the night against Lilly's will, he thought that the bird had burned him.

At the markets he did less and less and now it was Lilly who not only attracted the crowds but also took the money and kept time. He felt useless and hopeless, angry at himself that he was too stiff and unbending to do the things that he should to earn a living, resentful that his wife could do it all without appearing to try, angry that she should accept his withdrawal so readily, angry that she showed no guilt or remorse about a man's death, angry when she met his silences with her own, angry that he who hated the bird should continue to want the money it brought him.

They spent three hundred dollars on the car. Its radiator no longer boiled. A shiny new muffler was bolted securely into place. Yet the sight of that clean metal exhaust pipe sticking out from beneath the rear bumper made him close his eyes and suck in his breath.

He drank champagne without pleasure and made love with silent rage while Lilly's eyes followed invisible road maps on the ceiling.

With sticky tissues still between her legs she brought the bird to bed and stroked it till she drifted into sleep. Even the ease of her sleep enraged him, giving him further proof of her cold self-sufficiency.

And it was on one such night, with his wife asleep on the twin bed beside him, with a cheap air-conditioner rattling above his head, that he saw the current affairs bulletin on the latest quarantine breakdown. He watched it without alarm or even any particular interest. There had been many such breakdowns before and there would be many again in the future. As usual there were experts who were already crying catastrophe, and these were, of course, balanced by optimists who saw no serious threat to the terrestrial environment.

The breakdown in this case involved a tree, named by journalists as the Kennecott Rock-drill. The seeds of this tree took to their new home with a particular enthusiasm. Adapted for a harsh, rocky environment the seeds had a very specialized survival mechanism. Whereas a terrestial seed secreted mucus, the Kennecott Rock-drill secreted a strong acid much as a lichen did. When dropped on the rocky surfaces of its home planet the secreted acid produced a small hole. In this self-made bed the root tips expanded, using osmosis, and little by little cracked the rock, pushing a strong and complicated root system down a quarter of a mile if need be. In a terrestrial environment the whole process was speeded up, moisture and a less formidable ground surface accelerating the growth rate to such an extent that a single seed could emerge as a small tree on a busy freeway in less than seven days.

Mort watched the programme with the same detachment with which earlier generations had greeted oil spills or explosions in chemical plants.

Service stations in the north were overcome by green vegetation. Men in masks sprayed poisons which proved ineffective. People lay in hospital beds seriously ill from drinking water contaminated by this same herbicide. Fire, it seemed, rather than slowing the spread of the Rock-drill merely accelerated the germination of the seeds. Mort watched an overgrown house sacrificed to fire and then the result, a week later, when giant Rock-drills grew in the burnt-out ruins. He would have turned complacently to the late movie on another channel, had they not shown film of the Rock-drill's home environment.

There he watched the strange rocky outcrops of a Kennecott planet, saw the miners working beneath a merciless sun and silently thanked god he had not succeeded in getting a job there. He admired the beauty of the giant trees silhouetted against a purple sunset and then, sitting up with a cry of recognition, saw the flocks of birds that crowded the gnarled branches.

The birds were identical to the one which sat silently on the end of Lilly's bed.

He sat shaking his head, as puzzled and secretly pleased as any lost citizen who finds his hated neighbour on public television.

8.

The argument started the next morning at breakfast and flickered and flared for the next two days as they pursued an ever more erratic course, dictated more by Mort's perversity than the location of markets. His eyes blazed, bright, righteous and triumphant. A strange pallor lay like a sheet across his tucked-in face.

To Lilly he became a mosquito buzzing on the edges of an otherwise contented sleep. She slapped at the mosquito and wished it would go away. The bird, now officially outlawed for its role in spreading the Rock-drill seed, sat contentedly in her lap as she stroked it. The stroking rarely stopped now. It was as if she wanted nothing more from life than to stroke its blue jewelled back for ever and it seemed, for the bird, the arrangement was perfect.

"Are you listening to me?"

"Yes." She hadn't been.

"We'll have to hand it in."

"No we won't." There was no anger in her voice.

Mort sucked in breath through clenched teeth.

She heard the intake of air but it caused her no

concern. No matter how he shouted or hissed, no matter what he said about the bird, there was only one danger to Mort and it had nothing to do with quarantine breakdowns. From the depths of the blue well she now lived in, Lilly acknowledged the threat posed by the Kennecott Rock-drill and in her mind she had fulfilled her obligation to the world by collecting the bird's shit in a cardboard box. It was as simple as that. As for the potential violence of the bird, she saw no problem in that either. It was only violent when it was threatened. It was wiser not to threaten it.

These simple answers to the problem did not satisfy Mort and she concluded, correctly, that there must be other things which threatened him more directly.

"Do you know why you want me to get rid of this bird?" she said.

"Of course I bloody know."

"I don't think you do."

"Alright," he said slowly, "you tell me."

"First, you don't like the bird because you hate to see me being able to earn a living. Then you hate yourself because you can't. You're so fucked-up you can't see I'm doing it for both of us."

"Bullshit."

"No, Morty. Not bullshit, fact. But most of all," she paused, wondering if it was wise to say all this while he was driving.

"Yes, most of all . . ."

"Most of all it is because you're frightened of pleasure. You can't have pleasure yourself. You don't know how. You can't stand the sight of me having pleasure. You can't give me pleasure, so you're damned if anything else is going to."

The car swung off the road and onto the verge. It skidded in gravel. For a moment, as the wheels locked and the car slid sideways, she thought that it would roll. It turned 180 degrees and faced back the way it had come, its engine silent, red lights burning brightly on the dash.

"You're saying I'm a lousy fuck."

"I'm saying you give me no pleasure."

"You used to make enough noise."

"I loved you. I wanted to make you happy."

Mort didn't say anything for a moment. The silence was a tight pink membrane stretched through pale air.

She looked at the warning lights, thinking the ignition should be turned off.

She was expecting something, but when the blow came she did not know what happened. It felt like an ugly granite lump of hate, not a fist. Her head was hit sideways against the window.

Everything that happened then was slow and fast all at once. She felt wetness on her face and found tears rather than the blood she had expected. At the same time she saw the bird rise from her lap and fly at Mort. She saw Mort cower beneath the steering wheel and saw the bird peck at his head. She saw, like a slow motion replay, the policeman walk onto the road howling with pain. She quietly picked up the bird in both hands as she had done it a hundred times every day, and quietly wrung its neck.

She held the body on her lap, stroking it.

She watched Mort whom she did not love weep across the steering wheel.

9.

They drove in grey silence for there was nothing else to do. It was as if they travelled along the bottom of the ocean floor. If there was sun they didn't see it. If there were clouds they took no note of their shapes or colours.

If they had come to a motel first it is possible that the ending might have been different but, turning down a road marked A34, they came to their first forest of Kennecott Rock-drill. It grew across the road like a wall. It spread through a shopping complex and across a service station. Water gushed from broken pipes.

When they left the car the smell of gasoline enveloped them and in the service station they saw a huge underground tank pushed up through a tangle of roots and broken concrete, its ruptured skin veiled by an inflammable haze.

Lilly heard a sharp noise, a drumming, and looked to see Mort hammering on the car's bonnet with clenched fists, drumming like a child in a tantrum. He began screaming. There were no words at first. And then she saw what he had seen. Above their heads the branches of the trees were crowded with the birds, each one as blue and jewel-like as the dead body that lay in the front seat of the car. Through mists of gasoline Lilly saw, or imagined she saw, a curious arrogance in their movements, for all the world like troops who have just accomplished a complicated and elegant victory.

War Crimes

1.

In the end I shall be judged.

They will write about me in books and take care to explain me so badly that it is better that I do it myself. They will write with the stupid smugness of middle-class intellectuals, people of moral rectitude who have never seriously placed themselves at risk. They have supported wars they have not fought in, and damned companies they have not had the courage to destroy. Their skins are fair and pampered and their bellies are corseted by expensively-made jeans.

They will write about me as a tyrant, a psychopath, an aberrant accountant, and many other things but it would never once occur to them that I might know exactly what I am doing. Neither would they imagine that I might have feelings other than those of a mad dog.

But they do not have a monopoly on finer feelings, as you shall soon see.

I cannot begin to tell you how I loathe them, how I have, in weaker moments, envied them, how I longed to be accepted by them and how at the first hint of serious threat from them I would not have the faintest qualms about incarcerating them all.

The vermin, may they feast on this and cover it with their idiot foot notes.

2.

The most elegant Barto was driving the car, a Cadillac Eldorado with leaking airconditioning. In a purple T-shirt and waist-length fur coat, he looked the very embodiment of sexual decadence; his shoulder-length raven hair, his large nose and chin made him as severely handsome as an Indian on a postage stamp.

Beside him, I felt graceless and boring. My trousers were shapeless and baggy. My hair was tangled and knotted, my glasses filthy, and my unshaven face looked pasty, patchy and particularly unhealthy. It was a face made to appear in the dock, a poor man's face, squinting nervously into the future.

I had filled the trunk of the Eldorado with an armory of modern weapons but I carried a small .22 under my arm. The .22 is a punk's weapon. It was my secret and I shared it with no one.

Barto kept a Colt .45 in the glove box. It was big and heavy and perfectly melodramatic. "If it doesn't scare the cunts to death we can always shoot them."

It was a hard time and only the most unconventional methods were succeeding in business. Certainly we didn't look like the popular image of businessmen. We were special. Once you appreciated the power we held, you could only be astonished at our cleverness. For me, my grubbiness had become a habit so long ingrained that it is difficult to think back to how it started or why it continued. But it was, finally, a perverse identification with the poor people I was raised amongst. Excepting the years when I was a young accountant, I have continued to wear the marks of my caste for they are stamped, not only on my face, but also on my poorly fed bones. No matter what rich clothes I wore, I would deceive no one. So I wear them proudly. They stink. The most casual observer will know that I am someone of great note: to dress like a beggar and be given the accord due to a prince. It was a costume fit for an age which had begun by proudly proclaiming its lack of regimentation and ended railing at its own disarray.

Unemployment had become a way of life and the vagabonds had formed into bands with leaders, organizations and even, in some cases, apocalyptic religions whose leaders preached the coming of the millennium. These last were as rare as threatened species, cosseted, protected and filmed by bored journalists eager for symbols of the times. The rest of the bands roamed the country, godless, hungry and unpublicized.

We saw only one group on the six hundred mile journey north. They were camped by a bridge at the Thirty-Two Mile Creek. As we approached they attempted to drag a dead tree across the road.

I felt Bart hesitate. The cowboy boot came back off the accelerator, making a stoned decision at eighty miles an hour.

"Plant it," I said. I said it fast and hard.

He planted it. The Cadillac responded perfectly. I heard the crunch of breaking wood. Tearing noises. Looking back I saw two bundles of rags lying on the road.

"Shit." The word was very quiet. I looked at Bart. He looked a little pale.

"How did it feel?"

He considered my question. "I don't know," he drawled out the words, beginning to luxuriate in the puzzle they contained, "just sort of *soft*. Sort of. ." he furrowed his brow, "sort of did-it-happen, didn't-it-happen type of thing."

I leant into the back seat and pulled up a bag of dope and rolled an exceedingly large trumpet-shaped joint. The Cadillac devoured the miles while the faulty airconditioner dripped cold water onto Bart's cowboy boots, and I thought once again how genuinely strange our lives had become. I often stepped back and looked at myself from the outside. I was unthinkable to myself. Now I found it amazing to consider that only a week ago I had been making a most unconventional presentation to a highly conservative board of directors. The success of the presentation was the reason we were now heading north in this elegant motor car.

The board, of course, knew a great deal about us before we made the presentation. They were prepared for, and wanted, the unconventional. They expected to be frightened. They also expected to be given hope. Given their desire to believe in us, it would have been exceedingly difficult to do the presentation badly.

I dressed as badly as they would have expected me to, and spoke as arrogantly as they had been led to expect I would. There was nothing terribly original in the way we analysed the ills of the frozen meals subsidiary. It was simply professional, a quality that was lacking in the subsidiary's present management. We presented a market analysis, and pointed out that their company was in a unique position to take advantage of the present economic conditions. We presented a profit projection for the next twelve months and claimed a fee of half this figure, or whatever profit was finally delivered. If there was no profit we would ask for no fee. This money was to be delivered to us, in whatever way their lawyers could discover, tax free.

We demanded complete autonomy during those twelve months and asked the board's guarantee that they would not interfere.

It was not difficult to imagine that they would buy it. They were making heavy losses and we were obviously confident of making considerable profits. In addition I had two successes behind me: a pharmaceutical company and a supermarket chain, both of which had been rescued from the hands of the receivers and turned into profitable businesses.

It would never have occurred to them that now, on this road heading towards their factory, I would be so tense and nervous that my stomach would hurt. I had gained a perverse pleasure from their respect. Now I would live in terror of losing it.

Outside the car, the scrub was immersed in a hot haze. The world seemed full of poisonous spiders, venomous snakes, raw red clay, and the bitter desperate faces of disenfranchised men.

3.

The factory belched smoke into the sky and looked beyond saving. We parked by the bridge and watched white-coated men in an aluminium boat inspect the dead fish which were floating there.

The dead fish and the foul smoke from the plant assumed the nature of a feverish dream. Flies descended on our shirt backs and our faces. We waved at them distractedly. Through the heat-haze I observed the guard at the factory gate. His scuttling behaviour seemed as alien and inexplicable as that of a tropical crab. It took some time to realize that we were the object of his uncertain attentions: he kept walking out towards us and shouting. When we didn't respond, he quickly lost all courage and nervously scuttled back to his post.

The Cadillac was confusing him.

Around the plant the country was scrubby, dense, prickly and unattractive. Certain grasses betrayed the presence of swamp and the air itself was excessively humid and almost clinging. The prospect of spending twelve months here was not a pleasant one.

Behind the anxious guard the factory stood quietly rusting under a heavy grey sky. It looked like nothing more than a collection of eccentric tin huts. One might expect them to contain something dusty and rotten, the left-overs from a foreign war in disordered heaps, broken instruments with numbered dials and stiff canvas webbing left to slowly rust and decay.

Yet the plant was the largest frozen food processing and storage facility in the country. The storerooms, at this moment, contained one and a half million dollars worth of undistributed merchandise, household favourites that had lost their popularity in the market place. It was hard to reconcile the appearance of the plant with the neat spiral-bound report titled "Production and Storage Facilities".

I knew at that moment I didn't want to go anywhere near that plant. I wanted to be in a nice bar with soft music playing, the airconditioning humming, a little bowl of macadamia nuts and a very long gin and tonic in front of me. I got back into the Cadillac and took some Mylanta for my stomach.

At the gate the guard seemed reluctant to let us in and Bart pulled out the Colt. It was an unnecessary move but he enjoyed it. His gangster fantasies had never been allowed for in corporate life.

He looked like a prince of darkness, standing at the gate in a purple T-shirt, a fur coat, the finger-nails of his gun-hand painted in green and blue. I smiled watching him, thinking that capitalism had surely entered its most picturesque phase.

4.

The hate in the staff canteen was as palpable as the humidity outside. It buzzed and stung, finding weak spots in my carefully prepared defences. We had played the videotape with the chairman's speech to the employees but it did nothing to dilute the feelings of the office staff who behaved like a subject race.

The girls giggled rudely. The men glowered, pretending to misunderstand the nature of the orders we gave them. I felt that their threat might, at any instant, become physical and an attack be made. Barto, more agitated than usual, produced the .45.

He was laughed at. He stood there aghast, no longer feeling as cool as he would have liked.

It was a particularly bad start. I requested the sales, marketing and production managers to escort me to my new office where we could discuss their futures.

When I left the canteen I was burning with a quiet rage. My hands were wet. My stomach hurt. I was more than a little frightened. I began to understand why men raze villages and annihilate whole populations. The .22 under my arm nagged at me, producing feelings that were intense, unnameable, and not totally unpleasurable.

5.

I fed on my fear and used it to effect. It was my strength. It hardened me and kept my mind sharp and clear. It gave me the confidence of cornered men. It made sleep almost impossible.

We worked from the old general manager's office, the brown smudge of his suicide an unpleasant reminder of the possibility of failure. We found the floor more convenient than the desk and spread papers across it as we attempted to piece the mess together.

It became obvious very early that the marketing manager was a fool. His understanding of conditions in the market place was minimal. His foolishly optimistic report had been a major contributing factor in the present state of affairs.

He had taken too many store buyers to too many lunches. It must have been a little awkward for the buyers to tell him they weren't taking any more of his products.

It was also difficult for me to tell him that he could not continue as marketing manager. He was large and weak and watery. He had the softness of those who lie long hours in hot baths before dressing carefully in tailormade suits. He could not adjust to me. He could not think of me as a threat, merely as someone who needed a wash. When I dismissed him he did not understand. He returned to his office the next day and continued as usual.

When you kill flathead you put a knife in their foreheads. Their eyes roll and sometimes pop out. The marketing manager reacted in a similar manner when it occurred to him that he was being fired. His mouth opened wide with shock and I was reminded of a flathead when I looked at his eyes.

As with the fish, I found it necessary not to think too much about what I was doing. I consoled myself with the knowledge that there would have been no job for him if we had not arrived. He had been thorough enough to have destroyed any hope of his own survival. He had covered it from every angle.

With the marketing manager's departure I discovered a whole filing cabinet full of documents that he had withheld from me. As I examined them I felt like a surgeon who comes to remove a small growth and finds a body riddled with secondary cancers. I had promised the board of directors things which, given all the available information, had seemed reasonable at the time. But here the gap between the diseased body and my promises of glowing health seemed an inseparable gulf.

I began to feel that I might be less remarkable

than the glorious picture the board had of me. When I had presented my credentials and broad methods to them I had felt myself to be quite glamorous, a superior being who could succeed where they and their underlings had failed. It was a good picture. I preened myself before it as if it were a mirror.

I claimed to despise the board but I didn't want that mirror taken away from me. It was very important that they hold me in high esteem.

Incensed by the appalling news we found in marketing, we recalled the sales force and threatened them with violence and torture if they did not succeed. I am thin and not particularly strong but I had a gun and I had the genuine craziness of a man who will do anything to get what he wants. Anger filled me like electricity. My fingertips were full of it. They felt so tight and tense I couldn't keep them still. Bart stood smoking a joint and waving the Colt around the office with the most carefree abandon, sighting down the barrel at first one head and then another. We spoke to them quietly and politely about the sales targets we expected them to meet in the coming year.

Whether through accident or design Bart let off a shot into the ceiling and the sales manager involuntarily wet his pants. His staff laughed out loud at his misfortune. I thought how ugly they looked with their big cufflinks and silly grins.

It was not the ideal way to do business, but the times were hard, other job opportunities non-existent, and the competition in the trade intense. Our products had been de-listed by five major chains and were in danger of being kicked out of another three. Only our cheapest lines survived, and these — frozen dinners of exceptionally low quality and price — would have to spearhead our return to the market. They were cheap and filling and there were a lot of people who needed cheap filling meals.

I gave Bart control of the marketing function and watched him nervously like a driver who takes his hands from the wheel but is ready to take it back at any serious deviation. Apart from twelve months as a trainee product manager with Procter and Gamble, Bart's previous experience had been totally in advertising agencies. There was really nothing but my intuitive judgment to say that he'd be a success in this new role.

I needn't have worried. He had a business brain the like of which is rarely seen, as cool and clean as stainless steel and totally without compassion. It was Bart who dumped two warehouses full of frozen food straight into the river, thus clearing a serious bottleneck in the system and creating space for products that could actually be sold. He budgeted for the $800 fine and spent another $800 on the finest cocaine to celebrate with. I approved these expenses without question. The goods had been sitting in the warehouse for two years and had been written down in value by a thoughtful accountant who seemed the only person to have anticipated the company's present plight.

Bart doubled the advertising budget, a move which terrified me but which I approved. He planned to drop advertising altogether in the second half and plough an equivalent amount into promotions. It was pressure-cooked marketing. It was unorthodox and expensive but it was the sort of brutal tactic that could be necessary for our success.

Bart pursued the practice of business with the logic of an abstract artist. Things were, for him, problems of form, colour and design. He pursued cool acts with relentless enthusiasm.

From my office I watched him walk across the wide bitumen apron to fire the production manager. His hair was now dyed a henna red, and his cowboy boots made his out-turned toes look curiously elegant. He walked as casually as a man who has run out of cigarette papers taking a stroll to a corner shop.

6.

The typists had stopped staring at us and were actually managing to get some work done. However I still continued to have trouble with my secretary. She was nearly forty-five, matronly in style, and as the secretary to the most senior executive, she was the leader of the others. She was pursuing some guerilla war of her own, expressing her distaste for me in a hundred little ways which were almost impossible to confront directly.

On this occasion she found me alone in my office. I was sitting on the floor going through the computer print-outs from the Nielsen survey when she crept up behind me and hissed in my ear.

"May I have a word."

The bitch. She made me jump. I turned in time to catch the last sign of a smirk disappearing from her face.

I stood up. The idea of looking up her dress was

beyond contemplation. I thought, as I stumbled to my feet, that I should fire her or at least exchange her with someone who could handle her. As she continued to disapprove of me she was making me more and more irritable. Yet she seemed able to bully me. I felt awkward and embarrassed every time I talked to her.

"I think," she declared, "there is something you should know."

"Yes." I put the Nielsen survey carefully on the desk. Her face was pinched and her lips had become tightly pursed. If there had been a smirk it had well and truly been superseded by this angry, self-righteous expression.

"I have come to tell you that I can't work for you." I felt enormously relieved. "I'm sorry to hear that," I said.

"I don't suppose you'd be interested in why."

"Yes, of course I would."

This would be her moment and I would pay attention. I did as she wished.

"I cannot respect you." Her sanctimonious little face gave me the shits.

"Oh," I said, "and why not?"

"Because you are not worthy of respect." She stood stiffly upright, tapping her lolly pink suit with a ballpoint pen which was putting little blue flecks all over it.

"You don't respect yourself." She cast a derisive glance over me as if I were someone at the back door begging for sandwiches. So she didn't like the way I dressed. "You don't respect yourself, how can I respect you."

"Oh," I laughed, "I respect myself, please don't concern yourself on that one."

"You've obviously had a good education. Why don't you use it?"

She was beginning to push it a bit far. Her complete ridiculousness didn't stop her from upsetting me. I should have been beyond all this. "I'm your general manager," I said, "surely that's using my education."

She tossed her head. "Ah, but you're not the *real* general manager."

She shouldn't have upset me at all. Her values were nothing like mine. She was trapped and helpless and had to work for me. She had no education, no chance of change. All she had was the conviction that I was worthless. It shouldn't have upset me, but it is exactly the sort of thing that upsets me. The thing she wouldn't give me was the only thing I wanted from her. I felt my temper welling up.

"Do you realize the power I have over you?" I asked her.

"You have no power over me, young man."

She didn't understand me. She thought I was just a scruffy punk who had come to make a mess in her old boss's office. She couldn't know that I have a terrible character weakness, a temper that comes from nowhere and stuns even me with its ferocity and total unreasonableness.

She shouldn't have spoken to me like that, but she wouldn't stop. She wouldn't leave when I asked her to. I stood in my office and I asked the old bitch to leave. I asked her coolly and nicely and politely, but she continued to berate me.

I watched her mouth move. It became unreal. I

had the .22 under my arm, and my feelings were not like the real world, they were hot and pleasurable and electrically intense.

It was rage.

She had just repeated herself. She had just said something about respect when I drew the pistol and shot her in the foot.

She stopped talking. I watched the red mark on her stockinged foot and thought how amazingly accurate I had been.

She sat on the floor with surprise and a slight grunt.

Barto came running through the door and I stood there with the gun in my hand feeling stupid.

Later the incident made me think about myself and what I wanted from life.

7.

The provincial city nearest the plant was a most unappealing place, catering to the tastes of farmers and factory hands. We devised, therefore, quarters of our own at the plant itself and managed to create a very pleasant island within the administration block.

Here a quite unique little society began to evolve, hidden from a hostile environment by dull red brick walls. Here we devoted ourselves to the pursuit of good talk, fanciful ideas and the appreciation of good music.

We introduced fine old Belouch rugs, rich in colour, others from Shiraz, Luristan, old Khelims, mellow and pleasant, glowing like jewels. Here we had huge couches and leather armchairs, soft and old and vibrating with the dying snores of retired soldiers, the suppleness of ancient leathers a delight to the senses. We had low, slow, yellow lights, as gentle as moonlight and stereo equipment, its fidelity best evoked by considering the sound of Tibetan temple bells. The food, at first, was largely indifferent but the drugs and wine were always plentiful, of extraordinary variety and excellent quality.

In these conditions we marvelled at ourselves, that we, the sons of process workers and hotel-keepers, should live like this. We were still young enough to be so entranced by our success and Barto, whose father sold stolen goods in a series of hotels, was eager that a photograph be taken.

Barto seemed the most innocent of men. He approached life languidly, rarely rising before ten and never retiring before three. Ideas came from him in vast numbers and hardly ever appeared to be anything but wisps of smoke.

Lying on the great Belouch saddle bag, graceful as a cat in repose, he would begin by saying, "What if. . ." It was normally Bart who said "What if. . ." and normally me who said "yes" or "no". His mind was relentless in its logic, yet fanciful in style, so the most circuitous and fanciful plans would always, on examination, be found to have cold hard bones within their diaphanous folds.

We were all-powerful. We only had to dream and the dream could be made real. We planned the most unlikely strategies and carried them out, whole plots as involved and chancy as movie scenarios. It was our most remarkable talent. For instance, we evolved a plan for keeping a defecting product manager faithful by getting him a three-bag smack habit and then supplying it.

Our character judgment was perfect. We were delighted by our astuteness.

The product manager stayed but unfortunately killed himself a few months later, so not everything worked out as perfectly as we would have hoped.

We saw ourselves anew, mirrored in the eyes of each new arrival and we preened ourselves before their gaze.

Thelma was the first to arrive. She came to be with Bart and was astounded, firstly by the ugliness of the plant, secondly by the beauty of our private world, and thirdly by the change she claimed had occurred in Bart. She found him obsessed with the business enterprise and unbearably arrogant about his part in it. This she blamed me for. She sat in a corner whispering with Bart and I fretted lest she persuade him to go away with her. She was slender and elegant and dark as a gypsy. She had little needle tracks on her arms, so later on I was able to do a deal with her whereby she agreed to go away for a while.

Ian arrived to take over the sales force and we delighted in his company. He thought our methods of enthusing the salesmen historically necessary but not the most productive in the long term. He took them fifteen miles into town and got drunk with them for two days. He had two fist fights and, somewhere along the line, lost the representative for southern country districts, a point he continued to remain vague about.

He was the perfect chameleon and won them

over by becoming vulgar and loud-mouthed. He affected big cufflinks and changed his shirt twice a day. He had his hair cut perfectly and he looked handsome and macho with his smiling dark eyes.

The sales force loved him, having the mistaken idea that he was normal. Naturally he didn't discuss his enthusiastic appetite for a substance called ACP, a veterinary tranquillizer normally administered to nervous horses which he took, rather ostentatiously, from a teaspoon marked "Souvenir of Anglesea".

It was Ian who persuaded me to fly in Sergei from Hong Kong. With his arrival, a huge weight was lifted from my shoulders and I had more time to relax and enjoy the music and talk. Sergei was unknown to me and I found him, in some respects, alarming. It was as if he found nothing remarkable in our situation. He made no comment on the decor of our private quarters, our penchant for drugs, or the brilliance of our strategies. It was as if we stood before a mirror which reflected everything but ourselves. He made me nervous. I didn't know how I stood with him.

Yet he was the most ordinary of men: short, slim, and dark, moving with a preciseness which I found comforting in such a skilled accountant. He was eccentric in his dress, choosing neatly pressed grey flannel trousers, very expensive knitted shirts, and slip-on shoes of the softest leather. Only the small silver earring on his left earlobe gave an indication that he was not totally straight.

Sergei talked little but went quietly about the business of wrestling with our cash flow. In the first week he completely reprogrammed our computer to give us a simpler and faster idea of our situation. Each week's figures would be available on the Monday of the next week, which made life easier for all of us.

After three weeks I gave over the financial function almost completely to his care and tried to spend some time evolving a sensible long term strategy suited to the economic climate.

Whilst the unemployed continued to receive government assistance there would be a multi-million dollar business in satisfying their needs. Companies which should have had the sense to see this continued to ignore it. Obviously they viewed the present circumstances as some temporary aberration and were planning their long term strategies in the belief that we would shortly be returning to normal market conditions.

My view was that we were experiencing "normal" market conditions.

I instructed our new product development team to investigate the possibility of producing a range of very simple frozen meals which would be extremely filling, could be eaten cold when cooking facilities were not available, and would be lower in cost than anything comparable. I had a series of pie-like dishes in mind but I left the brief open. It seemed like a golden opportunity.

Whilst I was engaged in this, word came from Ian that they had had a highly successful sell-in of our existing lines of frozen meals. He had given the trade substantial discounts and we were operating on very low profit margins, hoping to achieve a very high volume turnover and, more importantly, get our relationship with the trade back to a healthier state.

The telex from Ian was very short: "They love us till their balls ache. Sell-in is 180 per cent of forecast."

I looked out my window as Barto and Sergei walked towards the storeroom which hid the plant itself from my view. Bart's Colt now sat snugly in a hand-tooled leather holster he had spent the last few nights making.

Beside Bart's pointy-toed languid walk, Sergei looked as strict as a wound-up toy.

I watched them thoughtfully, thinking that they had the comic appearance of truly lethal things.

8.
My father lost his hand in a factory. He carried the stump with him as a badge of his oppression by factories. When I was very small I saw that my father had no hand and concluded that my hand would also be cut off when the time came. I carried this belief quietly in the dark part of the mind reserved for dreadful truths. Thus it was with a most peculiar and personal interest that I watched the beheading of chickens, the amputation of fox-terriers' tails, and even the tarring of young lambs. My fear was so intense that all communication on the subject was unthinkable. It would be done just as they had mutilated my cock by cutting off the skin on its head.

I envied my two sisters, who, I was sure, would be allowed to have two hands like my mother.

The factories my father worked in were many and various. I remember only their dark cavernous doors, their dull, hot metal exteriors, the various stinks they left in my father's hair, and the tired sour smell of sweaty clothes that could never be washed often enough.

In the sleep-out behind the house I pinned pictures of motor cars to the walls and masturbated. The yellow walls were decorated with dull brown ageing cellotape and the breasts of impossible girls even less attainable than the motor cars. It was here that I waited to be sent to the factory. Here on hot, stinking afternoons I planned the most fantastic escapes and the most blood-curdling retaliations. It was here, at night, that I was struck dumb by nightmares. The nightmares that assailed me were full of factories which, never really seen and only imagined, were more horrifying than anything my father could have encountered. They cut and slashed at me with gleaming blades and their abysses and chasms gaped before my fearful feet. Their innards were vast and measureless, and they contained nothing but the machinery of mutilation.

The dreams pursued me throughout life and now, at thirty, I still have the same horrible nameless nightmare I first learned when I was five years old. I play it as if it were the music of hell, neatly notated, perfectly repeatable, and as horribly frightening as it was the first time. I am a rabbit caught in the headlights of my dream.

The time had now come to go and confront the factory which was mine. I had done everything in my power to stay away. It was easy enough to make decisions based on engineers' reports and the advice of the production manager. But finally the day came when the excuses began to look ridiculous.

When we left the central admin. block the heat came out of the scrubland and hung on us. I had not been outside for three weeks and the heat which I had seen as airconditioned sunshine now became a very raw reality. A northerly wind lifted stinging dust out of the scrub and flies tried to crawl up my nose and into my ears, as if they wished to lay eggs inside my brain.

The plant and storerooms blinded me with their metallic glare which was not diminished by the streaks of rust decorating their surfaces, hints of some internal disorder.

Barto, walking beside me on the soft, sticky bitumen, said: "How's your nightmare?"

His hair seemed surreal, haloed, blue sky above it and shining silver behind. Already I could hear the rumbling of the plant. A rivulet of dirty water came running from the No. 2 to meet us. Barto hopped across it nimbly, his cowboy boots still immaculately clean.

"Not good," I said. I regretted my confession most bitterly. A confession is nothing but a fart. I have despised those who make confessions of their fears and weaknesses. It is a game the middle class play but they are only manufacturing razor-blades which will be used to slash their own stupid white throats.

The door of the No. 2 yawned cavernous in front of me. The floor was an inch deep in filthy water.

Bart stopped. "Fuck, I can't go in there."

"Why not?" The bastard had to go with me. I wasn't going by myself. We stopped at the door. A foul smell of something cooking came out and engulfed us. I thought I was going to be sick. "Why not?" I asked. "What's the matter?" I tried to make my voice sound normal.

"I'll get my fucking boots fucked." Bart stood at the door, legs apart, a hand on his hip, a knee crooked, looking down at his cowboy boots. "Fuck," he said, "I'm sorry."

"I'll buy you a new pair." I shouldn't have said that.

"No, there's none left to buy. Shit, I'm sorry." I could see that he was. I could see that there was no way I could talk him into coming with me. I was going to have to do the factory tour alone.

"Fuck your fucking boots."

"I'm sorry. It's just that you can't buy them anymore."

I walked gingerly into the lake and kept going, leaving Bart to feel whatever guilt he was capable of.

In waking life it was not only the machinery I was frightened of, although it was terrifying enough. The vats were huge and their sheer bulk was so unrelated to anything human that I felt my throat block off at the consideration of the weight of food they would contain. The production line itself was also particularly old, clanking, wheezing, full of machinery that oozed grease and farted air, and which lifted and pulled and lifted without any regard for life and limb.

It was the people I didn't want to see.

The heat was impossible, far worse than outside.

It mixed with the noise to produce an almost palpable substance which should have suffocated all life. The belt stretched on through this giant corrugated-iron oven, and men and women in grubby white stood beside the line, doing operations that had been perfectly described on the production report.

Line No. 3: four female packers, one male supervisor.

The information on the report was enough. It didn't help me to know that one of the female packers was tall and thin with a baleful glare she directed accusingly at management, that her companion was just as tall but heavier, that next to her was a girl of sixteen with wire spectacles and a heat rash that extended from her forehead to her hands, that one other, an olive-skinned girl with a smooth Mediterranean Madonna face, would have the foolishness to smile at me. And so on.

I have seen enough factories, god knows, but they continue to be a problem to me. They should not be. My fear is irrational and should be overcome by habituation. But nothing dulls me to the assault of factories and I carry with me, still, the conviction that I will end up at the bottom of the shit pile, powerless against the machines in factories. So I look at the people a little too hard, too searchingly, wondering about them in a way that could make my job impossible. The fish in my hand cannot be thought of as anything more than an operation to be performed. The minute one considers the feelings of the fish the act becomes more difficult. So, in factories, I have a weakness, a hysterical tendency to become the people I see there, to enter their bodies and feel their feelings, and see the never-ending loud, metallic, boring days. And I become bitterly angry for them. And their anger, of course, is directed at me, who isn't them. It is a weakness. A folly. An idiot's hobby.

I got my arse out of the factory as fast as I could.

Bart met me at the door of the No. 2. "How's your nightmare?"

I was still in its grip. I was shaking and angry. "It's really shitty in there. It is *really* shitty."

Bart polished his cowboy boot, rubbing the right toe on the back of his left leg. "What are you going to do about it?" he asked, innocently enough.

A confession is a fart. You should never make a confession, no matter what dope you're on. "I'm not going to do anything, pig face. There's not a fucking thing to do, if I wanted to. That's what factories are like." My suede boots were soaked in muck. I flicked a pea off and watched it bounce across the bitumen.

"Listen," the word drawled out of Bart as slow and lazy as the kicking pointy-toed walk he was walking. The word was inquisitive, tentative, curious and also politely helpful. "Listen, do you think they hate you?"

"Yes." I said it before I had time to think.

"Well," the word came out as lazily as the "listen", "I'll tell you what I'll do in the next two months."

I grinned at him. "What'll you do, smart-arse?"

"I'll fucking make them love you, smart-arse, if that's what you want."

He was grinning delightedly, his hands in his

back pockets, his great Indian face turned up towards the screaming sun as if he was drinking power from it.

"And how will you do that?"

"Delegate, delegate," he drawled, "you've got to learn to delegate. Just leave it to me and I'll fix it for you." He finished the conversation in my office. "Easy," he said, "easy-peasy."

9.

Almost without noticing it, we became quite famous. This gave me a lot of pleasure, but also disappointed me. You imagine it will amount to more, that it will feel more substantial than it is. This, after all, is the bit you've dreamed of in all the grubby corners of your life. It is almost the reason you've done what you've done. This is where the world is forced to accept you no matter what you wear, no matter what you look like, no matter what your accent is. You re-define what is acceptable. This is when they ask you for your comments on the economy and war and peace, and beautiful girls want to fuck you because you are emanating power which has been the secret of all those strong physiques which you lack, which you needlessly envied. This is what you dreamed about jerking off in your stinking hot bungalow, treasuring your two hands. It is what you told the red-mouthed naked girl in the *Playboy* pin-up when you came all over the glossy page, and what you wished while you wiped the come off the printed image, so as to keep it in good condition for next time.

The middle-class intellectuals were the first to discover us and we were happy enough to have them around. They came up from the south pretending they weren't middle class. They drank our wine and smoked our dope and drove around in our Cadillac and did tours of the factory. They were most surprised to find that we dressed just like they did. We were flattered that they found us so fascinating and delighted when they were scandalized. In truth we despised them. They were comfortable and had fat-arsed ideas. They went to bed early to read books about people they would try to copy. They didn't know whether to love us or hate us.

We bought a French chef and we had long dinners with bottles of Chateau Latour, Corton, Chambertin, and old luscious vintages of Chateau d'Yquem. They couldn't get over the wine.

We discussed Dada, ecology, Virginia Woolf, Jean Paul Sartre, and the whole principle of making stacks of money and going to live in Penang or the south of France.

Occasionally we had rows on important issues and we normally resolved these by the use of violence.

The simplicity of this ploy struck me as obvious and delightful, yet they were too stupid to learn the lessons we could have taught them. They couldn't get past the style. They'd seen too many movies and hung around with too many wardrobe mistresses.

They couldn't see or understand that we were no different from Henry Ford or any of the other punks.

We were true artists. We showed them the bones of business and power. We instructed them in the uses of violence. Metaphorically, we shat with the door open.

They learned nothing, but were attracted to the power with the dumb misunderstanding of lost moths. They criticized us and asked us for jobs.

Finally, of course, the media arrived and allowed themselves to be publicly scandalized by the contradiction in our lives.

The "Late Night" man couldn't understand why we kept playing "Burning and a-Looting" by Bob Marley and the Wailers. I can still see his stupid good-looking face peering at me while he said: "But how can you listen to that type of material? They're singing about *you*. They want to burn and loot *you*."

The television audience was then treated to the sight of Ian, stoned out of his head on horse tranquillizer, smiling blissfully without even the politeness to act uncomfortable.

"We are," he said, "the Andy Warhols of business."

In the first six months we had achieved almost 100 per cent distribution, increased sales by 228 per cent, introduced a new line of low-price dinners, and, as the seventh month finished, we began to look as if we might meet the profit forecast we had made.

We entertained the board of directors at a special luncheon. They were delighted with us.

10.

The camp fires of the unemployed flicker around the perimeter. Tonight, once more, their numbers have increased. They grew from three, to six, to twenty. Now I choose not to count them. The unemployed have assumed the nature of a distinct and real threat. Yet they have done nothing. During grey days they have been nothing but poorly defined figures in a drab landscape, sitting, standing, concerned with matters I cannot imagine. They have done nothing to hamper trucks full of raw materials. Neither have they tried to intercept the freezer vans. Their inactivity sits most uneasily with their cancerous multiplication.

I can hear some of them singing. They sound like men on a bus coming home from a picnic.

The night buzzes with insects and great grey clouds roll across the sky, whipped across by a high, warm wind. Occasionally lightning flickers around the edge of the sky. Out in the scrub the mosquitoes must be fierce and relentless. It must be a poor feast for them.

Although the gate is guarded and the perimeter patrolled I have chosen to set up my own guard in this darkened window. It was not a popular decision. An open window makes the airconditioning behave badly. Sergei thinks that I am being an alarmist but I have always been an alarmist.

I have spent my life in a state of constant fear that could be understood by very few. I have anticipated disaster at every turn, physical attack at every instant. To be born small and thin and poor, one learns, very quickly, of one's vulnerability. My fear kept me in constant readiness and it also gave me fuel for my most incredible defence. My strength has been my preparedness to do anything, to be totally crazy, to go past the limits that even the strongest will dare to contemplate. The extent of my terrible quaking fear was in exact correspondence with the degree of my craziness. For I performed unthinkable acts of cruelty to others, total bluffs that would prevent all thought of retaliation.

I learnt this early, as a child, when I got my nose busted up by a boy four years older and much, much bigger. I can still remember the bastard. He had wire-framed glasses and must have been blind in one eye because he had white tape obscuring one lens. I can remember the day after he bashed me. I can remember as if it were yesterday. I waited for him just around the side of the Catholic Church. There was a lane there which he always walked down and beside the lane was a big pile of house bricks, neatly stacked. I was eight years old. I waited for the bastard as he came down the lane kicking a small stone. He looked arrogant and self-confident and I knew I couldn't afford to fail. As he passed me I stood up and threw the first brick. It sounded soft and quiet as it hit his shoulder, but I'd thrown it so hard it knocked him over. He looked round with astonishment but I already had the second brick in the air. It gashed his arm. He started crying. His glasses had gone. They were on the ground. I stood on them. Then I kicked him for good measure.

The effectiveness of this action was greatly enhanced by the fact that I had been seen by others. It helped me get a reputation. I built on this with other bricks and great lumps of wood. I cut and burned and slashed. I pursued unthinkable actions with the fearful skill and sensitivity of someone who can't afford to have his bluff called. I developed the art of rages and found a way to let my eyes go slightly mad and, on occasions, to dribble a little. It was peculiar that these theatrical effects often became real. I forgot I was acting.

But there was no real defence against the fires of the unemployed. They were nothing more than threatening phantoms licking at the darkness. My mind drifted in and out of fantasies about them and ended, inevitably, with the trap corridors of a maze, at the place where they killed or tortured me.

Below me Bart was sitting on the steps. I could hear him fiddling with his weapon. All week he has been working on a new, better, hand-tooled leather holster. Now it is finished he wears it everywhere. He looks good enough for the cover of *Rolling Stone*.

The unemployed are singing "Blowing in the Wind". Bart starts to hum the tune along with them, then decides not to. I can hear him shifting around uncomfortably, but there is nothing I can say to him that would make his mind any more at ease.

The unemployed will have the benefit of their own holy rage.

It is difficult to see across the plant. The spotlights we rigged up seem to create more darkness than light. I stare into the darkness, imagining movements, and thinking about my day's work. Today I went through the last three months' cost reports and discovered that our raw material costs are up over 10 per cent on eight of our lines. This is making me edgy. Something nags at me about it. I feel irritable that no one has told me. But there is nothing that can be done until tomorrow.

The movement across the face of the No. 1 store is vague and uncertain. I rub my eyes and squint. Below me I can hear Bart shift. He has taken off his boots and now he moves out towards the No. 1, sleek as a night cat, his gun hand out from his side like a man in a movie. I hold my breath. He fades into almost-dark. The figure near the No. 1 stops and becomes invisible to me. At that moment there is a shot. The figure flows out of the dark, dropping quietly like a shadow to the ground.

I am running down the stairs and am halfway across the apron before Bart has reached the No. 1. I pray to god he hasn't shot a guard.

"Not bad, eh? That's about fifty yards."

I don't say anything. He is fussing over his gun, replacing the dead shell with a live bullet. I let him walk ahead. I'm not going to get any fun out of this. He walks forward, as nonchalant as if he were going to change a record or go and get another drink.

I see his flashlight turn on and then a pause as he kneels to look at the body. And then the light goes out and he is running around and around in circles. He is yelping and running like a dog whose foot has been run over. As he circles he says, "Shit, Shit, Shit, oh fucking Christ." He looks comical and terrible dancing in his bare feet. He can't stay still. He runs around saying shit.

Then I am looking at the body. In the yellow light of my flashlight I see the face of a sixteen-year-old boy. I notice strange things, small details: golden down on the cheeks, bad pimples, and something else. At first, in dumb shock, I think it's his guts coming up. And a pea rolls out. In his mouth is a chunk of TV dinner, slowly thawing.

11.

When I was six years old I threw a cat into an incinerator. It wasn't until the cat came running out the grate at the bottom, burning, screaming, that I had any comprehension of what I had done.

The burning cat still runs through my dreams searing me with its dreadful knowledge.

When I saw the dead boy I knew it was Bart's burning cat.

He is like the girls in *Vogue*, wearing combat clothes and carrying guns and smoking pink cigarettes. He is like the intellectuals: he lives on the wrong side of the chasm between ideas and action. The gap is exactly equal to the portion of time that separates the live cat from the burning cat.

That is the difference between us.

It should be said to him: "If you wear guns on your hip you will need to see young boys lying dead at your feet and confront what 'dead' is. That is what it takes to live that fantasy. If you cannot do this, you should take off your uniform. Others will perform the unpleasant acts for you. It is the nature of business that as a result of your decisions some people will starve and others be killed. It is simply a matter of confronting the effects of your actions. If you can grasp this nettle you will be strong. If you cannot, you are a fool and are deluding yourself."

12.
Our burning cats are loose.

Bart's is sedated, slowed down, held tightly on a fearful leash by Mandies or some other downer. Perhaps he has been shooting up with morphine. His eyes are dull and his movements clumsy but his cat stirs threateningly within him, intimidating him with its most obvious horror.

My cat is loose and raging and my eyes are wide. Black smoke curls like friendly poison through my veins and bubbles of rage course through my brain. My cat is clawing and killing, victim and killer. I am in an ecstasy. I can't say. My eyes stretch wide and nostrils, also, are flaring.

Oh, the electricity. The batteries of torches firing little hits of electricity behind the eyes. To stretch my fingers and feel the tautness behind the knuckles like full sails under heavy wind.

For I have found out.

I have discovered a most simple thing. The little bastard Sergei has been cheating me in such a foolish and simple way that I cannot contain my rage at the insult to my intelligence. He has been siphoning funds like a punk. A dull stupid punk without inventiveness. He is someone trying to club a knife-fighter to death. He is so stupid I cannot believe it.

Ah, the rage. The rage, the fucking rage. He has no sense. He hasn't even the sense to be afraid. He stands before me, Bart by his side. Bart does not live here. He is away on soft beds of morphine which cannot ease his pain. Sergei is threatening. He is being smart. He thinks I'm a fool. He casts collusive glances towards Bart who is like a man lobotomized. Smiling vaguely, insulated by blankets of morphine from my rage, like a man in an asbestos suit in the middle of a terrible fire.

Oh, and fire it is.

For the cost of raw materials has not risen by 10 per cent. The cost of raw materials has not risen at all. Sergei, the fool, has been paying a fictitious company on his cheque butts and using the actual cheques to pay both the real suppliers and himself.

I only do this for the profit, for the safety, for the armour and strength that money gives. That I may be insulated from disaster and danger and threats and little bastards who are trying to subvert my friends and take my money.

And now there will be an example.

For he is trying to place me in a factory. He is trying to take my power. He shall be fucking well cut, and slashed, and shall not breathe to spread his hurt,

He is smart and self-contained. He speaks with the voice of the well-educated and powerful. His eyebrows meet across his forehead.

It took me three hours to trace his schoolboy fiddle. And it only took that long because the bastards who were doing the company's search took so long to confirm that the company he's been writing on his cheque butts doesn't exist. It took me five minutes to check that his prices were inflated. Five minutes to guess what he was up to.

The body of Bart's victim has been tied to the top of the perimeter fence. Let that warn the bastards. Even the wind will not keep down the flies. The unemployed shall buzz with powerless rage.

And now Sergei. An example will be made. I have called for his suit and his white business shirt and black shoes. The suit is being pressed. The shoes are being polished. It will be a most inventive execution, far more interesting than his dull childish cheating.

Under my surveillance his hair is being cut. Very neat. He is shaved cleanly. He is shaved twice. The poor idiot does not know what is happening. Bart watches with dumb incomprehension, helping the girl who is cutting the hair. He holds the bowl of hot water. He brings a towel. He points out a little bit of side-burn that needs trimming better. He is stumbling and dazed. Only I know. I have Bart's gun, just in case.

The suit is pressed. Bart helps with the tie. He fusses, tying and re-tying. Sergei's eyes have started to show fear. He tries to talk casually to me, to Bart. He is asking what is happening but Bart is so far away that his mind is totally filled with the simple problem of tying the tie, its loops and folds provide intricate problems of engineering and aesthetics.

I never liked Sergei. He never treated me with respect. He showed disdain.

I will donate him a briefcase. I have a beautiful one left me by the old general manager. It is slim and black with smart snappy little chrome clips on

276

it. In it I place Sergei's excellent references and about five hundred dollars worth of cash. It is a shame about the money, but no one must ever think him poor or helpless.

I order him to hold the briefcase. He looks so dapper. Who could not believe he was a senior executive? Who indeed!

It is time now for the little procession to the gate. The knowledge of what is happening hits Sergei on this, his walk to the scaffold. He handles it well enough, saying nothing I remember.

High on the wire the dead boy stands like a casualty of an awkward levitation trick.

I have the main gate opened and Sergei walks out of it. The guards stand dumbly like horses in a paddock swishing flies away. I am watching Bart's eyes but they are clouded from me. He has become a foreign world veiled in mists. I know now that we will not discuss Kandinsky again or get stoned together. But he will do what I want because he knows I am crazy and cannot be deceived.

He seems to see nothing as the great wire mesh gate is rolled back into place and locked with chains. Sergei walks slowly down the gravel road away from us.

A grey figure slides out from the scrub a mile or so away. They will welcome him soon, this representative of management with his references in his briefcase.

The fact of Sergei's execution could not possibly be nearly as elegant as my plan. I return to my office, leaving the grisly reality of it to the watchers at the gate.

13.

In the night they put Sergei's head on the wire. It stares towards my office in fear and horror, a reminder of my foolishness.

For now it appears that I misunderstood the situation. It appears that he was acting on Bart's instructions, that the siphoned funds were being used to rebuild the inside of the factory.

To please me, dear god.

How could I have guarded against Bart's "What if. . ." or protected us all from his laconic "easy-peasy". If one lives with dreamers and encourages their aberrations something is bound to go wrong. Now I understand what it is to be the parent of brilliant children, children reared with no discipline, their every fantasy pandered to. Thus one creates one's own assassins.

The factory tour is over now and Bart sits in my office eyeing me with the cunning of a dog, pretending servility, but with confused plans and strategies showing in his dog-wet eyes.

He understood nothing of factories nor my fear of them. His model factory is a nightmare far more obscene that anything my simple mind could have created.

For they have made a factory that is quiet. They have worried about aesthetics.

Areas of peaceful blue and whole fields of the most lyrical green. In these ideal conditions people perform insulting functions, successfully imitating the functions of mid-twentieth century machinery.

This is Bart and Sergei's masterpiece, their gift to me. They have the mentality of art students who think they can change the world by spraying their hair silver.

They make me think of other obscenities. For instance: a Georg Jensen guillotine made from the finest silver and shaped with due concern for function and aesthetic appeal. Alternatively: condemned cells decorated with pretty blue bunny patterns from children's nurseries.

In order to achieve these effects they have reduced profit by 6.5 per cent.

In here it is very quiet. No noise comes from the staff outside. I have seen them, huddled together in little groups at the windows staring at Sergei. They seem anesthetized. They have the glazed eyes of people too frightened to see anything that might get them into trouble. Thus they avoided Bart's eyes. He pranced through like a spider, his hand on his gun, the fury in his veins bursting to fill the room like black ink in water.

Now in the silence of my office I see the extent to which he is afflicted by hurt and misunderstanding. Trying to talk to him, I put my hand on his arm. He flinches from me. In that terrible instant I am alone on the pack ice, the string inside me taut and all that lonely ice going in front of me no matter which way I turn. And he, Bart, looking at me guilty and afraid and angry and does he want to kill me?

Yes, he does.

He will learn to use his burning cat. He hates me because I killed his friend. It was a misunderstanding. It was his fault, not mine. If they hadn't cheated I would never have made the mistake. His friend Sergei, the little turd, he thought he was clever but he was a fool. Sergei, his stupid mouth dribbling black blood on the top of the wire fence. If only his siphoning of funds had been more subtle. There were two other ways to do it, but he did it like a petty cash clerk. It was this which upset me the most. It was this which put me over the line and left me here, alone, threatened by the one person I thought my friend.

He may wish to kill me.

But I, alone on the ice, have eyes like the headlights of a truck. I have power. I will do anything. And I have made enough bad dreams that one more dying face will make not the slightest scrap of difference. Anyone who wants to cling onto their life won't fuck around with me too willingly, though their hand might easily encircle my wrist, though they have the strength to crush me with their bare arms, for I am fearful and my fear makes me mighty.

And I am not mad, but rather I have opened the door you all keep locked with frightened bolts and little prayers. I am more like you than you know. You have not inspected the halls and attics. You haven't got yourself grubby in the cellars. Instead you sit in the front room in worn blue jeans, reading about atrocities in the Sunday papers.

Now Bart will do as I wish for he wishes to live and is weak because of it. I am a freight train, black smoke curling back, thundering down the steel lines of terrible logic.

So now I speak to him so quietly that I am forcing him to strain towards me. Trucks have been destroyed attempting to enter the plant. It is time, I tell him, that the scrub be cleared of unemployed.

It will give him something to do. It will give him

a use for his rage. He can think about his friend, whom I didn't kill. He was killed by the people in the scrub, whoever they are. They are the ones holding up trucks and stopping business, and business must go on. BUSINESS MUST GO ON. That is what the hell we are here for. There is no other reason for this. This is the time that is sold to the devil. It is time lost, never to be re-lived, time stolen so it can be OK later and I can live in white sheets and ironed shirts and drink gin and tonic in long glasses, well away from all this.

Then I can have the luxury of nightmares, and pay the price gladly, for it will only be my sleep which will be taken and not my waking hours as well.

14.

All around the plant seemed very, very still. The sun had gone down, leaving behind a sky of the clearest blue I had ever seen. But even as I watched, this moment passed and darkness claimed it.

I watched Bart lead his contingent of workers through the dusk in the direction of the front gate. Each man had a flamethrower strapped to his back and I smiled to think that these men had been producing food to feed those whom they would now destroy.

I watched the operation from the roof of the canteen, using binoculars Sergei had left behind.

As I watched men run through the heat burning other men alive, I knew that thousands of men had stood on hills or roofs and watched such scenes of terrible destruction, the result of nothing more than their fear and their intelligence.

In the scrub the bodies of those who hated me were charred and smouldering.

I touched my arm, marvelling at the fineness of hairs and skin, the pretty pinkness glowing through the fingernails, the web-like mystery of the palm, the whiteness underneath the fore-arm and the curious sensitivity where the arm bends.

I wished I had been born a great painter. I would have worn fine clothes and celebrated the glories of man. I would have stood aloft, a judge, rather than wearily kept vigil on this hill, hunchbacked, crippled, one more guilty fool with blood on his hands.

Other books by

PETER CAREY

THE TAX INSPECTOR

The audit of Catchprice Motors looks like the least challenging assignment of the Tax Inspector's life, but once behind the cyclone fence she is going to find the Catchprice family have dangerous dreams the Tax Office were not previously aware of.

Granny Catchprice always wanted a flower farm.

Her forty-seven-year-old daughter wants to be a country singer.

And sixteen-year-old Benny is about to turn himself into an angel.

The Tax Inspector is a dark and brilliant achievement that is illuminated, even at its darkest moments, with a rare humour and compassion. Set in 1990s Sydney, it is a work of astonishing originality by a master of the contemporary novel.

"Peter Carey is a brilliant, powerful and dangerous writer. Dangerous because to read this book involves a loss of innocence. One can never pretend the world is exactly as one imagined it before."

Sue Gough, *Courier-Mail*

"It is quintessential Carey and in Australia we can read it before anyone else in the world. This is our good fortune. For it's a work for us, about us, now."

Diana Giese, *Australian*

"*The Tax Inspector* is an unusual, at times absurd, look at ourselves. It is peopled by the sensuous, wilful characters we've come to expect from Peter Carey."

Phil Holcroft, *Sunday Sun*

The Fat Man in History

A landmark in contemporary Australian literature, *The Fat Man in History* has brought widespread acclaim to Peter Carey for his brilliant and ingenious fiction. These twelve stories introduce visionary landscapes of intense clarity, where the rules of the game are bizarre, and yet chillingly familiar.

"Peter Carey is a surrealist, a maker of fables, myths, allegories, dreams, nightmares, fantasies."

Douglas Stewart, *Sydney Morning Herald*

"One of the outstanding writers to have emerged during this period."

Peter Lewis, *Times Literary Supplement*

"Carey is that rarity, a highly imaginative writer, verging sometimes on science fiction but writing with verbal economy and a tight narrative grip."

New Statesman

"The most genuinely original of our story tellers — a fabulist and, in some corners of his imagination, a surrealist of disturbing power."

Australian Book Review

Exotic Pleasures

This dazzling collection of fables and fantasies opens with Peter Carey's most famous short story — "The Fat Man in History" — and closes with another, "War Crimes". In between are people caught on the edge of the near future, careless of the past, consumed by their weird fears and deluded passions.

"If you never read another short story collection read this one."

Woman's Journal

"Peter Carey writes an intelligent, sizzling, and rapid narrative. He will also do allegories, fables, and astonishing tricks . . . I recommend his work to you with great enthusiasm."

Frank Moorhouse

"Impressive and entertaining . . . Each story ends on a melancholy but powerful note, like the sudden discharge of electrical energy which illuminates all that it touches."

Peter Ackroyd, *Sunday Times*

Bliss

"Harry Joy was to die three times, but it was his first death which was to have the greatest effect on him, and it is this first death which we shall now witness."

So begins this masterpiece of illusion which marked Peter Carey's brilliant debut as a novelist. The dilemma of Harry Joy is both funny and terrifying, for Harry wakes up in Hell, tortured by those he loves, and by the dreams and nightmares he once created for profit.

"*Bliss* is outrageous perfection . . . madcap, adventurous, engaging, compelling, shocking, moving, funny, sad and inventive."

San Francisco Bay Area Reporter

"Peter Carey's first novel is a marvel to read . . . it's one 'hell' of a good book."

Margaret Smith, *Weekend Australian*

Illywhacker

"*Illywhacker* is such an astonishing novel, of such major proportions, that before saying anything else one must record gratitude for its existence."

Geoffrey Dutton, *Bulletin*

"Awesome breadth, ambition and downright narrative joy . . . *Illywhacker* is a triumph."

Curt Suplee, *Washington Post*

"It is impossible to convey in a review the cumulative brilliance and accelerating hilarity of the prose."

Nicholas Spice, *London Review of Books*

"The finest and funniest picaresque novel yet written in Australia."

Peter Pierce, *National Times*

Winner

AGE BOOK OF THE YEAR AWARD, 1985
NBC AWARD FOR AUSTRALIAN LITERATURE, 1985
FAW BARBARA RAMSDEN AWARD, 1985
NATIONAL SCIENCE FICTION CONVENTION AWARD, 1986
SHORTLISTED BOOKER PRIZE, 1985

Oscar and Lucinda